THOMAS HARDY'S
TALES FROM WESSEX

Thomas Hardy was born in 1840 at Upper Bockhampton in Dorset, the Wessex of his books, son of a builder and descendant of Nelson's famous flag-captain. He was educated at a private school in Dorchester and then from 1856 to 1861 was apprentice to an ecclesiastical architect in the same town. The following year he moved to London where for five years he studied architecture under Sir Arthur Blomfield, at the same time attending classes at King's College. In 1863 he was awarded a medal of the Institute of British Architects.

His first published work was a sketch entitled *How I Built Myself a House*, which appeared in *Chambers's Journal* in 1865. In 1871, at his own expense, he published his first novel, a murder story called *Desperate Remedies*. His first great novel, *Far from the Madding Crowd*, appeared in 1874, and was soon followed by *The Return of the Native* and *The Trumpet Major*. *The Mayor of Casterbridge*, published in 1886 marked a turning point in his life, for it was then that he moved into Max Gate, his house near Dorchester, where he spent the rest of his life.

Tess of the D'Urbervilles and *Jude the Obscure* aroused so much hostility and disgust in many quarters that Thomas Hardy gave up writing novels, though a fantasy, *The Well-beloved*, appeared in 1897.

His collections of short stories include *Wessex Tales*, *A Group of Noble Dames*, *Life's Little Ironies* and *A Changed Man*.

The Dynasts, his epic drama, is considered by some to be his greatest work. Hardy stands high also as a nature poet with verse whose strength redeems its ruggedness and which, it is thought, may well outlast his novels. He was twice married, to Emma Gifford in 1874, and after her death to Florence Dugdale. He died in 1928.

THOMAS HARDY'S
TALES FROM WESSEX

Contains the six stories used for the
BBC Television Series WESSEX TALES,
with an Introduction by the producer, Irene Shubik

UNABRIDGED

PAN BOOKS LTD : LONDON

'The Withered Arm', 'Fellow-Townsmen' and 'An Imaginative Woman' from *Wessex Tales* first published 1888; 'A Tragedy of Two Ambitions' and 'The Melancholy Hussar of the German Legion' from *Life's Little Ironies* first published 1894; and 'Barbara of the House of Grebe' from *A Group of Noble Dames* first published 1891

This edition first published 1973 by Pan Books Ltd, 33 Tothill Street, London SW1

ISBN 0 330 23776 4

Introduction © Irene Shubik 1973

*Printed and bound in England by
Hazell Watson & Viney Ltd,
Aylesbury, Bucks*

Contents

Introduction

The six stories in this volume were selected for presentation on television. They were a personal choice guided by two considerations: would they work dramatically on the screen? and would they provide the viewer with sufficient variety? – for Hardy, like many great writers, can be repetitive.

Hardy's work bestows on the television- or film-maker a wealth of evocative visual images. No one can remain unmoved by his depiction of the countryside and the seasons and their powerful effect upon human emotions. Nor can one fail to respond to his sense of the past and the eternal passage of time. In the opening lines of *The Melancholy Hussar of the German Legion* one has a most perfect illustration of these characteristics: 'Here stretch the downs, high and breezy and green, absolutely unchanged since those eventful days ... At night, when I walk across the lonely place, it is impossible to avoid hearing, amid the scourings of the wind over the grass-bents and thistles, the old trumpets and bugle calls, the rattle of the halters; to help seeing rows of spectral tents and the *impedimenta* of the soldiery.' The landscapes of Dorset are transmuted by Hardy into his own inner, imaginary world of Wessex.

Hardy summons his characters from the past, tells their tale, and banishes them again. He presents them in many dimensions, viewing them with a profoundly ironic and very modern eye. His attitudes to women, religion and class could well be those of now. Even in those most melodramatic tales of witchcraft and horror, *The Withered Arm* and *Barbara of the House of Grebe*, no characters behave other than believably in terms of modern psychology. Barbara is easily recognizable as the spoiled deb who soon regrets her hasty elopement. Equally recognizable is the tragi-comic plight of the two sons in *A Tragedy of Two Ambitions*, as they try to escape from their disreputable father and cross the class barrier via religion. Ella Marchmill in *An Imaginative Woman* is surely a 'captive wife' longing for self-expression.

To all those concerned in filming these stories, the problem has been to re-create Hardy's world. The reader will find that world for himself in the pages that follow.

1973   IRENE SHUBIK

The Withered Arm

I

A Lorn Milkmaid

It was an eighty-cow dairy, and the troop of milkers, regular and supernumerary, were all at work; for, though the time of year was as yet but early April, the feed lay entirely in water-meadows, and the cows were 'in full pail'. The hour was about six in the evening, and three-fourths of the large, red, rectangular animals having been finished off, there was opportunity for a little conversation.

'He do bring home his bride tomorrow, I hear. They've come as far as Anglebury today.'

The voice seemed to proceed from the belly of the cow called Cherry, but the speaker was a milking-woman, whose face was buried in the flank of that motionless beast.

'Hav' anybody seen her?' said another.

There was a negative response from the first. 'Though they say she's a rosy-cheeked, tisty-tosty little body enough,' she added; and as the milkmaid spoke she turned her face so that she could glance past her cow's tail to the other side of the barton, where a thin, fading woman of thirty milked somewhat apart from the rest.

'Years younger than he, they say,' continued the second, with also a glance of reflectiveness in the same direction.

'How old do you call him, then?'

'Thirty or so.'

'More like forty,' broke in an old milkman near, in a long white pinafore or 'wropper', and with the brim of his hat tied down, so that he looked like a woman. ' 'A was born before our Great Weir was builded, and I hadn't man's wages when I laved water there.'

The discussion waxed so warm that the purr of the milk streams became jerky, till a voice from another cow's belly cried with authority, 'Now then, what the Turk do it matter to us about Farmer Lodge's age, or Farmer Lodge's new mis'ess? I shall have to pay him nine pound a year for the rent of every one of these milchers, whatever his age or hers. Get on with your work, or 'twill be dark afore we have done. The evening is pinking in a'ready.' This speaker was the dairyman himself, by whom the milkmaids and men were employed.

Nothing more was said publicly about Farmer Lodge's wedding, but the first woman murmured under her cow to her next neighbour. ' 'Tis hard for *she*,' signifying the thin worn milkmaid aforesaid.

'O no,' said the second. 'He ha'n't spoke to Rhoda Brook for years.'

When the milking was done they washed their pails and hung them on a many-forked stand made as usual of the peeled limb of an oak-tree, set upright in the earth, and resembling a colossal antlered horn. The majority then dispersed in various directions homeward. The thin woman who had not spoken was joined by a boy of twelve or thereabout, and the twain went away up the field also.

Their course lay apart from that of the others, to a lonely spot high above the water-meads, and not far from the border of Egdon Heath, whose dark countenance was visible in the distance as they drew nigh to their home.

'They've just been saying down in barton that your father brings his young wife home from Anglebury tomorrow,' the woman observed. 'I shall want to send you for a few things to market, and you'll be pretty sure to meet 'em.'

'Yes, Mother,' said the boy. 'Is Father married then?'

'Yes . . . You can give her a look, and tell me what she's like, if you do see her.'

'Yes, Mother.'

'If she's dark or fair, and if she's tall – as tall as I. And if she seems like a woman who has ever worked for a living, or one that has been always well off, and has never done anything, and shows marks of the lady on her, as I expect she do.'

'Yes.'

They crept up the hill in the twilight and entered the cottage. It was built of mud-walls, the surface of which had been washed by many rains into channels and depressions that left none of the orginal flat face visible, while here and there in the thatch above a rafter showed like a bone protruding through the skin.

She was kneeling down in the chimney-corner, before two pieces of turf laid together with the heather inwards, blowing at the red-hot ashes with her breath till the turves flamed. The radiance lit her pale cheek, and made her dark eyes, that had once been handsome, seem handsome anew. 'Yes,' she resumed, 'see if she is dark or fair, and if you can, notice if her hands be white; if not, see if they look as though she had ever done housework, or are milker's hands like mine.'

The boy again promised, inattentively this time, his mother not observing that he was cutting a notch with his pocket-knife in the beech-backed chair.

II

The Young Wife

The road from Anglebury to Holmstoke is in general level, but there is one place where a sharp ascent breaks its monotony. Farmers homeward-bound from the former market-town, who trot all the rest of the way, walk their horses up this short incline.

The next evening while the sun was yet bright a handsome new gig, with a lemon-coloured body and red wheels, was spinning westward along the level highway at the heels of a powerful mare. The driver was a yeoman in the prime of life, cleanly shaven like an actor, his face being toned to that bluish-vermilion hue which so often graces a thriving farmer's features when returning home after successful dealings in the town. Beside him sat a woman, many years his junior – almost, indeed, a girl. Her face too was fresh in colour, but it was of a totally different quality – soft and evanescent, like the light under a heap of rose-petals.

Few people travelled this way, for it was not a main road; and the long white riband of gravel that stretched before them was empty, save of one small scarce-moving speck, which presently resolved itself into the figure of a boy, who was creeping on at a snail's pace, and continually looking behind him – the heavy bundle he carried being some excuse for, if not the reason of, his dilatoriness. When the bouncing gig-party slowed at the bottom of the incline above mentioned, the pedestrian was only a few yards in front. Supporting the large bundle by putting one hand on his hip, he turned and looked straight at the farmer's wife as though he would read her through and through, pacing along abreast of the horse.

The low sun was full in her face, rendering every feature,

shade, and colour distinct, from the curve of her little nostril to the colour of her eyes. The farmer, though he seemed annoyed at the boy's persistent presence, did not order him to get out of the way; and thus the lad preceded them, his hard gaze never leaving her, till they reached the top of the ascent, when the farmer trotted on with relief in his lineaments – having taken no outward notice of the boy whatever.

'How that poor lad stared at me!' said the young wife.

'Yes, dear; I saw that he did.'

'He is one of the village, I suppose?'

'One of the neighbourhood. I think he lives with his mother a mile or two off.'

'He knows who we are, no doubt?'

'O yes. You must expect to be stared at just at first, my pretty Gertrude.'

'I do – though I think the poor boy may have looked at us in the hope we might relieve him of his heavy load, rather than from curiosity.'

'O no,' said her husband off-handedly. 'These country lads will carry a hundredweight once they get it on their backs; besides his pack had more size than weight in it. Now, then, another mile and I shall be able to show you our house in the distance – if it is not too dark before we get there.' The wheels spun round, and particles flew from their periphery as before, till a white house of ample dimensions revealed itself, with farm-buildings and ricks at the back.

Meanwhile the boy had quickened his pace, and turning up a by-lane some mile-and-a-half short of the white farmstead, ascended towards the leaner pastures, and so on to the cottage of his mother.

She had reached home after her day's milking at the outlying dairy, and was washing cabbage at the doorway in the declining light. 'Hold up the net a moment,' she said, without preface, as the boy came up.

He flung down his bundle, held the edge of the cabbage-net, and as she filled its meshes with the dripping leaves she went on, 'Well, did you see her?'

'Yes; quite plain.'

'Is she ladylike?'

'Yes; and more. A lady complete.'

'Is she young?'

'Well, she's growed up, and her ways be quite a woman's.'

'Of course. What colour is her hair and face?'

'Her hair is lightish, and her face as comely as a live doll's.'

'Her eyes, then, are not dark like mine?'

'No – of a bluish turn, and her mouth is very nice and red; and when she smiles, her teeth show white.'

'Is she tall?' said the woman sharply.

'I couldn't see. She was sitting down.'

'Then do you go to Holmstoke church tomorrow morning: she's sure to be there. Go early and notice her walking in, and come home and tell me if she's taller than I.'

'Very well, Mother. But why don't you go and see for yourself?'

'*I* go to see her! I wouldn't look up at her if she were to pass my window this instant. She was with Mr Lodge, of course. What did he say or do?'

'Just the same as usual.'

'Took no notice of you?'

'None.'

Next day the mother put a clean shirt on the boy, and started him off for Holmstoke church. He reached the ancient little pile when the door was just being opened, and he was the first to enter. Taking his seat by the font, he watched all the parishioners file in. The well-to-do Farmer Lodge came nearly last; and his young wife, who accompanied him, walked up the aisle with the shyness natural to a modest woman who had appeared thus for the first time. As all other eyes were fixed upon her, the youth's stare was not noticed now.

When he reached home his mother said, 'Well?' before he had entered the room.

'She is not tall. She is rather short,' he replied.

'Ah!' said his mother, with satisfaction.

'But she's very pretty – very. In fact, she's lovely.' The

youthful freshness of the yeoman's wife had evidently made an impression even on the somewhat hard nature of the boy.

'That's all I want to hear,' said his mother quickly. 'Now, spread the table-cloth. The hare you wired is very tender; but mind nobody catches you. You've never told me what sort of hands she had.'

'I have never seen 'em. She never took off her gloves.'

'What did she wear this morning?'

'A white bonnet and a silver-coloured gownd. It whewed and whistled so loud when it rubbed against the pews that the lady coloured up more than ever for very shame at the noise, and pulled it in to keep it from touching; but when she pushed into her seat, it whewed more than ever. Mr Lodge, he seemed pleased, and his waistcoat stuck out, and his great golden seals hung like a lord's; but she seemed to wish her noisy gownd anywhere but on her.'

'Not she! However, that will do now.'

These descriptions of the newly married couple were continued from time to time by the boy at his mother's request, after any chance encounter he had had with them. But Rhoda Brook, though she might easily have seen young Mrs Lodge for herself by walking a couple of miles, would never attempt an excursion towards the quarter where the farm-house lay. Neither did she, at the daily milking in the dairy-man's yard on Lodge's outlying second farm, ever speak on the subject of the recent marriage. The dairyman, who rented the cows of Lodge, and knew perfectly the tall milk-maid's history, with manly kindness always kept the gossip in the cow-barton from annoying Rhoda. But the atmosphere thereabout was full of the subject the first days of Mrs Lodge's arrival; and fom her boy's description and the casual words of the other milkers, Rhoda Brook could raise a mental image of the unconscious Mrs Lodge that was realistic as a photograph.

III

A Vision

One night, two or three weeks after the bridal return, when the boy had gone to bed, Rhoda sat a long time over the turf ashes that she had raked out in front of her to extinguish them. She contemplated so intently the new wife, as presented to her in her mind's eye over the embers, that she forgot the lapse of time. At last, wearied by her day's work, she too retired.

But the figure which had occupied her so much during this and the previous days was not to be banished at night. For the first time Gertrude Lodge visited the supplanted woman in her dreams. Rhoda Brook dreamed – since her assertion that she really saw, before falling asleep, was not to be believed – that the young wife, in the pale silk dress and white bonnet, but with features shockingly distorted, and wrinkled as by age, was sitting upon her chest as she lay. The pressure of Mrs Lodge's person grew heavier; the blue eyes peered cruelly into her face; and then the figure thrust forward its left hand mockingly, so as to make the wedding-ring it wore glitter in Rhoda's eyes. Maddened mentally, and nearly suffocated by pressure, the sleeper struggled; the incubus, still regarding her, withdrew to the foot of the bed, only, however, to come forward by degrees, resume her seat, and flash her left hand as before.

Gasping for breath, Rhoda, in a last desperate effort, swung out her right hand, seized the confronting spectre by its obtrusive left arm, and whirled it backward to the floor, starting up herself as she did so with a low cry.

'O, merciful heaven!' she cried, sitting on the edge of the bed in a cold sweat; 'that was not a dream – she was here!'

She could feel her antagonist's arm within her grasp even

now – the very flesh and bone of it, as it seemed. She looked on the floor whither she had whirled the spectre, but there was nothing to be seen.

Rhoda Brook slept no more that night, and when she went milking at the next dawn they noticed how pale and haggard she looked. The milk that she drew quivered into the pail; her hand had not calmed even yet, and still retained the feel of the arm. She came home to breakfast as wearily as if it had been supper-time.

'What was that noise in your chimmer, mother, last night?' said her son. 'You fell off the bed, surely?'

'Did you hear anything fall? At what time?'

'Just when the clock struck two.'

She could not explain, and when the meal was done went silently about her household works, the boy assisting her, for he hated going afield on the farms, and she indulged his reluctance. Between eleven and twelve the garden-gate clicked, and she lifted her eyes to the window. At the bottom of the garden, within the gate, stood the woman of her vision. Rhoda seemed transfixed.

'Ah, she said she would come!' exclaimed the boy, also observing her.

'Said so – when? How does she know us?'

'I have seen and spoken to her. I talked to her yesterday.'

'I told you,' said the mother, flushing indignantly, 'never to speak to anybody in that house, or go near the place.'

'I did not speak to her till she spoke to me. And I did not go near the place. I met her in the road.'

'What did you tell her?'

'Nothing. She said, "Are you the poor boy who had to bring the heavy load from market?" And she looked at my boots, and said they would not keep my feet dry if it came on wet, because they were so cracked. I told her I lived with my mother, and we had enough to do to keep ourselves, and that's how it was; and she said then: "I'll come and bring you some better boots, and see your mother." She gives away things to other folks in the meads besides us.'

Mrs Lodge was by this time close to the door – not in her

silk, as Rhoda had dreamt of in the bed-chamber, but in a morning hat, and gown of common light material, which became her better than silk. On her arm she carried a basket.

The impression remaining from the night's experience was still strong. Brook had almost expected to see the wrinkles, the scorn and the cruelty on her visitor's face. She would have escaped an interview, had escape been possible. There was, however, no backdoor to the cottage, and in an instant the boy had lifted the latch to Mrs Lodge's gentle knock.

'I see I have come to the right house,' said she, glancing at the lad, and smiling. 'But I was not sure till you opened the door.'

The figure and action were those of the phantom; but her voice was so indescribably sweet, her glance so winning, her smile so tender, so unlike that of Rhoda's midnight visitant, that the latter could hardly believe the evidence of her senses. She was truly glad that she had not hidden away in sheer aversion, as she had been inclined to do. In her basket Mrs Lodge brought the pair of boots that she had promised to the boy, and other useful articles.

At these proofs of a kindly feeling towards her and hers Rhoda's heart reproached her bitterly. This innocent young thing should have her blessing and not her curse. When she left them a light seemed gone from the dwelling. Two days later she came again to know if the boots fitted; and less than a fortnight after paid Rhoda another call. On this occasion the boy was absent.

'I walk a good deal,' said Mrs Lodge, 'and your house is the nearest outside our own parish. I hope you are well. You don't look quite well.'

Rhoda said she was well enough; and, indeed, though the paler of the two, there was more of the strength that endures in her well-defined features and large frame than in the soft-cheeked young woman before her. The conversation became quite confidential as regarded their powers and weaknesses; and when Mrs Lodge was leaving, Rhoda said, 'I hope you will find this air agree with you, ma'am, and not suffer from the damp of the water-meads.'

The younger one replied that there was not much doubt of it, her general health being usually good. 'Though, now you remind me,' she added, 'I have one little ailment which puzzles me. It is nothing serious, but I cannot make it out.'

She uncovered her left hand and arm; and their outline confronted Rhoda's gaze as the exact original of the limb she had beheld and seized in her dream. Upon the pink round surface of the arm were faint marks of an unhealthy colour, as if produced by a rough grasp. Rhoda's eyes became riveted on the discolorations; she fancied that she discerned in them the shape of her own four fingers.

'How did it happen?' she said mechanically.

'I cannot tell,' replied Mrs Lodge, shaking her head. 'One night when I was sound asleep, dreaming I was away in some strange place, a pain suddenly shot into my arm there, and was so keen as to awaken me. I must have struck it in the daytime, I suppose, though I don't remember doing so.' She added, laughing, 'I tell my dear husband that it looks just as if he had flown into a rage and struck me there. O, I daresay it will soon disappear.'

'Ha, ha! Yes . . . On what night did it come?'

Mrs Lodge considered, and said it would be a fortnight ago on the morrow. 'When I awoke I could not remember where I was,' she added, 'till the clock striking two reminded me.'

She had named the night and hour of Rhoda's spectral encounter, and Brook felt like a guilty thing. The artless disclosure startled her; she did not reason on the freaks of coincidence; and all the scenery of that ghastly night returned with double vividness to her mind.

'O, can it be,' she said to herself, when her visitor had departed, 'that I exercise a malignant power over people against my own will?' She knew that she had been slyly called a witch since her fall; but never having understood why that particular stigma had been attached to her, it had passed disregarded. Could this be the explanation, and had such things as this ever happened before?

IV

A Suggestion

The summer drew on, and Rhoda Brook almost dreaded to meet Mrs Lodge again, notwithstanding that her feeling for the young wife amounted well-nigh to affection. Something in her own individuality seemed to convict Rhoda of crime. Yet a fatality sometimes would direct the steps of the latter to the outskirts of Holmstoke whenever she left her house for any other purpose than her daily work; and hence it happened that their next encounter was out of doors. Rhoda could not avoid the subject which had so mystified her, and after the first few words she stammered, 'I hope your – arm is well again, ma'm?' She had perceived with consternation that Gertrude Lodge carried her left arm stiffly.

'No; it not quite well. Indeed it is no better at all; it is rather worse. It pains me dreadfully sometimes.'

'Perhaps you had better go to a doctor, ma'am.'

She replied that she had already seen a doctor. Her husband had insisted upon her going to one. But the surgeon had not seemed to understand the afflicted limb at all; he had told her to bathe it in hot water, and she had bathed it, but the treatment had done no good.

'Will you let me see it?' said the milkwoman.

Mrs Lodge pushed up her sleeve and disclosed the place, which was a few inches above the wrist. As soon as Rhoda Brook saw it, she could hardly preserve her composure. There was nothing of the nature of a wound, but the arm at that point had a shrivelled look, and the outline of the four fingers appeared more distinct than at the former time. Moreover, she fancied that they were imprinted in precisely the relative position of her clutch upon the arm in the trance;

the first finger towards Gertrude's wrist, and the fourth towards her elbow.

What the impress resembled seemed to have struck Gertrude herself since their last meeting. 'It looks almost like finger-marks,' she said; adding with a faint laugh, 'my husband says it is as if some witch, or the devil himself, had taken hold of me there, and blasted the flesh.'

Rhoda shivered. 'That's fancy,' she said hurriedly. 'I wouldn't mind it, if I were you.'

'I shouldn't so much mind it,' said the younger, with hesitation, 'if – if I hadn't a notion that it makes my husband – dislike me – no, love me less. Men think so much of personal appearance.'

'Some do – he for one.'

'Yes; and he was very proud of mine, at first.'

'Keep your arm covered from his sight.'

'Ah – he knows the disfigurement is there!' She tried to hide the tears that filled her eyes.

'Well, ma'am, I earnestly hope it will go away soon.'

And so the milkwoman's mind was chained anew to the subject by a horrid sort of spell as she returned home. The sense of having been guilty of an act of malignity increased, affect as she might to ridicule her superstition. In her secret heart Rhoda did not altogether object to a slight diminution of her successor's beauty, by whatever means it had come about; but she did not wish to inflict upon her physical pain. For though this pretty young woman had rendered impossible any reparation which Lodge might have made Rhoda for his past conduct, everything like resentment at the unconscious usurpation had quite passed away from the elder's mind.

If the sweet and kindly Gertrude Lodge only knew of the dream-scene in the bed-chamber, what would she think? Not to inform her of it seemed treachery in the presence of her friendliness; but tell she could not of her own accord – neither could she devise a remedy.

She mused upon the matter the greater part of the night; and the next day, after the morning milking, set out to obtain another glimpse of Gertrude Lodge if she could, being held to her by a gruesome fascination. By watching the house from a distance the milkmaid was presently able to discern the farmer's wife in a ride she was taking alone – probably to join her husband in some distant field. Mrs Lodge perceived her, and cantered in her direction.

'Good morning, Rhoda!' Gertrude said, when she had come up. 'I was going to call.'

Rhoda noticed that Mrs Lodge held the reins with some difficulty.

'I hope – the bad arm,' said Rhoda.

'They tell me there is possibly one way by which I might be able to find out the cause, and so perhaps the cure of it,' replied the other anxiously. 'It is by going to some clever man over in Egdon Heath. They did not know if he was still alive – and I cannot remember his name at this moment; but they said that you knew more of his movements than anybody else hereabout, and could tell me if he were still to be consulted. Dear me – what was his name? But you know.'

'Not Conjuror Trendle?' said her thin companion, turning pale.

'Trendle – yes. Is he alive?'

'I believe so,' said Rhoda, with reluctance.

'Why do you call him conjuror?'

'Well – they say – they used to say he was a – he had powers other folks have not.'

'O, how could my people be so superstitious as to recommend a man of that sort! I thought they meant some medical man. I shall think no more of him.'

Rhoda looked relieved, and Mrs Lodge rode on. The milkwoman had inwardly seen, from the moment she heard of her having been mentioned as a reference for this man, that there must exist a sarcastic feeling among the workfolk that a sorceress would know the whereabouts of the exorcist. They suspected her, then. A short time ago this would have given no concern to a woman of her common sense. But she had a haunting reason to be superstitious now;

and she had been seized with sudden dread that this Conjuror Trendle might name her as the malignant influence which was blasting the fair person of Gertrude, and so lead her friend to hate her for ever, and to treat her as some fiend in human shape.

But all was not over. Two days after, a shadow intruded into the window-pattern thrown on Rhoda Brook's floor by the afternoon sun. The woman opened the door at once, almost breathlessly.

'Are you alone?' said Gertrude. She seemed to be no less harassed and anxious than Brook herself.

'Yes,' said Rhoda.

'The place on my arm seems worse, and troubles me!' the young farmer's wife went on. 'It is so mysterious! I do hope it will not be an incurable wound. I have again been thinking of what they said about Conjuror Trendle. I don't really believe in such men, but I should not mind just visiting him, from curiosity – though on no account must my husband know. Is it far to where he lives?'

'Yes – five miles,' said Rhoda backwardly. 'In the heart of Egdon.'

'Well, I should have to walk. Could not you go with me to show me the way – say tomorrow afternoon?'

'O, not I; that is—,' the milkwoman murmured, with a start of dismay. Again the dread seized her that something to do with her fierce act in the dream might be revealed, and her character in the eyes of the most useful friend she had ever had be ruined irretrievably.

Mrs Lodge urged, and Rhoda finally assented, though with much misgiving. Sad as the journey would be to her, she could not conscientiously stand in the way of a possible remedy for her patron's strange affliction. It was agreed that, to escape suspicion of their mystic intent, they should meet at the edge of the heath at the corner of a plantation which was visible from the spot where they now stood.

V

Conjuror Trendle

By the next afternoon Rhoda would have done anything to escape this inquiry. But she had promised to go. Moreover, there was a horrid fascination at times in becoming instrumental in throwing such possible light on her own character as would reveal her to be something greater in the occult world than she had ever herself suspected.

She started just before the time of day mentioned between them, and half an hour's brisk walking brought her to the south-eastern extension of the Egdon tract of country, where the fir plantation was. A slight figure, cloaked and veiled, was already there. Rhoda recognized, almost with a shudder, that Mrs Lodge bore her left arm in a sling.

They hardly spoke to each other, and immediately set out on their climb into the interior of this solemn country, which stood high above the rich alluvial soil they had left half an hour before. It was a long walk; thick clouds made the atmosphere dark, though it was as yet only early afternoon; and the wind howled dismally over the slopes of the heath – not improbably the same heath which had witnessed the agony of the Wessex King Ina, presented to after-ages as Lear. Gertrude Lodge talked most, Rhoda replying with monosyllabic preoccupation. She had a strange dislike to walking on the side of her companion where hung the afflicted arm, moving round to the other when inadvertently near it. Much heather had been brushed by their feet when they descended upon a cart-track, beside which stood the house of the man they sought.

He did not profess his remedial practices openly, or care anything about their continuance, his direct interests being those of a dealer in furze, turf, 'sharp sand', and other local products. Indeed, he affected not to believe largely in his own powers, and when warts that had been shown him for cure miraculously disappeared – which it must be owned they infallibly did – he would say lightly, 'O, I only drink a glass of grog upon 'em at your expense – perhaps it's all chance', and immediately turn the subject.

He was at home when they arrived, having in fact seen them descending into his valley. He was a grey-bearded man, with a reddish face, and he looked singularly at Rhoda the first moment he beheld her. Mrs Lodge told him her errand; and then with words of self-disparagement he examined her arm.

'Medicine can't cure it,' he said promptly. ' 'Tis the work of an enemy.'

Rhoda shrank into herself, and drew back.

'An enemy? What enemy?' asked Mrs Lodge.

He shook his head. 'That's best known to yourself,' he said. 'If you like, I can show the person to you, though I shall not myself know who it is. I can do no more; and don't wish to do that.'

She pressed him; on which he told Rhoda to wait outside where she stood, and took Mrs Lodge into the room. It opened immediately from the door; and, as the latter remained ajar, Rhoda Brook could see the proceedings without taking part in them. He brought a tumbler from the dresser, nearly filled it with water, and fetching an egg, prepared it in some private way; after which he broke it on the edge of the glass, so that the white went in and the yolk remained. As it was getting gloomy, he took the glass and its contents to the window, and told Gertrude to watch the mixture closely. They leant over the table together, and the milkwoman could see the opaline hue of the egg-fluid changing form as it sank in the water, but she was not near enough to define the shape that it assumed.

'Do you catch the likeness of any face or figure as you look?' demanded the conjuror of the young woman.

She murmured a reply, in tones so low as to be inaudible

to Rhoda, and continued to gaze intently into the glass.
Rhoda turned, and walked a few steps away.

When Mrs Lodge came out, and her face was met by the
light, it appeared exceedingly pale – as pale as Rhoda's –
against the sad dun shades of the upland's garniture. Trendle
shut the door behind her, and they at once started homeward together. But Rhoda perceived that her companion
had quite changed.

'Did he charge much?' she asked tentatively.

'O no – nothing. He would not take a farthing,' said Gertrude.

'And what did you see?' inquired Rhoda.

'Nothing I – care to speak of.' The constraint in her manner was remarkable; her face was so rigid as to wear an
oldened aspect, faintly suggestive of the face in Rhoda's
bed-chamber.

'Was it you who first proposed coming here?' Mrs Lodge
suddenly inquired, after a long pause. 'How very odd, if you
did!'

'No. But I am not very sorry we have come, all things
considered,' she replied. For the first time a sense of triumph
possessed her, and she did not altogether deplore that the
young thing at her side should learn that their lives had been
antagonized by other influences than their own.

The subject was no more alluded to during the long and
dreary walk home. But in some way or other a story was
whispered about the many-dairied lowland that winter that
Mrs Lodge's gradual loss of the use of her left arm was
owing to her being 'overlooked' by Rhoda Brook. The latter
kept her own counsel about the incubus, but her face grew
sadder and thinner; and in the spring she and her boy disappeared from the neighbourhood of Holmstoke.

VI

A Second Attempt

Half a dozen years passed away, and Mr and Mrs Lodge's married experience sank into prosiness, and worse. The farmer was usually gloomy and silent: the woman whom he had wooed for her grace and beauty was contorted and disfigured in the left limb; moreover, she had brought him no child, which rendered it likely that he would be the last of a family who had occupied that valley for some two hundred years. He thought of Rhoda Brook and her son; and feared this might be a judgement from heaven upon him.

The once blithe-hearted and enlightened Gertrude was changing into an irritable, superstitious woman, whose whole time was given to experimenting upon her ailment with every quack remedy she came across. She was honestly attached to her husband, and was ever secretly hoping against hope to win back his heart again by regaining some at least of her personal beauty. Hence it arose that her closet was lined with bottles, packets, and ointment-pots of every description – nay, bunches of mystic herbs, charms, and books of necromancy, which in her schoolgirl time she would have ridiculed as folly.

'Damned if you won't poison yourself with these apothecary messes and witch mixtures some time or other,' said her husband, when his eye chanced to fall upon the multitudinous array.

She did not reply, but turned her sad, soft glance upon him in such heart-swollen reproach that he looked sorry for his words, and added, 'I only meant it for your good, you know, Gertrude.'

'I'll clear out the whole lot, and destroy them,' said she huskily, 'and try such remedies no more!'

'You want somebody to cheer you,' he observed. 'I once thought of adopting a boy; but he is too old now. And he is gone away I don't know where.'

She guessed to whom he alluded; for Rhoda Brook's story had in the course of years become known to her; though not a word had ever passed between her husband and herself on the subject. Neither had she ever spoken to him of her visit to Conjuror Trendle, and of what was revealed to her, or she thought was revealed to her, by that solitary heathman.

She was now five-and-twenty; but she seemed older. 'Six years of marriage, and only a few months of love,' she sometimes whispered to herself. And then she thought of the apparent cause, and said, with a tragic glance at her withering limb, 'If I could only be again as I was when he first saw me!'

She obediently destroyed her nostrums and charms; but there remained a hankering wish to try something else – some other sort of cure altogether. She had never revisited Trendle since she had been conducted to the house of the solitary by Rhoda against her will; but it now suddenly occurred to Gertrude that she would, in a last desperate effort at deliverance from this seeming curse, again seek out the man, if he yet lived. He was entitled to a certain credence, for the indistinct form he had raised in the glass had undoubtedly resembled the only woman in the world who – as she now knew, though not then – could have a reason for bearing her ill-will. The visit should be paid.

This time she went alone, though she nearly got lost on the heath, and roamed a considerable distance out of her way. Trendle's house was reached at last, however: he was not indoors, and instead of waiting at the cottage, she went to where his bent figure was pointed out to her at work a long way off. Trendle remembered her, and laying down the handful of furze-roots which he was gathering and throwing into a heap, he offered to accompany her in the homeward direction, as the distance was considerable and the days were short. So they walked together, his head bowed nearly to the earth, and his form of a colour with it.

'You can send away warts and other excrescences, I know,' she said; 'why can't you send away this?' And the arm was uncovered.

'You think too much of my powers!' said Trendle; 'and I am old and weak now, too. No, no; it is too much for me to attempt in my own person. What have ye tried?'

She named to him some of the hundred medicaments and counterspells which she had adopted from time to time. He shook his head.

'Some were good enough,' he said approvingly; 'but not many of them for such as this. This is of the nature of a blight, not of the nature of a wound; and if you ever do throw it off, it will be all at once.'

'If I only could!'

'There is only one chance of doing it known to me. It has never failed in kindred afflictions – that I can declare. But it is hard to carry out, and especially for a woman.'

'Tell me!' said she.

'You must touch with the limb the neck of a man who's been hanged.'

She started a little at the image he had raised.

'Before he's cold – just after he's cut down,' continued the conjuror impassively.

'How can that do good?'

'It will turn the blood and change the constitution. But, as I say, to do it is hard. You must go to the jail when there's a hanging, and wait for him when he's brought off the gallows. Lots have done it, though perhaps not such pretty women as you. I used to send dozens for skin complaints. But that was in former times. The last I sent was in '13 – near twelve years ago.'

He had no more to tell her; and, when he had put her into a straight track homeward, turned and left her, refusing all money as at first.

VII

A Ride

The communication sank deep into Gertrude's mind. Her nature was rather a timid one; and probably of all remedies that the white wizard could have suggested there was not one which would have filled her with so much aversion as this, not to speak of the immense obstacles in the way of its adoption.

Casterbridge, the county-town, was a dozen or fifteen miles off; and though in those days, when men were executed for horse-stealing, arson, and burglary, an assize seldom passed without a hanging, it was not likely that she could get access to the body of the criminal unaided. And the fear of her husband's anger made her reluctant to breathe a word of Trendle's suggestion to him or to anybody about him.

She did nothing for months, and patiently bore her disfigurement as before. But her woman's nature, craving for renewed love, through the medium of renewed beauty (she was but twenty-five), was ever stimulating her to try what, at any rate, could hardly do her any harm. 'What came by a spell will go by a spell surely,' she would say. Whenever her imagination pictured the act she shrank in terror from the possibility of it : then the words of the conjuror, 'It will turn your blood', were seen to be capable of a scientific no less than ghastly interpretation; the mastering desire returned, and urged her on again.

There was at this time but one county paper, and that her husband only occasionally borrowed. But old-fashioned days had old-fashioned means, and news was extensively conveyed by word of mouth from market to market, or from fair to fair, so that, whenever such an event as an execution was about to take place, few within a radius of twenty miles were ignorant of the coming sight; and, so far as Holmstoke was concerned, some enthusiasts had been known to walk all the way to Casterbridge and back in one day, solely to witness the spectacle. The next assizes were in March; and when Gertrude Lodge heard that they had been held, she inquired stealthily at the inn as to the result, as soon as she could find opportunity.

She was, however, too late. The time at which the sentences were to be carried out had arrived, and to make the journey and obtain permission at such short notice required at least her husband's assistance. She dared not tell him, for she had found by delicate experiment that these smouldering village beliefs made him furious if mentioned, partly because he half entertained them himself. It was therefore necessary to wait for another opportunity.

Her determination received a fillip from learning that two epileptic children had attended from this very village of Holmstoke many years before with beneficial results, though the experiment had been strongly condemned by the neighbouring clergy. April, May, June, passed; and it is no overstatement to say that by the end of the last-named month Gertrude well-nigh longed for the death of a fellow-creature. Instead of her formal prayers each night, her unconscious prayer was, 'O Lord, hang some guilty or innocent person soon!'

This time she made earlier inquiries, and was altogether more systematic in her proceedings. Moreover the season was summer, between the haymaking and the harvest, and in the leisure thus afforded him her husband had been holiday-taking away from home.

The assizes were in July, and she went to the inn as before. There was to be one execution – only one – for arson.

Her greatest problem was not how to get to Casterbridge, but what means she should adopt for obtaining admission to the jail. Though access for such purposes had formerly never been denied, the custom had fallen into desuetude; and in contemplating her possible difficulties, she was again almost driven to fall back upon her husband. But, on sounding him about the assizes, he was so uncommunicative, so more than usually cold, that she did not proceed, and decided that whatever she did she would do alone.

Fortune, obdurate hitherto, showed her unexpected favour. On the Thursday before the Saturday fixed for the execution, Lodge remarked to her that he was going away from home for another day or two on business at a fair, and that he was sorry he could not take her with him.

She exhibited on this occasion so much readiness to stay at home that he looked at her in surprise. Time had been when she would have shown deep disappointment at the loss of such a jaunt. However, he lapsed into his usual taciturnity, and on the day named left Holmstoke.

It was now her turn. She at first had thought of driving, but on reflection held that driving would not do, since it would necessitate her keeping to the turnpike-road, and so increase by tenfold the risk of her ghastly errand being found out. She decided to ride, and avoid the beaten track, notwithstanding that in her husband's stables there was no animal just at present which by any stretch of imagination could be considered a lady's mount, in spite of his promise before marriage to always keep a mare for her. He had, however, many cart-horses, fine ones of their kind; and among the rest was a serviceable creature, an equine Amazon, with a back as broad as a sofa, on which Gertrude had occasionally taken an airing when unwell. This horse she chose.

On Friday afternoon one of the men brought it round. She was dressed, and before going down looked at her shrivelled arm. 'Ah!' she said to it, 'if it had not been for you this terrible ordeal would have been saved me!'

When strapping up the bundle in which she carried a few articles of clothing, she took occasion to say to the servant, 'I take these in case I should not get back tonight from the person I am going to visit. Don't be alarmed if I am not in by ten, and close up the house as usual. I shall be home tomorrow for certain.' She meant then to tell her husband privately: the deed accomplished was not like the deed projected. He would almost certainly forgive her.

And then the pretty palpitating Gertrude Lodge went from her husband's homestead; but though her goal was Casterbridge she did not take the direct route thither through Stickleford. Her cunning course at first was in precisely the opposite direction. As soon as she was out of sight, however, she turned to the left, by a road which led into Egdon, and on entering the heath wheeled round, and set out in the true course, due westerly. A more private way down the county could not be imagined; and as to direction, she had merely to keep her horse's head to a point a little to the right of the sun. She knew that she would light upon a furze-cutter or cottager of some sort from time to time, from whom she might correct her bearing.

Though the date was comparatively recent, Egdon was much less fragmentary in character than now. The attempts – successful and otherwise – at cultivation on the lower slopes, which intrude and break up the original heath into small detached heaths, had not been carried far; Enclosure Acts had not taken effect, and the banks and fences which now exclude the cattle of those villagers who formerly enjoyed rights of commonage thereon, and the carts of those who had turbary privileges which kept them in firing all the year round, were not erected. Gertrude, therefore, rode along with no other obstacles than the prickly furze-bushes, the mats of heather, the white water-courses, and the natural steeps and declivities of the ground.

Her horse was sure, if heavy-footed and slow, and though a draught animal, was easy-paced; had it been otherwise, she was not a woman who could have ventured to ride over such a bit of country with a half-dead arm. It was therefore nearly eight o'clock when she drew rein to breathe her bearer on the last outlying high point of heath-land towards Casterbridge, previous to leaving Egdon for the cultivated valleys.

She halted before a pool called Rushy-pond, flanked by the ends of two hedges; a railing ran through the centre of the pond, dividing it in half. Over the railing she saw the low green country; over the green trees the roofs of the town; over the roofs a white flat façade, denoting the entrance to the county jail. On the roof of this front specks were moving about; they seemed to be workmen erecting something. Her flesh crept. She descended slowly, and was soon amid corn-fields and pastures. In another half-hour, when it was almost dusk, Gertrude reached the White Hart, the first inn of the town on that side.

Little surprise was excited by her arrival; farmers' wives rode on horseback then more than they do now; though, for that matter, Mrs Lodge was not imagined to be a wife at all; the innkeeper supposed her some harum-skarum young woman who had come to attend 'hang-fair' next day. Neither her husband nor herself ever dealt in Casterbridge market, so that she was unknown. While dismounting she beheld a crowd of boys standing at the door of a harness-maker's shop just above the inn, looking inside it with deep interest.

'What is going on there?' she asked of the ostler.

'Making the rope for tomorrow.'

She throbbed responsively, and contracted her arm.

' 'Tis sold by the inch afterwards,' the man continued. 'I could get you a bit, miss, for nothing, if you'd like?'

She hastily repudiated any such wish, all the more from a curious creeping feeling that the condemned wretch's destiny was becoming interwoven with her own; and having engaged a room for the night, sat down to think.

Up to this time she had formed but the vaguest notions about her means of obtaining access to the prison. The words of the cunning-man returned to her mind. He had implied that she should use her beauty, impaired though it was, as a pass-key. In her inexperience she knew little about jail functionaries; she had heard of a high-sheriff and an under-sheriff, but dimly only. She knew, however, that there must be a hangman, and to the hangman she determined to apply.

VIII

A Water-side Hermit

A T this date, and for several years after, there was a hangman to almost every jail. Gertrude found, on inquiry, that the Casterbridge official dwelt in a lonely cottage by a deep slow river flowing under the cliff on which the prison buildings were situate – the stream being the self-same one, though she did not know it, which watered the Stickleford and Holmstoke meads lower down in its course.

Having changed her dress, and before she had eaten or drunk – for she could not take her ease till she had ascertained some particulars – Gertrude pursued her way by a path along the water-side to the cottage indicated. Passing thus the outskirts of the jail, she discerned on the level roof over the gateway three rectangular lines against the sky, where the specks had been moving in her distant view; she recognized what the erection was, and passed quickly on. Another hundred yards brought her to the executioner's house, which a boy pointed out. It stood close to the same stream, and was hard by a weir, the waters of which emitted a steady roar.

While she stood hesitating the door opened, and an old man came forth shading a candle with one hand. Locking the door on the outside, he turned to a flight of wooden steps fixed against the end of the cottage, and began to ascend them, this being evidently the staircase to his bedroom. Gertrude hastened forward, but by the time she reached the foot of the ladder he was at the top. She called to him loudly enough to be heard above the roar of the weir; he looked down and said, 'What d'ye want here?'

'To speak to you a minute.'

The candle-light, such as it was, fell upon her imploring,

pale, upturned face, and Davies (as the hangman was called) backed down the ladder. 'I was just going to bed,' he said; ' "Early to bed and early to rise", but I don't mind stopping a minute for such a one as you. Come into house.' He re-opened the door, and preceded her to the room within.

The implements of his daily work, which was that of a jobbing gardener, stood in a corner, and seeing probably that she looked rural, he said, 'If you want me to undertake country work I can't come, for I never leave Casterbridge for gentle nor simple – not I. My real calling is officer of justice,' he added formally.

'Yes, yes! That's it. Tomorrow!'

'Ah! I thought so. Well, what's the matter about that? 'Tis no use to come here about the knot – folks do come continually, but I tell 'em one knot is as merciful as another if ye keep it under the ear. Is the unfortunate man a relation; or, I should say, perhaps' (looking at her dress) 'a person who's been in your employ?'

'No. What time is the execution?'

'The same as usual – twelve o'clock, or as soon after as the London mail-coach gets in. We always wait for that, in case of a reprieve.'

'O – a reprieve – I hope not!' she said involuntarily.

'Well, – hee, hee! – as a matter of business, so do I! But still, if ever a young fellow deserved to be let off, this one does; only just turned eighteen, and only present by chance when the rick was fired. Howsomever, there's not much risk of that, as they are obliged to make an example of him, there having been so much destruction of property that way lately.'

'I mean,' she explained, 'that I want to touch him for a charm, a cure of an affliction, by the advice of a man who has proved the virtue of the remedy.'

'O yes, miss! Now I understand. I've had such people come in past years. But it didn't strike me that you looked of a sort to require blood-turning. What's the complaint? The wrong kind for this, I'll be bound.'

'My arm.' She reluctantly showed the withered skin.

'Ah! – 'tis all a-scram!' said the hangman, examining it.

'Yes,' said she.

'Well,' he continued, with interest, 'that *is* the class o' subject, I'm bound to admit! I like the look of the wownd; it is truly as suitable for the cure as any I ever saw. 'Twas a knowing-man that sent 'ee, whoever he was.'

'You can contrive for me all that's necessary?' she said breathlessly.

'You should really have gone to the governor of the jail, and your doctor with 'ee, and given your name and address – that's how it used to be done, if I recollect. Still, perhaps, I can manage it for a trifling fee.'

'O, thank you! I would rather do it this way, as I should like it kept private.'

'Lover not to know, eh?'

'No – husband.'

'Aha! Very well. I'll get 'ee a touch of the corpse.'

'Where is it now?' she said, shuddering.

'It? – *he*, you mean; he's living yet. Just inside that little small winder up there in the glum.' He signified the jail on the cliff above.

She thought of her husband and her friends. 'Yes, of course,' she said; 'and how am I to proceed?'

He took her to the door. 'Now, do you be waiting at the little wicket in the wall, that you'll find up there in the lane, not later than one o'clock. I will open it from the inside, as I shan't come home to dinner till he's cut down. Goodnight. Be punctual; and if you don't want anybody to know 'ee, wear a veil. Ah – once I had such a daughter as you!'

She went away, and climbed the path above, to assure herself that she would be able to find the wicket next day. Its outline was soon visible to her – a narrow opening in the outer wall of the prison precincts. The steep was so great that, having reached the wicket, she stopped a moment to breathe; and, looking back upon the water-side cot, saw the hangman again ascending his outdoor staircase. He entered the loft or chamber to which it led, and in a few minutes extinguished his light.

The town clock struck ten, and she returned to the White Hart as she had come.

IX

A Rencounter

IT was one o'clock on Saturday. Gertrude Lodge, having been admitted to the jail as above described, was sitting in a waiting-room within the second gate, which stood under a classic archway of ashlar, then comparatively modern, and bearing the inscription, 'COVNTY JAIL : 1793.' This had been the façade she saw from the heath the day before. Near at hand was a passage to the roof on which the gallows stood.

The town was thronged, and the market suspended; but Gertrude had seen scarcely a soul. Having kept her room till the hour of the appointment, she had proceeded to the spot by a way which avoided the open space below the cliff where the spectators had gathered; but she could, even now, hear the multitudinous babble of their voices, out of which rose at intervals the hoarse croak of a single voice uttering the words, 'Last dying speech and confession!' There had been no reprieve, and the execution was over; but the crowd still waited to see the body taken down.

Soon the persistent woman heard a trampling overhead, then a hand beckoned to her, and, following directions, she went out and crossed the inner paved court beyond the gate-house, her knees trembling so that she could scarcely walk. One of her arms was out of its sleeve, and only covered by her shawl.

On the spot at which she had now arrived were two trestles, and before she could think of their purpose she heard heavy feet descending stairs somewhere at her back. Turn her head she would not, or could not, and, rigid in this position, she was conscious of a rough coffin passing her shoulder, borne by four men. It was open, and in it lay the body of a young man, wearing the smockfrock of a rustic, and fustian breeches. The corpse had been thrown into the coffin so hastily that the skirt of the smockfrock was hanging over. The burden was temporarily deposited on the trestles.

By this time the young woman's state was such that a grey mist seemed to float before her eyes, on account of which, and the veil she wore, she could scarcely discern anything: it was as though she had nearly died, but was held up by a sort of galvanism.

'Now!' said a voice close at hand, and she was just conscious that the word had been addressed to her.

By a last strenuous effort she advanced, at the same time hearing persons approaching behind her. She bared her poor curst arm; and Davies, uncovering the face of the corpse, took Gertrude's hand, and held it so that her arm lay across the dead man's neck, upon a line the colour of an unripe blackberry, which surrounded it.

Gertrude shrieked: 'the turn o' the blood', predicted by the conjuror, had taken place. But at that moment a second shriek rent the air of the enclosure: it was not Gertrude's, and its effect upon her was to make her start round.

Immediately behind her stood Rhoda Brook, her face drawn, and her eyes red with weeping. Behind Rhoda stood Gertrude's own husband; his countenance lined, his eyes dim, but without a tear.

'D—n you! what are you doing here?' he said hoarsely.

'Hussy – to come between us and our child now!' cried Rhoda. 'This is the meaning of what Satan showed me in the vision! You are like her at last!' And clutching the bare arm of the younger woman, she pulled her unresistingly back against the wall. Immediately Brook had loosened her hold the fragile young Gertrude slid down against the feet of her husband. When he lifted her up she was unconscious.

The mere sight of the twain had been enough to suggest to her that the dead young man was Rhoda's son. At that time the relatives of an executed convict had the privilege of claiming the body for burial, if they chose to do so; and it was for this purpose that Lodge was awaiting the inquest with Rhoda. He had been summoned by her as soon as the young man was taken in the crime, and at different times since; and he had attended in court during the trial. This was the 'holiday' he had been indulging in of late. The two wretched parents had wished to avoid exposure; and hence had come themselves for the body, a wagon and sheet for its conveyance and covering being in waiting outside.

Gertrude's case was so serious that it was deemed advisable to call to her the surgeon who was at hand. She was taken out of the jail into the town; but she never reached home alive. Her delicate vitality, sapped perhaps by the paralysed arm, collapsed under the double shock that followed the severe strain, physical and mental, to which she had subjected herself during the previous twenty-four hours. Her blood had been 'turned' indeed – too far. Her death took place in the town three days after.

Her husband was never seen in Casterbridge again; once only in the old market-place at Anglebury, which he had so much frequented, and very seldom in public anywhere. Burdened at first with moodiness and remorse, he eventually changed for the better, and appeared as a chastened and thoughtful man. Soon after attending the funeral of his poor wife he took steps towards giving up the farms in Holmstoke and the adjoining parish, and, having sold every head of his stock, he went away to Port-Bredy, at the other end of the county, living there in solitary lodgings till his death two years later of a painless decline. It was then found that he had bequeathed the whole of his not inconsiderable property to a reformatory for boys, subject to the payment of a small annuity to Rhoda Brook, if she could be found to claim it.

For some time she could not be found; but eventually she reappeared in her old parish – absolutely refusing, however, to have anything to do with the provision made for her. Her monotonous milking at the dairy was resumed, and followed for many long years, till her form became bent, and her once abundant dark hair white and worn away at the forehead – perhaps by long pressure against the cows. Here, sometimes, those who knew her experiences would stand and observe her, and wonder what sombre thoughts were beating inside that impassive, wrinkled brow, to the rhythm of the alternating milk-streams.

Blackwood's Magazine, January 1888

Fellow-Townsmen

I

THE shepherd on the east hill could shout out lambing intelligence to the shepherd on the west hill, over the intervening town chimneys, without great inconvenience to his voice, so nearly did the steep pastures encroach upon the burghers' backyards. And at night it was possible to stand in the very midst of the town and hear from their native paddocks on the lower levels of greensward the mild lowing of the farmer's heifers, and the profound, warm blowings of breath in which those creatures indulge. But the community which had jammed itself in the valley thus flanked formed a veritable town, with a real mayor and corporation, and a staple manufacture.

During a certain damp evening five-and-thirty years ago, before the twilight was far advanced, a pedestrian of professional appearance, carrying a small bag in his hand and an elevated umbrella, was descending one of these hills by the turnpike road when he was overtaken by a phaeton.

'Hullo, Downe – is that you?' said the driver of the vehicle, a young man of pale and refined appearance. 'Jump up here with me, and ride down to your door.'

The other turned a plump, cheery, rather self-indulgent face over his shoulder towards the hailer.

'O, good evening, Mr Barnet – thanks,' he said, and mounted beside his acquaintance.

They were fellow-burgesses of the town which lay beneath them, but though old and very good friends they were differently circumstanced. Barnet was a richer man than the struggling young lawyer Downe, a fact which was to some extent perceptible in Downe's manner towards his companion, though nothing of it ever showed in Barnet's manner towards the solicitor. Barnet's position in the town was none of his own making; his father had been a very successful flax-merchant in the same place, where the trade was still carried on as briskly as the small capacities of its quarters would allow. Having acquired a fair fortune, old Mr Barnet had retired from business, bringing up his son as a gentleman-burgher, and, it must be added, as a well-educated, liberal-minded young man.

'How is Mrs Barnet?' asked Downe.

'Mrs Barnet was very well when I left home,' the other answered constrainedly, exchanging his meditative regard of the horse for one of self-consciousness.

Mr Downe seemed to regret his inquiry, and immediately took up another thread of conversation. He congratulated his friend on his election as a councilman; he thought he had not seen him since that event took place; Mrs Downe had meant to call and congratulate Mrs Barnet, but he feared that she had failed to do so as yet.

Barnet seemed hampered in his replies. 'We should have been glad to see you. I – my wife would welcome Mrs Downe at any time, as you know ... Yes, I am a member of the corporation – rather an inexperienced member, some of them say. It is quite true; and I should have declined the honour as premature – having other things on my hands just now, too – if it had not been pressed upon me so very heartily.'

'There is one thing you have on your hands which I can never quite see the necessity for,' said Downe, with good-humoured freedom. 'What the deuce do you want to build that new mansion for, when you have already got such an excellent house as the one you live in?'

Barnet's face acquired a warmer shade of colour; but as the question had been idly asked by the solicitor while regarding the surrounding flocks and fields, he answered after a moment with no apparent embarrassment:

'Well, we wanted to get out of the town, you know; the house I am living in is rather old and inconvenient.'

Mr Downe declared that he had chosen a pretty site for the new building. They would be able to see for miles and miles from the windows. Was he going to give it a name? He supposed so.

Barnet thought not. There was no other house near that was likely to be mistaken for it. And he did not care for a name.

'But I think it has a name!' Downe observed: 'I went past – when was it? – this morning; and I saw something – "Château Ringdale", I think it was, stuck up on a board!'

'It was an idea she – we had for a short time,' said Barnet hastily. 'But we have decided finally to do without a name – at any rate such a name as that. It must have been a week ago that you saw it. It was taken down last Saturday ... Upon that matter I am firm!' he added grimly.

Downe murmured in an unconvinced tone that he thought he had seen it yesterday.

Talking thus, they drove into the town. The street was unusually still for the hour of seven in the evening; an increasing drizzle from the sea had prevailed since the afternoon, and now formed a gauze across the yellow lamps, and trickled with a gentle rattle down the heavy roofs of stone tile, that bent the house-ridges hollow-backed with its weight, and in some instances caused the walls to bulge outwards in the upper storey. Their route took them past the little town hall, the Black Bull Hotel, and onward to the junction of a small street on the right, consisting of a row of those two-and-two windowed brick residences of no particular age, which are exactly alike wherever found, except in the people they contain.

'Wait – I'll drive you up to your door,' said Barnet, when Downe prepared to alight at the corner. He thereupon turned into the narrow street, when the faces of three little girls could be discerned close to the panes of a lighted window a few yards ahead, surmounted by that of a young matron, the gaze of all four being directed eagerly up the empty street. 'You are a fortunate fellow, Downe,' Barnet continued, as mother and children disappeared from the window to run to the door. 'You must be happy if any man is. I would give a hundred such houses as my new one to have a home like yours.'

'Well – yes, we get along pretty comfortably,' replied Downe complacently.

'That house, Downe, is none of my ordering,' Barnet broke out, revealing a bitterness hitherto suppressed, and checking the horse a moment to finish his speech before delivering up his passenger. 'The house I have already is good enough for me, as you supposed. It is my own freehold; it was built by my grandfather, and is stout enough for a castle. My father was born there, lived there, and died there. I was born there, and have always lived there; yet I must needs build a new one.'

'Why do you?' said Downe.

'Why do I? To preserve peace in the household. I do anything for that; but I don't succeed. I was firm in resisting "Château Ringdale", however; not that I would not have put up with the absurdity of the name, but it was too much to have your house christened after Lord Ringdale, because your wife once had a fancy for him. If you only knew everything, you would think all attempt at reconciliation hopeless. In your happy home you have had no such experiences; and God forbid that you ever should. See, here they are all ready to receive you!'

'Of course! And so will your wife be waiting to receive you,' said Downe. 'Take my word for it she will! And with a dinner prepared for you far better than mine.'

'I hope so,' Barnet replied dubiously.

He had moved on to Downe's door, which the solicitor's

family had already opened. Downe descended, but being encumbered with his bag and umbrella, his foot slipped, and he fell upon his knees in the gutter.

'O, my dear Charles!' said his wife, running down the steps; and, quite ignoring the presence of Barnet, she seized hold of her husband, pulled him to his feet, and kissed him, exclaiming, 'I hope you are not hurt, darling!' The children crowded round, chiming in piteously, 'Poor papa!'

'He's all right,' said Barnet, perceiving that Downe was only a little muddy, and looking more at the wife than at the husband. Almost at any other time – certainly during his fastidious bachelor years – he would have thought her a too demonstrative woman; but those recent circumstances of his own life to which he had just alluded made Mrs Downe's solicitude so affecting that his eye grew damp as he witnessed it. Bidding the lawyer and his family goodnight he left them, and drove slowly into the main street towards his own house.

The heart of Barnet was sufficiently impressionable to be influenced by Downe's parting prophecy that he might not be so unwelcome home as he imagined: the dreary night might, at least on this one occasion, make Downe's forecast true. Hence it was in a suspense that he could hardly have believed possible that he halted at his door. On entering his wife was nowhere to be seen, and he inquired for her. The servant informed him that her mistress had the dressmaker with her, and would be engaged for some time.

'Dressmaker at this time of day!'

'She dined early, sir, and hopes you will excuse her joining you this evening.'

'But she knew I was coming tonight?'

'O yes, sir.'

'Go up and tell her I am come.'

The servant did so; but the mistress of the house merely transmitted her former words.

Barnet said nothing more, and presently sat down to his lonely meal, which was eaten abstractedly, the domestic scene he had lately witnessed still impressing him by its contrast with the situation here. His mind fell back into past years upon a certain pleasing and gentle being whose face would loom out of their shades at such times as these. Barnet turned in his chair, and looked with unfocused eyes in a direction southward from where he sat, as if he saw not the room but a long way beyond. 'I wonder if she lives there still!' he said.

II

H E rose with a sudden rebelliousness, put on his hat and coat, and went out of the house, pursuing his way along the glistening pavement while eight o'clock was striking from St Mary's tower, and the apprentices and shopmen were slamming up the shutters from end to end of the town. In two minutes only those shops which could boast of no attendant save the master or the mistress remained with open eyes. These were ever somewhat less prompt to exclude customers than the others: for their owners' ears the closing hour had scarcely the cheerfulness that it possessed for the hired servants of the rest. Yet the night being dreary the delay was not for long, and their windows, too, blinked together one by one.

During this time Barnet had proceeded with decided step in a direction at right angles to the broad main thoroughfare of the town, by a long street leading due southward. Here, though his family had no more to do with the flax manufacture, his own name occasionally greeted him on gates and warehouses, being used allusively by small rising tradesmen as a recommendation, in such words as 'Smith, from Barnet & Co' – 'Robinson, late manager at Barnet's'. The sight led him to reflect upon his father's busy life, and he questioned if it had not been far happier than his own.

The houses along the road became fewer, and presently open ground appeared between them on either side, the track on the right hand rising to a higher level till it merged in a knoll. On the summit a row of builders' scaffold-poles probed the indistinct sky like spears, and at their bases could be discerned the lower courses of a building lately begun. Barnet slackened his pace and stood for a few moments without leaving the centre of the road, apparently not much interested in the sight, till suddenly his eye was caught by a post in the fore part of the ground bearing a white board at the top. He went to the rails, vaulted over, and walked in far enough to discern painted upon the board 'Château Ringdale'.

A dismal irony seemed to lie in the words, and its effect was to irritate him. Downe, then, had spoken truly. He stuck his umbrella into the sod, and seized the post with both hands, as if intending to loosen and throw it down. Then, like one bewildered by an opposition which would exist none the less though its manifestations were removed, he allowed his arms to sink to his side.

'Let it be,' he said to himself. 'I have declared there shall be peace – if possible.'

Taking up his umbrella he quietly left the enclosure, and went on his way, still keeping his back to the town. He had advanced with more decision since passing the new building, and soon a hoarse murmur rose upon the gloom; it was the sound of the sea. The road led to the harbour, at a distance of a mile from the town, from which the trade of the district was fed. After seeing the obnoxious name-board Barnet had forgotten to open his umbrella, and the rain tapped smartly on his hat, and occasionally stroked his face as he went on.

Though the lamps were still continued at the roadside they stood at wider intervals than before, and the pavement had given place to rough gravel. Every time he came to a lamp an increasing shine made itself visible upon his shoulders, till at last they quite glistened with wet. The murmur from the shore grew stronger, but it was still some distance off when he paused before one of the smallest of the detached houses by the wayside, standing in its own garden, the latter being divided from the road by a row of wooden palings. Scrutinizing the spot to ensure that he was not mistaken, he opened the gate and gently knocked at the cottage door.

When he had patiently waited minutes enough to lead any

man in ordinary cases to knock again, the door was heard to open, though it was impossible to see by whose hand, there being no light in the passage. Barnet said at random, 'Does Miss Savile live here?'

A youthful voice assured him that she did live there, and by a sudden afterthought asked him to come in. It would soon get a light, it said : but the night being wet, Mother had not thought it worth while to trim the passage lamp.

'Don't trouble yourself to get a light for me,' said Barnet hastily; 'it is not necessary at all. Which is Miss Savile's sitting-room?'

The young person, whose white pinafore could just be discerned, signified a door in the side of the passage, and Barnet went forward at the same moment, so that no light should fall upon his face. On entering the room he closed the door behind him, pausing till he heard the retreating footsteps of the child.

He found himself in an apartment which was simply and neatly, though not poorly furnished; everything, from the miniature chiffonnier to the shining little daguerreotype which formed the central ornament of the mantelpiece, being in scrupulous order. The picture was enclosed by a frame of embroidered card-board – evidently the work of feminine hands and it was the portrait of a thin-faced, elderly lieutenant in the navy. From behind the lamp on the table a female form now rose into view, that of a young girl, and a resemblance between her and the portrait was early discoverable. She had been so absorbed in some occupation on the other side of the lamp as to have barely found time to realize her visitor's presence.

They both remained standing for a few seconds without speaking. The face that confronted Barnet had a beautiful outline; the Raffaelesque oval of its contour was remarkable for an English countenance, and that countenance housed in a remote country-road to an unheard-of harbour. But her features did not do justice to this splendid beginning : Nature had recollected that she was not in Italy; and the young lady's lineaments, though not so inconsistent as to make her plain, would have been accepted rather as pleasing than as correct. The preoccupied expression which, like images on the retina, remained with her for a moment after the state that caused it had ceased, now changed into a reserved, half-proud, and slightly indignant look, in which the blood diffused itself quickly across her cheek, and additional brightness broke the shade of her rather heavy eyes.

'I know I have no business here,' he said, answering the look. 'But I had a great wish to see you, and inquire how you were. You can give your hand to me, seeing how often I have held it in past days?'

'I would rather forget than remember all that, Mr Barnet,' she answered, as she coldly complied with the request. 'When I think of the circumstances of our last meeting, I can hardly consider it kind of you to allude to such a thing as our past – or, indeed, to come here at all.'

'There was no harm in it surely? I don't trouble you often, Lucy.'

'I have not had the honour of a visit from you for a very long time, certainly, and I did not expect it now,' she said, with the same stiffness in her air. 'I hope Mrs Barnet is very well?'

'Yes, yes!' he impatiently returned. 'At least I suppose so – thought I only speak from inference!'

'But she is your wife, sir,' said the young girl tremulously.

The unwonted tones of a man's voice in that feminine chamber had startled a canary that was roosting in its cage by the window; the bird awoke hastily, and fluttered against the bar. She went and stilled it by laying her face against the cage and murmuring a coaxing sound. It might partly have been done to still herself.

'I didn't come to talk of Mrs Barnet,' he pursued; 'I came to talk of you, of yourself alone; to inquire how you are getting on since your great loss.' And he turned towards the portrait of her father.

'I am getting on fairly well, thank you.'

The force of her utterance was scarcely borne out by her look; but Barnet courteously reproached himself for not having guessed a thing so natural; and to dissipate all embarrassment added, as he bent over the table, 'What were you doing when I came in? – painting flowers, and by candlelight?'

'O no,' she said, 'not painting them – only sketching the outlines. I do that at night to save time – I have to get three dozen done by the end of the month.'

Barnet looked as if he regretted it deeply. 'You will wear your poor eyes out,' he said, with more sentiment than he had hitherto shown. 'You ought not to do it. There was a time when I should have said you must not. Well – I almost wish I had never seen light with my own eyes when I think of that!'

'Is this a time or place for recalling such matters?' she asked, with dignity. 'You used to have a gentlemanly respect for me, and for yourself. Don't speak any more as you have spoken, and don't come again. I cannot think that this visit is serious, or was closely considered by you.'

'Considered: well, I came to see you as an old and good friend – not to mince matters, to visit a woman I loved. Don't be angry! I could not help doing it, so many things brought you into my mind ... This evening I fell in with an acquaintance, and when I saw how happy he was with his wife and family welcoming him home, though with only one-tenth of my income and chances, and thought what might have been in my case, it fairly broke down my discretion, and off I came here. Now I am here I feel that I am wrong to some extent. But the feeling that I should like to see you, and talk of those we used to know in common, was very strong.'

'Before that can be the case a little more time must pass,' said Miss Savile quietly; 'a time long enough for me to regard with some calmness what at present I remember far too impatiently – though it may be you almost forget it. Indeed you must have forgotten it long before you acted as you did.' Her voice grew stronger and more vivacious as she added: 'But I am doing my best to forget it too, and I know I shall succeed from the progress I have made already!'

She had remained standing till now, when she turned and sat down, facing half away from him.

Barnet watched her moodily. 'Yes, it is only what I deserve,' he said. 'Ambition pricked me on – no, it was not ambition, it was wrongheadedness! Had I but reflected ...' He broke out vehemently: 'But always remember this, Lucy: if you had written to me only one little line after that misunderstanding, I declare I should have come back to you. That ruined me!' He slowly walked as far as the little room would allow him to go, and remained with his eyes on the skirting.

'But, Mr Barnet, how could I write to you? There was no opening for my doing so.'

'Then there ought to have been,' said Barnet, turning. 'That was my fault!'

'Well, I don't know anything about that; but as there had been nothing said by me which required any explanation by letter, I did not send one. Everything was so indefinite, and feeling your position to be so much wealthier than mine, I fancied I might have mistaken your meaning. And when I heard of the other lady – a woman of whose family even you might be proud – I thought how foolish I had been, and said nothing.'

'Then I suppose it was destiny – accident – I don't know what, that separated us, dear Lucy. Anyhow you were the woman I ought to have made my wife – and I let you slip, like the foolish man that I was!'

'O, Mr Barnet,' she said, almost in tears, 'don't revive the subject to me; I am the wrong one to console you – think, sir – you should not be here – it would be so bad for me if it were known!'

'It would – it would, indeed,' he said hastily. 'I am not right in doing this, and I won't do it again.'

'It is a very common folly of human nature, you know, to think the course you did *not* adopt must have been the best,' she continued, with gentle solicitude, as she followed him to the door of the room. 'And you don't know that I should have accepted you, even if you had asked me to be your wife.' At this his eye met hers, and she dropped her gaze. She knew that her voice belied her. There was a silence till she looked up to add, in a voice of soothing playfulness, 'My family was so much poorer than yours, even before I lost my dear father, that – perhaps your companions would have made it unpleasant for us on account of my deficiencies.'

'Your disposition would soon have won them round,' said Barnet.

She archly expostulated: 'Now, never mind my disposition; try to make it up with your wife! Those are my commands to you. And now you are to leave me at once.'

'I will. I must make the best of it all, I suppose,' he replied, more cheerfully than he had as yet spoken. 'But I shall never again meet with such a dear girl as you!' And he suddenly opened the door, and left her alone. When his glance again fell on the lamps that were sparsely ranged along the dreary level road, his eyes were in a state which showed straw-like motes of light radiating from each flame into the surrounding air.

On the other side of the way Barnet observed a man under an umbrella, walking parallel with himself. Presently this man left the footway, and gradually converged on Barnet's course. The latter then saw that it was Charlson, a surgeon of the town, who owed him money. Charlson was a man not without ability; yet he did not prosper. Sundry circumstances stood in his way as a medical practitioner: he was needy; he was not a coddle; he gossiped with men instead of with women; he had married a stranger instead of one of the town young ladies; and he was given to conversational buffoonery. Moreover, his look was quite erroneous. Those only proper features in the family doctor, the quiet eye, and the thin straight passionless lips which never curl in public either for laughter or for scorn, were not his; he had a full-curved mouth, and a bold black eye that made timid people nervous. His companions were what in old times would have been called boon companions – an expression which, though of irreproachable root, suggests fraternization carried to the point of unscrupulousness. All this was against him in the little town of his adoption.

Charlson had been in difficulties, and to oblige him Barnet

had put his name to a bill; and, as he had expected, was called upon to meet it when it fell due. It had been only a matter of fifty pounds, which Barnet could well afford to lose, and he bore no ill-will to the thriftless surgeon on account of it. But Charlson had a little too much brazen indifferentism in his composition to be altogether a desirable acquaintance.

'I hope to be able to make that little bill-business right with you in the course of three weeks, Mr Barnet,' said Charlson with hail-fellow friendliness.

Barnet replied good-naturedly that there was no hurry.

This particular three weeks had moved on in advance of Charlson's present with the precision of a shadow for some considerable time.

'I've had a dream,' Charlson continued. Barnet knew from his tone that the surgeon was going to begin his characteristic nonsense, and did not encourage him. 'I've had a dream,' repeated Charlson, who required no encouragement. 'I dreamed that a gentleman, who has been very kind to me, married a haughty lady in haste, before he had quite forgotten a nice little girl he knew before, and that one wet evening, like the present, as I was walking up the harbour-road, I saw him come out of that dear little girl's present abode.'

Barnet glanced towards the speaker. The rays from a neighbouring lamp struck through the drizzle under Charlson's umbrella, so as just to illumine his face against the shade behind, and show that his eye was turned up under the outer corner of its lid, whence it leered with impish jocoseness as he thrust his tongue into his cheek.

'Come,' said Barnet gravely, 'we'll have no more of that.'

'No, no – of course not,' Charlson hastily answered, seeing that his humour had carried him too far, as it had done many times before. He was profuse in his apologies, but Barnet did not reply. Of one thing he was certain – that scandal was a plant of quick root, and that he was bound to obey Lucy's injunction for Lucy's own sake.

III

H E did so, to the letter; and though, as the crocus followed
the snowdrop and the daffodil the crocus in Lucy's garden,
the harbour-road was a not unpleasant place to walk in, Barnet's feet never trod its stones, much less approached her
door. He avoided a saunter that way as he would have
avoided a dangerous dram, and took his airings a long distance northward, among severely square and brown
ploughed fields, where no other townsman came. Sometimes
he went round by the lower lanes of the borough, where the
rope-walks stretched in which his family formerly had share,
and looked at the rope-makers walking backwards, overhung
by apple-trees and bushes, and intruded on by cows and
calves, as if trade had established itself there at considerable
inconvenience to Nature.

One morning, when the sun was so warm as to raise a
steam from the south-western slopes of those flanking hills
that looked so lovely above the old roofs, but made every
low-chimneyed house in the town as smoky at Tophet, Barnet
glanced from the windows of the town-council room for lack
of interest in what was proceeding within. Several members
of the corporation were present, but there was not much
business doing, and in a few minutes Downe came leisurely
across to him, saying that he seldom saw Barnet now.

Barnet owned that he was not often present.

Downe looked at the crimson curtain which hung down
beside the panes, reflecting its hot hues into their faces, and
then out of the window. At that moment there passed along
the street a tall commanding lady, in whom the solicitor
recognized Barnet's wife. Barnet had done the same thing,
and turned away.

'It will be all right some day,' said Downe, with cheering
sympathy.

'You have heard, then, of her last outbreak?'

Downe depressed his cheerfulness to its very reverse in a

moment. 'No, I have not heard of anything serious,' he said, with as long a face as one naturally round could be turned into at short notice. 'I only hear vague reports of such things.'

'You may think it will be all right,' said Barnet drily. 'But I have a different opinion ... No, Downe, we must look the thing in the face. Not poppy nor mandragora – however, how are your wife and children?'

Downe said that they were all well, thanks; they were out that morning somewhere; he was just looking to see if they were walking that way. Ah, there they were, just coming down the street; and Downe pointed to the figures of two children with a nursemaid, and a lady walking behind them.

'You will come out and speak to her?' he asked.

'Not this morning. The fact is I don't care to speak to anybody just now.'

'You are too sensitive, Mr Barnet. At school I remember you used to get as red as a rose if anybody uttered a word that hurt your feelings.'

Barnet mused. 'Yes,' he admitted, 'there is a grain of truth in that. It is because of that I often try to make peace at home. Life would be tolerable then at any rate, even if not particularly bright.'

'I have thought more than once of proposing a little plan to you,' said Downe with some hesitation. 'I don't know whether it will meet your views, but take it or leave it, as you choose. In fact, it was my wife who suggested it : that she would be very glad to call on Mrs Barnet and get into her confidence. She seems to think that Mrs Barnet is rather alone in the town, and without advisers. Her impression is that your wife will listen to reason. Emily has a wonderful way of winning the hearts of people of her own sex.'

'And of the other sex too, I think. She is a charming woman, and you were a lucky fellow to find her.'

'Well, perhaps I was,' simpered Downe, trying to wear an aspect of being the last man in the world to feel pride. 'However, she will be likely to find out what ruffles Mrs Barnet. Perhaps it is some misunderstanding, you know – something that she is too proud to ask you to explain, or some little thing in your conduct that irritates her because she does not fully comprehend you. The truth is, Emily would have been more ready to make advances if she had been quite sure of her fitness for Mrs Barnet's society, who has of course been accustomed to London people of good position, which made Emily fearful of intruding.'

Barnet expressed his warmest thanks for the well-intentioned proposition. There was reason in Mrs Downe's fear – that he owned. 'But do let her call,' he said. 'There is no woman in England I would so soon trust on such an errand. I am afraid there will not be any brilliant result; still I shall take it as the kindest and nicest thing if she will try it, and not be frightened at a repulse.'

When Barnet and Downe had parted, the former went to the Town Savings-Bank, of which he was a trustee, and endeavoured to forget his troubles in the contemplation of low sums of money, and figures in a network of red and blue lines. He sat and watched the working-people making their deposits, to which at intervals he signed his name. Before he left in the afternoon Downe put his head inside the door.

'Emily has seen Mrs Barnet,' he said, in a low voice. 'She has got Mrs Barnet's promise to take her for a drive down to the shore tomorrow, if it is fine. Good afternoon!'

Barnet shook Downe by the hand without speaking, and Downe went away.

IV

THE next day was as fine as the arrangement could possibly require. As the sun passed the meridian and declined westward, the tall shadows from the scaffold-poles of Barnet's rising residence streaked the ground as far as to the middle of the highway. Barnet himself was there inspecting the progress of the works for the first time during several weeks. A building in an old-fashioned town five-and-thirty years ago did not, as in the modern fashion, rise from the sod like a booth at a fair. The foundations and lower courses were put in and allowed to settle for many weeks before the super-structure was built up, and a whole summer of drying was hardly sufficient to do justice to the important issues involved. Barnet stood within a window-niche which had as yet received no frame, and thence looked down a slope into the road. The wheels of a chaise were heard, and then his handsome Xantippe, in the company of Mrs Downe, drove past on their way to the shore. They were driving slowly; there was a pleasing light in Mrs Downe's face, which seemed faintly to reflect itself upon the countenance of her companion – that *politesse du cœur* which was so natural to her having possibly begun already to work results. But whatever the situation, Barnet resolved not to interfere, or do anything to hazard the promise of the day. He might well afford to trust the issue to another when he could never direct it but to ill himself. His wife's clenched rein-hand in its lemon-coloured glove, her stiff erect figure, clad in velvet and lace, and her boldly outlined face, passed on, exhibiting their owner as one fixed for ever above the level of her companion – socially by her early breeding, and materially by her higher cushion.

Barnet decided to allow them a proper time to themselves, and then stroll down to the shore and drive them home. After lingering on at the house for another hour he started with this intention. A few hundred yards below 'Château Ringdale' stood the cottage in which the late lieutenant's daughter had her lodging. Barnet had not been so far that way for a long time, and as he approached the forbidden ground a curious warmth passed into him, which led him to perceive that, unless he were careful, he might have to fight the battle with himself about Lucy over again. A tenth of his present excuse would, however, have justified him in travelling by that road today.

He came opposite the dwelling, and turned his eyes for a momentary glance into the little garden that stretched from the palings to the door. Lucy was in the enclosure; she was walking and stooping to gather some flowers, possibly for the purpose of painting them, for she moved about quickly, as if anxious to save time. She did not see him; he might have passed unnoticed; but a sensation which was not in strict unison with his previous sentiments that day led him to pause in his walk and watch her. She went nimbly round and round the beds of anemones, tulips, jonquils, polyanthuses, and other old-fashioned flowers, looking a very charming figure in her half-mourning bonnet, and with an incomplete nosegay in her left hand. Raising herself to pull down a lilac blossom she observed him.

'Mr Barnet!' she said, innocently smiling. 'Why, I have been thinking of you many times since Mrs Barnet went by in the pony-carriage, and now here you are!'

'Yes, Lucy,' he said.

Then she seemed to recall particulars of their last meeting, and he believed that she flushed, though it might have been only the fancy of his own super-sensitiveness.

'I am going to the harbour,' he added.

'Are you?' Lucy remarked simply. 'A great many people begin to go there now the summer is drawing on.'

Her face had come more into his view as she spoke, and he noticed how much thinner and paler it was than when he had seen it last. 'Lucy, how weary you look! tell me, can I help you?' he was going to cry out. – 'If I do,' he thought, 'it will be the ruin of us both!' He merely said that the afternoon was fine, and went on his way.

As he went a sudden blast of air came over the hill as if in contradiction to his words, and spoilt the previous quiet of the scene. The wind had already shifted violently, and now smelt of the sea.

The harbour-road soon began to justify its name. A gap appeared in the rampart of hills which shut out the sea, and on the left of the opening rose a vertical cliff, coloured a burning orange by the sunlight, the companion cliff on the right being livid in shade. Between these cliffs, like the Libyan bay which sheltered the shipwrecked Trojans, was a little haven, seemingly a beginning made by Nature herself of a perfect harbour, which appealed to the passer-by as only requiring a little human industry to finish it and make it famous, the ground on each side as far back as the daisied slopes that bounded the interior valley being a mere layer of blown sand. But the Port-Bredy burgesses a mile inland had, in the course of ten centuries, responded many times to that mute appeal, with the result that the tides had invariably choked up their works with sand and shingle as soon as completed. There were but few houses here: a rough pier, a few boats, some stores, an inn, a residence or two, a ketch unloading in the harbour, were the chief features of the settlement. On the open ground by the shore stood his wife's pony-carriage, empty, the boy in attendance holding the horse.

When Barnet drew nearer, he saw an indigo-coloured spot moving swiftly along beneath the radiant base of the eastern cliff, which proved to be a man in a jersey, running with all his might. He held up his hand to Barnet, as it seemed, and they approached each other. The man was local, but a stranger to him.

'What is it, my man?' said Barnet.

'A terrible calamity!' the boatman hastily explained. Two ladies had been capsized in a boat – they were Mrs Downe and Mrs Barnet of the old town; they had driven down there that afternoon – they had alighted, and it was so fine, that, after walking about a little while, they had been tempted to go out for a short sail round the cliff. Just as they were putting in to the shore, the wind shifted with a sudden gust, the boat listed over, and it was thought they were both drowned. How it could have happened was beyond his mind to fathom, for John Green knew how to sail a boat as well as any man there.

'Which is the way to the place?' said Barnet.

It was just round the cliff.

'Run to the carriage and tell the boy to bring it to the place as soon as you can. Then go to the Harbour Inn and tell them to ride to town for a doctor. Have they been got out of the water?'

'One lady has.'

'Which?'

'Mrs Barnet. Mrs Downe, it is feared, has fleeted out to sea.'

Barnet ran to that part of the shore which the cliff had hitherto obscured from his view, and there discerned, a long way ahead, a group of fishermen standing. As soon as he came up one or two recognized him, and, not liking to meet his eye, turned aside with misgiving. He went amidst them and saw a small sailing-boat lying draggled at the water's edge; and, on the sloping shingle beside it, a soaked and sandy woman's form in the velvet dress and yellow gloves of his wife.

V

ALL had been done that could be done. Mrs Barnet was in her own house under medical hands, but the result was still uncertain. Barnet had acted as if devotion to his wife were the dominant passion of his existence. There had been much to decide – whether to attempt restoration of the apparently lifeless body as it lay on the shore – whether to carry her to the Harbour Inn – whether to drive with her at once to his own house. The first course, with no skilled help or appliances near at hand, had seemed hopeless. The second course would have occupied nearly as much time as a drive to the town, owing to the intervening ridges of shingle, and the necessity of crossing the harbour by boat to get to the house, added to which much time must have elapsed before a doctor could have arrived down there. By bringing her home in the carriage some precious moments had slipped by; but she had been laid in her own bed in seven minutes, a doctor called to her side, and every possible restorative brought to bear upon her.

At what a tearing pace he had driven up that road, through the yellow evening sunlight, the shadows flapping irksomely into his eyes as each wayside object rushed past between him and the west! Tired workmen with their baskets at their backs had turned on their homeward journey to wonder at his speed. Halfway between the shore and Port-Bredy town he had met Charlson, who had been the first surgeon to hear of the accident. He was accompanied by his assistant in a gig. Barnet had sent on the latter to the coast in case that Downe's poor wife should by that time have been reclaimed from the waves, and had brought Charlson back with him to the house.

Barnet's presence was not needed here, and he felt it to be his next duty to set off at once and find Downe, that no other than himself might break the news to him.

He was quite sure that no chance had been lost for Mrs Downe by his leaving the shore. By the time that Mrs Barnet had been laid in the carriage a much larger group had assembled to lend assistance in finding her friend, rendering his own help superfluous. But the duty of breaking the news was made doubly painful by the circumstance that the catastrophe which had befallen Mrs Downe was solely the result of her own and her husband's loving-kindness towards himself.

He found Downe in his office. When the solicitor comprehended the intelligence he turned pale, stood up, and remained for a moment perfectly still, as if bereft of his faculties; then his shoulders heaved, he pulled out his handkerchief and began to cry like a child. His sobs might have been heard in the next room. He seemed to have no idea of going to the shore, or of doing anything; but when Barnet took him gently by the hand and proposed to start at once, he quietly acquiesced, neither uttering any further word nor making any effort to repress his tears.

Barnet accompanied him to the shore, where, finding that no trace had as yet been seen of Mrs Downe, and that his stay would be of no avail, he left Downe with his friends and the young doctor, and once more hastened back to his own house.

At the door he met Charlson. 'Well!' Barnet said.

'I have just come down,' said the doctor; 'we have done everything, but without result. I sympathize with you in your bereavement.'

Barnet did not much appreciate Charlson's sympathy, which sounded to his ears as something of a mockery from the lips of a man who knew what Charlson knew about his domestic relations. Indeed there seemed an odd spark in Charlson's full black eye as he said the words; but that might have been imaginary.

'And, Mr Barnet,' Charlson resumed, 'that little matter between us – I hope to settle it finally in three weeks at least.'

'Never mind that now,' said Barnet abruptly. He directed the surgeon to go to the harbour in case his services might even now be necessary there: and himself entered the house.

The servants were coming from his wife's chamber, looking helplessly at each other and at him. He passed them by and entered the room, where he stood regarding the shape on the bed for a few minutes, after which he walked into his own dressing-room adjoining, and there paced up and down. In a minute or two he noticed what a strange and total silence had come over the upper part of the house; his own movements, muffled as they were by the carpet, seemed noisy, and his thoughts to disturb the air like articulate utterances. His eye glanced through the window. Far down the road to the harbour a roof detained his gaze: out of it rose a red chimney, and out of the red chimney a curl of smoke, as from a fire newly kindled. He had often seen such a sight before. In that house lived Lucy Savile; and the smoke was from the fire which was regularly lighted at this time to make her tea.

After that he went back to the bedroom, and stood there some time regarding his wife's silent form. She was a woman some years older than himself, but had not by any means overpassed the maturity of good looks and vigour. Her passionate features, well-defined, firm, and statuesque in life, were doubly so now: her mouth and brow, beneath her purplish black hair, showed only too clearly that the turbulency of character which had made a bear-garden of his house had been no temporary phase of her existence. While he reflected, he suddenly said to himself, I wonder if all has been done?

The thought was led up to by his having fancied that his wife's features lacked in its completeness the expression which he had been accustomed to associate with the faces of those whose spirits have fled for ever. The effacement of life was not so marked but that, entering uninformed, he might have supposed her sleeping. Her complexion was that seen in the numerous faded portraits by Sir Joshua Reynolds; it was pallid in comparison with life, but there was visible on a close inspection the remnant of what had once been a flush; the keeping between the cheeks and the hollows of the face being thus preserved, although positive colour was gone. Long orange rays of evening sun stole in through chinks in the blind, striking on the large mirror, and being thence reflected upon the crimson hangings and woodwork of the heavy bedstead, so that the general tone of light was remarkably warm; and it was probable that something might be due to this circumstance. Still the fact impressed him as strange. Charlson had been gone more than a quarter of an hour: could it be possible that he had left too soon, and that his attempts to restore her had operated so sluggishly as only now to have made themselves felt? Barnet laid his hand upon her chest, and fancied that ever and anon a faint flutter of palpitation, gentle as that of a butterfly's wing, disturbed the stillness there – ceasing for a time, then struggling to go on, then breaking down in weakness and ceasing again.

Barnet's mother had been an active practitioner of the healing art among her poorer neighbours, and her inspirations had all been derived from an octavo volume of Domestic Medicine, which at this moment was lying, as it had lain for many years, on a shelf in Barnet's dressing-room. He hastily fetched it, and there read under the head 'Drowning':

Exertions for the recovery of any person who has not been immersed for a longer period than half an hour should be continued for at least four hours, as there have been many cases in which returning life has made itself visible even after a longer interval.

Should, however, a weak action of any of the organs show itself when the case seems almost hopeless, our efforts must be redoubled; the feeble spark in this case requires to be solicited; it will certainly disappear under a relaxation of labour.

Barnet looked at his watch; it was now barely two hours and a half from the time when he had first heard of the accident. He threw aside the book and turned quickly to reach a stimulant which had previously been used. Pulling up the blind for more light, his eye glanced out of the window. There he saw that red chimney still smoking cheerily, and that roof, and through the roof that somebody. His mechanical movements stopped, his hand remained on the blind-cord, and he seemed to become breathless, as if he had suddenly found himself treading a high rope.

While he stood a sparrow lighted on the window-sill, saw him, and flew away. Next a man and a dog walked over one of the green hills which bulged above the roofs of the town. But Barnet took no notice.

We may wonder what were the exact images that passed through his mind during those minutes of gazing upon Lucy Savile's house, the sparrow, the man and the dog, and Lucy Savile's house again. There are honest men who will not admit to their thoughts, even as idle hypotheses, views of the future that assume as done a deed which they would recoil from doing; and there are other honest men for whom morality ends at the surface of their own heads, who will deliberate what the first will not so much as suppose. Barnet had a wife whose presence distracted his home; she now lay as in death; by merely doing nothing – by letting the intelligence which had gone forth to the world lie undisturbed – he would effect such a deliverance for himself as he had never hoped for, and open up an opportunity of which till now he had never dreamed. Whether the conjecture had arisen through any unscrupulous, ill-considered impulse of

Charlson to help out of a strait the friend who was so kind as never to press him for what was due could not be told; there was nothing to prove it; and it was a question which could never be asked. The triangular situation – himself – his wife – Lucy Savile – was the one clear thing.

From Barnet's actions we may infer that he *supposed* such and such a result, for a moment, but did not deliberate. He withdrew his hazel eyes from the scene without, calmly turned, rang the bell for assistance, and vigorously exerted himself to learn if life still lingered in that motionless frame. In a short time another surgeon was in attendance; and then Barnet's surmise proved to be true. The slow life timidly heaved again; but much care and patience were needed to catch and retain it, and a considerable period elapsed before it could be said with certainty that Mrs Barnet lived. When this was the case, and there was no further room for doubt, Barnet left the chamber. The blue evening smoke from Lucy's chimney had died down to an imperceptible stream, and as he walked about downstairs he murmured to himself, 'My wife was dead, and she is alive again.'

It was not so with Downe. After three hours' immersion his wife's body had been recovered, life, of course, being quite extinct. Barnet on descending, went straight to his friend's house, and there learned the result. Downe was helpless in his wild grief, occasionally even hysterical. Barnet said little, but finding that some guiding hand was necessary in the sorrow-stricken household, took upon him to supervise and manage till Downe should be in a state of mind to do so for himself.

VI

ONE September evening, four months later, when Mrs Barnet was in perfect health, and Mrs Downe but a weakening memory, an errand-boy paused to rest himself in front of Mr Barnet's old house, depositing his basket on one of the window-sills. The street was not yet lighted, but there were lights in the house, and at intervals a flitting shadow fell upon the blind at his elbow. Words also were audible from the same apartment, and they seemed to be those of persons in violent altercation. But the boy could not gather their purport, and he went on his way.

Ten minutes afterwards the door of Barnet's house opened, and a tall, closely veiled lady in a travelling-dress came out and descended the freestone steps. The servant stood in the doorway watching her as she went with a measured tread down the street. When she had been out of sight for some minutes Barnet appeared at the door from within.

'Did your mistress leave word where she was going?' he asked.

'No, sir.'

'Is the carriage ordered to meet her anywhere?'

'No, sir.'

'Did she take a latch-key?'

'No, sir.'

Barnet went in again, sat down in his chair, and leaned back. Then in solitude and silence he brooded over the bitter emotions that filled his heart. It was for this that he had gratuitously restored her to life, and made his union with another impossible! The evening drew on, and nobody came to disturb him. At bedtime he told the servants to retire, that he would sit up for Mrs Barnet himself; and when they were gone he leaned his head upon his hand and mused for hours.

The clock struck one, two; still his wife came not, and, with impatience added to depression, he went from room to room till another weary hour had passed. This was not altogether a new experience for Barnet; but she had never before so prolonged her absence. At last he sat down again and fell asleep.

He awoke at six o'clock to find that she had not returned. In searching about the rooms he discovered that she had taken a case of jewels which had been hers before her marriage. At eight a note was brought him; it was from his wife, in which she stated that she had gone by coach to the house of a distant relative near London, and expressed a wish that certain boxes, articles of clothing, and so on, might be sent to her forthwith. The note was brought to him by a waiter at the Black Bull Hotel, and had been written by Mrs Barnet immediately before she took her place in the stage.

By the evening this order was carried out, and Barnet, with a sense of relief, walked out into the town. A fair had been held during the day, and the large clear moon which rose over the most prominent hill flung its light upon the booths and standings that still remained in the street, mixing its rays curiously with those from the flaring naphtha lamps. The town was full of country-people who had come in to enjoy themselves, and on this account Barnet strolled through the streets unobserved. With a certain recklessness he made for the harbour-road, and presently found himself by the shore, where he walked on till he came to the spot near which his friend, the kindly Mrs Downe, had lost her life, and his own wife's life had been preserved. A tremulous pathway of bright moonshine now stretched over the water which had engulfed them, and not a living soul was near.

Here he ruminated on their characters, and next on the young girl in whom he now took a more sensitive interest than at the time when he had been free to marry her. Nothing, so far as he was aware, had ever appeared in his own conduct to show that such an interest existed. He had made it a point of the utmost strictness to hinder that feeling from influencing in the faintest degree his attitude towards his wife; and this was made all the more easy for him by the small demand Mrs Barnet made upon his attentions, for which she ever evinced the greatest contempt; thus unwittingly giving him the satisfaction of knowing that their severance owed nothing to jealousy, or, indeed, to any personal behaviour of his at all. Her concern was not with him or his feelings, as she frequently told him; but that she had, in a moment of weakness, thrown herself away upon a common burgher when she might have aimed at, and possibly brought down, a peer of the realm. Her frequent depreciation of Barnet in these terms had at times been so intense that he was sorely tempted to retaliate on her egotism by owning that he loved at the same low level on which he lived; but prudence had prevailed, for which he was now thankful.

Something seemed to sound upon the shingle behind him over and above the raking of the wave. He looked round, and a slight girlish shape appeared quite close to him. He could not see her face because it was in the direction of the moon.

'Mr Barnet?' the rambler said, in timid surprise. The voice was the voice of Lucy Savile.

'Yes,' said Barnet. 'How can I repay you for this pleasure?'

'I only came because the night was so clear. I am now on my way home.'

'I am glad we have met. I want to know if you will let me do something for you, to give me an occupation, as an idle man? I am sure I ought to help you, for I know you are almost without friends.'

She hesitated. 'Why should you tell me that?' she said.

'In the hope that you will be frank with me.'

'I am not altogether without friends here. But I am going to make a little change in my life – to go out as a teacher of freehand drawing and practical perspective, of course I mean on a comparatively humble scale, because I have not been specially educated for that profession. But I am sure I shall like it much.'

'You have an opening?'

'I have not exactly got it, but I have advertised for one.'

'Lucy, you must let me help you!'

'Not at all.'

'You need not think it would compromise you, or that I am indifferent to delicacy. I bear in mind how we stand. It is very unlikely that you will succeed as teacher of the class you mention, so let me do something of a different kind for you. Say what you would like, and it shall be done.'

'No; if I can't be a drawing-mistress or governess, or

something of that sort, I shall go to India and join my brother.'

'I wish I could go abroad, anywhere, everywhere with you, Lucy, and leave this place and its associations for ever!'

She played with the end of her bonnet-string, and hastily turned aside. 'Don't ever touch upon that kind of topic again,' she said, with a quick severity not free from anger. 'It simply makes it impossible for me to see you, much less receive any guidance from you. No, thank you, Mr Barnet; you can do nothing for me at present; and as I suppose my uncertainty will end in my leaving for India, I fear you never will. If ever I think you *can* do anything, I will take the trouble to ask you. Till then, goodbye.'

The tone of her latter words was equivocal, and while he remained in doubt whether a gentle irony was or was not inwrought with their sound, she swept lightly round and left him alone. He saw her form get smaller and smaller along the damp belt of sea-sand between ebb and flood; and when she had vanished round the cliff into the harbour-road he himself followed in the same direction.

That her hopes from an advertisement should be the single thread which held Lucy Savile in England was too much for Barnet. On reaching the town he went straight to the residence of Downe, now a widower with four children. The young motherless brood had been sent to bed about a quarter of an hour earlier, and when Barnet entered he found Downe sitting alone. It was the same room as that from which the family had been looking out for Downe at the beginning of the year, when Downe had slipped into the gutter and his wife had been so enviably tender towards him. The old neatness had gone from the house; articles lay in places which could show no reason for their presence, as if momentarily deposited there some months ago, and forgotten ever since; there were no flowers; things were jumbled together on the furniture which should have been in cupboards; and the place in general had that stagnant, unrenovated air which usually pervades the maimed home of the widower.

Downe soon renewed his customary full-worded lament over his wife, and even when he had worked himself up to tears, went on volubly, as if a listener were a luxury to be enjoyed whenever he could be caught.

'She was a treasure beyond compare, Mr Barnet! I shall never see such another. Nobody now to nurse me – nobody to console me in those daily troubles, you know, Barnet, which make consolation so necessary to a nature like mine. It would be unbecoming to repine, for her spirit's home was elsewhere – the tender light in her eyes always showed it; but it is a long dreary time that I have before me, and nobody else can ever fill the void left in my heart by her loss – nobody – nobody!' And Downe wiped his eyes again.

'She was a good woman in the highest sense,' gravely answered Barnet, who, though Downe's words drew genuine compassion from the heart, could not help feeling that a tender reticence would have been a finer tribute to Mrs Downe's really sterling virtues than such a second-class lament as this.

'I have something to show you,' Downe resumed, producing from a drawer a sheet of paper on which was an elaborate design for a canopied tomb. 'This has been sent me by the architect, but it is not exactly what I want.'

'You have got Jones to do it, I see, the man who is carrying out my house,' said Barnet, as he glanced at the signature to the drawing.

'Yes, but it is not quite what I want. I want something more striking – more like a tomb I have seen in St Paul's Cathedral. Nothing less will do justice to my feelings, and how far short of them that will fall!'

Barnet privately thought the design a sufficiently imposing one as it stood, even extravagantly ornate; but, feeling that he had no right to criticize, he said gently, 'Downe, should you not live more in your children's lives at the present time, and soften the sharpness of regret for your own past by thinking of their future?'

'Yes, yes; but what can I do more?' asked Downe, wrinkling his forehead hopelessly.

It was with anxious slowness that Barnet produced his

reply – the secret object of his visit tonight. 'Did you not say one day that you ought by rights to get a governess for the children?'

Downe admitted that he had said so, but that he could not see his way to it. 'The kind of woman I should like to have,' he said, 'would be rather beyond my means. No; I think I shall send them to school in the town when they are old enough to go out alone.'

'Now, I know of something better than that. The late Lieutenant Savile's daughter, Lucy, wants to do something for herself in the way of teaching. She would be inexpensive, and would answer your purpose as well as anybody for six or twelve months. She would probably come daily if you were to ask her, and so your housekeeping arrangements would not be much affected.'

'I thought she had gone away,' said the solicitor, musing. 'Where does she live?'

Barnet told him, and added that, if Downe should think of her as suitable, he would do well to call as soon as possible, or she might be on the wing. 'If you do see her,' he said, 'it would be advisable not to mention my name. She is rather stiff in her ideas of me, and it might prejudice her against a course if she knew that I recommended it.'

Downe promised to give the subject his consideration, and nothing more was said about it just then. But when Barnet rose to go, which was not till nearly bedtime, he reminded Downe of the suggestion and went up the street to his own solitary home with a sense of satisfaction at his promising diplomacy in a charitable cause.

VII

THE walls of his new house were carried up nearly to their full height. By a curious though not infrequent reaction, Barnet's feelings about that unnecessary structure had undergone a change; he took considerable interest in its progress

as a long-neglected thing, his wife before her departure having grown quite weary of it as a hobby. Moreover, it was an
excellent distraction for a man in the unhappy position of
having to live in a provincial town with nothing to do. He
was probably the first of his line who had ever passed a day
without toil, and perhaps something like an inherited instinct
disqualifies such men for a life of pleasant inaction, such as
lies in the power of those whose leisure is not a personal
accident, but a vast historical accretion which has become
part of their natures.

Thus Barnet got into a way of spending many of his
leisure hours on the site of the new building, and he might
have been seen on most days at this time trying the temper
of the mortar by punching the joints with his stick, looking
at the grain of a floor-board, and meditating where it grew,
or picturing under what circumstances the last fire would be
kindled in the at present sootless chimneys. One day when
thus occupied he saw three children pass by in the company
of a fair young woman, whose sudden appearance caused
him to flush perceptibly.

'Ah, she is there,' he thought. 'That's a blessed thing.'

Casting an interested glance over the rising building and
the busy workmen, Lucy Savile and the little Downes passed
by; and after that time it became a regular though almost
unconscious custom of Barnet to stand in the half-completed
house and look from the ungarnished windows at the governess as she tripped towards the sea-shore with her young
charges, which she was in the habit of doing on most fine
afternoons. It was on one of these occasions, when he had
been loitering on the first-floor landing, near the hole left for
the staircase, not yet erected, that there appeared above the
edge of the floor a little hat, followed by a little head.

Barnet withdrew through a doorway, and the child came
to the top of the ladder, stepping on to the floor and crying
to her sisters and Miss Savile to follow. Another head rose
above the floor, and another, and then Lucy herself came
into view. The troop ran hither and thither through the
empty, shaving-strewn rooms, and Barnet came forward.

Lucy uttered a small exclamation: she was very sorry that she had intruded; she had not the least idea that Mr Barnet was there: the children had come up, and she had followed.

Barnet replied that he was only too glad to see them there. 'And now, let me show you the rooms,' he said.

She passively assented, and he took her round. There was not much to show in such a bare skeleton of a house, but he made the most of it, and explained the different ornamental fittings that were soon to be fixed here and there. Lucy made but few remarks in reply, though she seemed pleased with her visit, and stole away down the ladder, followed by her companions.

After this the new residence became yet more of a hobby for Barnet. Downe's children did not forget their first visit, and when the windows were glazed, and the handsome staircase spread its broad low steps into the hall, they came again, prancing in unwearied succession through every room from ground floor to attics, while Lucy stood waiting for them at the door. Barnet, who rarely missed a day in coming to inspect progress, stepped out from the drawing-room.

'I could not keep them out,' she said, with an apologetic blush. 'I tried to do so very much: but they are rather wilful, and we are directed to walk this way for the sea air.'

'Do let them make the house their regular playground, and you yours,' said Barnet. 'There is no better place for children to romp and take their exercise in than an empty house, particularly in muddy or damp weather such as we shall get a good deal of now; and this place will not be furnished for a long long time – perhaps never. I am not at all decided about it.'

'O, but it must!' replied Lucy, looking round at the hall. 'The rooms are excellent, twice as high as ours; and the views from the windows are so lovely.'

'I daresay, I daresay,' he said absently.

'Will all the furniture be new?' she asked.

'All the furniture be new – that's a thing I have not thought of. In fact I only come here and look on. My father's house would have been large enough for me, but another person had a voice in the matter, and it was settled that we should build. However, the place grows upon me; its recent associations are cheerful, and I am getting to like it fast.'

A certain uneasiness in Lucy's manner showed that the conversation was taking too personal a turn for her. 'Still, as modern tastes develop, people require more room to gratify them in,' she said, withdrawing to call the children; and serenely bidding him good afternoon she went on her way.

Barnet's life at this period was singularly lonely, and yet he was happier than he could have expected. His wife's estrangement and absence, which promised to be permanent, left him free as a boy in his movements, and the solitary walks that he took gave him ample opportunity for chastened reflection on what might have been his lot if he had only shown wisdom enough to claim Lucy Savile when there was no bar between their lives, and she was to be had for the asking. He would occasionally call at the house of his friend Downe; but there was scarcely enough in common between their two natures to make them more than friends of that excellent sort whose personal knowledge of each other's history and character is always in excess of intimacy, whereby they are not so likely to be severed by a clash of sentiment as in cases where intimacy springs up in excess of knowledge. Lucy was never visible at these times, being either engaged in the school-room, or in taking an airing out of doors; but, knowing that she was now comfortable, and had given up the, to him, depressing idea of going off to the other side of the globe, he was quite content.

The new house had so far progressed that the gardeners were beginning to grass down the front. During an afternoon which he was passing in marking the curve for the carriage-drive, he beheld her coming in boldly towards him from the road. Hitherto Barnet had only caught her on the premises by stealth; and this advance seemed to show that at last her reserve had broken down.

A smile gained strength upon her face as she approached, and it was quite radiant when she came up, and said, without a trace of embarrassment, 'I find I owe you a hundred thanks – and it comes to me quite as a surprise! It was through your kindness that I was engaged by Mr Downe. Believe me, Mr Barnet, I did not know it until yesterday, or I should have thanked you long and long ago!'

'I had offended you – just a trifle – at the time, I think?' said Barnet, smiling, 'and it was best that you should not know.'

'Yes, yes,' she returned hastily. 'Don't allude to that; it is past and over, and we will let it be. The house is finished almost, is it not? How beautiful it will look when the evergreens are grown! Do you call the style Palladian, Mr Barnet?'

'I – really don't quite know what it is. Yes, it must be Palladian, certainly. But I'll ask Jones, the architect; for, to tell the truth, I had not thought much about the style: I had nothing to do with choosing it, I am sorry to say.'

She would not let him harp on this gloomy refrain, and talked on bright matters till she said, producing a small roll of paper which he had noticed in her hand all the while, 'Mr Downe wished me to bring you this revised drawing of the late Mrs Downe's tomb, which the architect has just sent him. He would like you to look it over.'

The children came up with their hoops, and she went off with them down the harbour-road as usual. Barnet had been glad to get those words of thanks; he had been thinking for many months that he would like her to know of his share in finding her a home such as it was; and what he could not do for himself, Downe had now kindly done for him. He returned to his desolate house with a lighter tread; though in reason he hardly knew why his tread should be light.

On examining the drawing, Barnet found that, instead of the vast altar-tomb and canopy Downe had determined on at their last meeting, it was to be a more modest memorial even than had been suggested by the architect; a coped tomb of good solid construction, with no useless elaboration at all. Barnet was truly glad to see that Downe had come to reason of his own accord; and he returned the drawing with a note of approval.

He followed up the house-work as before, and as he walked up and down the rooms, occasionally gazing from the windows over the bulging green hills and the quiet harbour that lay between them, he murmured words and fragments of words, which, if listened to, would have revealed all the secrets of his existence. Whatever his reason in going there, Lucy did not call again: the walk to the shore seemed to be abandoned: he must have thought it as well for both that it should be so, for he did not go anywhere out of his accustomed ways to endeavour to discover her.

VIII

THE winter and the spring had passed, and the house was complete. It was a fine morning in the early part of June, and Barnet, though not in the habit of rising early, had taken a long walk before breakfast; returning by way of the new building. A sufficiently exciting cause of his restlessness to-day might have been the intelligence which had reached him the night before, that Lucy Savile was going to India after all, and notwithstanding the representations of her friends that such a journey was unadvisable in many ways for an unpractised girl, unless some more definite advantage lay at the end of it than she could show to be the case. Barnet's walk up the slope to the building betrayed that he was in a dissatisfied mood. He hardly saw that the dewy time of day lent an unusual freshness to the bushes and trees which had so recently put on their summer habit of heavy leafage, and made his newly laid lawn look as well established as an old manorial meadow. The house had been so adroitly placed between six tall elms which were growing on the site beforehand, that they seemed like real ancestral trees; and the rooks, young and old, cawed melodiously to their visitor.

The door was not locked, and he entered. No workmen appeared to be present, and he walked from sunny window to sunny window of the empty rooms, with a sense of seclusion which might have been very pleasant but for the antecedent knowledge that his almost paternal care of Lucy Savile was to be thrown away by her wilfulness. Footsteps echoed through an adjoining room; and bending his eyes in that direction, he perceived Mr Jones, the architect. He had come to look over the building before giving the contractor his final certificate. They walked over the house together. Everything was finished except the papering: there were the latest improvements of the period in bell-hanging, ventilating, smoke-jacks, fire-grates, and french windows. The business was soon ended, and Jones, having directed Barnet's attention to a book of wall-paper patterns which lay on a bench for his choice, was leaving to keep another engagement, when Barnet said, 'Is the tomb finished yet for Mrs Downe?'

'Well – yes: it is at last,' said the architect, coming back and speaking as if he were in a mood to make a confidence. 'I have had no end of trouble in the matter, and, to tell the truth, I am heartily glad it is over.'

Barnet expressed his surprise. 'I thought poor Downe had given up those extravagant notions of his? Then he has gone back to the altar and canopy after all? Well, he is to be excused, poor fellow!'

'O no – he has not at all gone back to them – quite the reverse,' Jones hastened to say. 'He has so reduced design after design, that the whole thing has been nothing but waste labour for me; till in the end it has become a common headstone, which a mason put up in half a day.'

'A common headstone?' said Barnet.

'Yes. I held out for some time for the addition of a footstone at least. But he said, O no – he couldn't afford it'.

'Ah, well – his family is growing up, poor fellow, and his expenses are getting serious.'

'Yes, exactly,' said Jones, as if the subject were none of his. And again directing Barnet's attention to the wall-papers, the bustling architect left him to keep some other engagement.

'A common headstone,' murmured Barnet, left again to

himself. He mused a minute or two, and next began looking over and selecting from the patterns; but had not long been engaged in the work when he heard another footstep on the gravel without, and somebody enter the open porch.

Barnet went to the door – it was his manservant in search of him.

'I have been trying for some time to find you, sir,' he said. 'This letter has come by the post, and it is marked immediate. And there's this one from Mr Downe, who called just now wanting to see you.' He searched his pocket for the second.

Barnet took the first letter – it had a black border, and bore the London postmark. It was not in his wife's handwriting, or in that of any person he knew; but conjecture soon ceased as he read the page, wherein he was briefly informed that Mrs Barnet had died suddenly on the previous day, at the furnished villa she had occupied near London.

Barnet looked vaguely round the empty hall, at the blank walls, out of the doorway. Drawing a long palpitating breath, and with eyes downcast, he turned and climbed the stairs slowly, like a man who doubted their stability. The fact of his wife having, as it were, died once already, and lived on again, had entirely dislodged the possibility of her actual death from his conjecture. He went to the landing, leant over the balusters, and after a reverie, of whose duration he had but the faintest notion, turned to the window and stretched his gaze to the cottage further down the road, which was visible from his landing, and from which Lucy still walked to the solicitor's house by a cross path. The faint words that came from his moving lips were simply, 'At last!'

Then, almost involuntarily, Barnet fell down on his knees and murmured some incoherent words of thanksgiving. Surely his virtue in restoring his wife to life had been rewarded! But, as if the impulse struck uneasily on his conscience, he quickly rose, brushed the dust from his trousers, and set himself to think of his next movements. He could not start for London for some hours; and as he had no preparations to make that could not be made in half an hour, he mechanically descended and resumed his occupation of turning over the wall-papers. They had all got brighter for him, those papers. It was all changed – who would sit in the rooms that they were to line? He went on to muse upon Lucy's conduct in so frequently coming to the house with the children; her occasional blush in speaking to him; her evident interest in him. What woman can in the long run avoid being interested in a man whom she knows to be devoted to her? If human solicitation could ever effect anything, there should be no going to India for Lucy now. All the papers previously chosen seemed wrong in their shades, and he began from the beginning to choose again.

While entering on the task he heard a forced 'Ahem!' from without the porch, evidently uttered to attract his attention, and footsteps again advancing to the door. His man, whom he had quite forgotten in his mental turmoil, was still waiting there.

'I beg your pardon, sir,' the man said from round the doorway; 'but here's the note from Mr Downe that you didn't take. He called just after you went out, and as he couldn't wait, he wrote this on your study-table.'

He handed in the letter – no black-bordered one now, but a practical-looking note in the well-known writing of the solicitor.

DEAR BARNET – it ran – Perhaps you will be prepared for the information I am about to give – that Lucy Savile and myself are going to be married this morning. I have hitherto said nothing as to my intention to any of my friends, for reasons which I am sure you will fully appreciate. The crisis has been brought about by her expressing her intention to join her brother in India. I then discovered that I could not do without her.

It is to be quite a private wedding; but it is my particular wish that you come down here quietly at ten, and go to church with us; it will add greatly to the pleasure I shall experience in the ceremony, and, I believe, to Lucy's also. I have called on you very early to make the request, in the

belief that I should find you at home; but you are beforehand with me in your early rising. – Yours sincerely,

C. DOWNE.

'Need I wait, sir?' said the servant after a dead silence.

'That will do, William. No answer,' said Barnet calmly.

When the man had gone Barnet re-read the letter. Turning
eventually to the wall-papers, which he had been at such
pains to select, he deliberately tore them into halves and
quarters, and threw them into the empty fireplace. Then he
went out of the house, locked the door, and stood in the front
awhile. Instead of returning into the town he went down the
harbour-road and thoughtfully lingered about by the sea,
near the spot where the body of Downe's late wife had been
found and brought ashore.

Barnet was a man with a rich capacity for misery, and
there is no doubt that he exercised it to its fullest extent
now. The events that had, as it were, dashed themselves together into one half-hour of this day showed that curious
refinement of cruelty in their arrangement which often proceeds from the bosom of the whimsical god at other times
known as blind Circumstance. That his few minutes of hope,
between the reading of the first and second letters, had carried him to extraordinary heights of rapture was proved by
the immensity of his suffering now. The sun blazing into his
face would have shown a close watcher that a horizontal line,
which had never been seen before, but which was never to
be gone thereafter, was somehow gradually forming itself in
the smooth of his forehead. His eyes, of a light hazel, had a
curious look which can only be described by the word
bruised; the sorrow that looked from them being largely
mixed with the surprise of a man taken unawares.

The secondary particulars of his present position, too,
were odd enough, though for some time they appeared to
engage little of his attention. Not a soul in the town knew,
as yet, of his wife's death; and he almost owed Downe the
kindness of not publishing it till the day was over: the con-
juncture, taken with that which had accompanied the death

of Mrs Downe, being so singular as to be quite sufficient to darken the pleasure of the impressionable solicitor to a cruel extent, if made known to him. But as Barnet could not set out on his journey to London, where his wife lay, for some hours (there being at this date no railway within a distance of many miles), no great reason existed why he should leave the town.

Impulse in all its forms characterized Barnet, and when he heard the distant clock strike the hour of ten his feet began to carry him up the harbour-road with the manner of a man who must do something to bring himself to life. He passed Lucy Savile's old house, his own new one, and came in view of the church. Now he gave a perceptible start, and his mechanical condition went away. Before the church-gate were a couple of carriages, and Barnet then could perceive that the marriage between Downe and Lucy was at that moment being solemnized within. A feeling of sudden, proud self-confidence, an indocile wish to walk unmoved in spite of grim environments, plainly possessed him, and when he reached the wicket-gate he turned in without apparent effort. Pacing up the paved footway he entered the church and stood for a while in the nave passage. A group of people was standing round the vestry door; Barnet advanced through these and stepped into the vestry.

There they were, busily signing their names. Seeing Downe about to look round Barnet averted his somewhat disturbed face for a second or two; when he turned again front to front he was calm and quite smiling; it was a creditable triumph over himself, and deserved to be remembered in his native town. He greeted Downe heartily, offering his congratulations.

It seemed as if Barnet expected a half-guilty look upon Lucy's face; but no; save the natural flush and flurry engendered by the service just performed, there was nothing whatever in her bearing which showed a disturbed mind: her grey-brown eyes carried in them now as at other times the well-known expression of common-sensed rectitude which never went so far as to touch on hardness. She shook hands with him, and Downe said warmly, 'I wish you could have come sooner: I called on purpose to ask you. You'll drive back with us now?'

'No, no,' said Barnet; 'I am not at all prepared; but I thought I would look in upon you for a moment, even though I had not time to go home and dress. I'll stand back and see you pass out, and observe the effect of the spectacle upon myself as one of the public.'

Then Lucy and her husband laughed, and Barnet laughed and retired; and the quiet little party went gliding down the nave and towards the porch, Lucy's new silk dress sweeping with a smart rustle round the base-mouldings of the ancient font, and Downe's little daughters following in a state of round-eyed interest in their position, and that of Lucy, their teacher and friend.

So Downe was comforted after his Emily's death, which had taken place twelve months, two weeks, and three days before that time.

When the two flys had driven off and the spectators had vanished, Barnet followed to the door, and went out into the sun. He took no more trouble to preserve a spruce exterior; his step was unequal, hesitating, almost convulsive; and the slight changes of colour which went on in his face seemed refracted from some inward flame. In the churchyard he became pale as a summer cloud, and finding it not easy to proceed he sat down on one of the tombstones and supported his head with his hand.

Hard by was a sexton filling up a grave which he had not found time to finish on the previous evening. Observing Barnet, he went up to him, and recognizing him, said, 'Shall I help you home, sir?'

'O no, thank you,' said Barnet, rousing himself and standing up. The sexton returned to his grave, followed by Barnet, who, after watching him awhile, stepped into the grave, now nearly filled, and helped to tread in the earth.

The sexton apparently thought his conduct a little singular, but he made no observation, and when the grave was full, Barnet suddenly stopped, looked far away, and with a decided step proceeded to the gate and vanished. The sexton rested on his shovel and looked after him for a few moments, and then began banking up the mound.

In those short minutes of treading in the dead man Barnet had formed a design, but what it was the inhabitants of that town did not for some long time imagine. He went home, wrote several letters of business, called on his lawyer, an old man of the same place who had been the legal adviser of Barnet's father before him, and during the evening overhauled a large quantity of letters and other documents in his possession. By eleven o'clock the heap of papers in and before Barnet's grate had reached formidable dimensions, and he began to burn them. This, owing to their quantity, it was not so easy to do as he had expected, and he sat long into the night to complete the task.

The next morning Barnet departed for London, leaving a note for Downe to inform him of Mrs Barnet's sudden death, and that he was going to bury her; but when a thrice-sufficient time for that purpose had elapsed, he was not seen again in his accustomed walks, or in his new house, or in his old one. He was gone for good, nobody knew whither. It was soon discovered that he had empowered his lawyer to dispose of all his property, real and personal, in the borough, and pay in the proceeds to the account of an unknown person at one of the large London banks. The person was by some supposed to be himself under an assumed name; but few, if any, had certain knowledge of that fact.

The elegant new residence was sold with the rest of his possessions; and its purchaser was no other than Downe, now a thriving man in the borough, and one whose growing family and new wife required more roomy accommodation than was afforded by the little house up the narrow side street. Barnet's old habitation was bought by the trustees of the Congregational Baptist body in that town, who pulled down the time-honoured dwelling and built a new chapel on its site. By the time the last hour of that, to Barnet, eventful year had chimed, every vestige of him had disappeared from the precincts of his native place, and the name became extinct in the borough of Port-Bredy, after having been a living force therein for more than two hundred years.

IX

TWENTY-ONE years and six months do not pass without setting a mark even upon durable stone and triple brass; upon humanity such a period works nothing less than transformation. In Barnet's old birthplace vivacious young children with bones like india-rubber had grown up to be stable men and women, men and women had dried in the skin, stiffened, withered, and sunk into decrepitude; while selections from every class had been consigned to the outlying cemetery. Of inorganic differences the greatest was that a railway had invaded the town, tying it on to a main line at a junction a dozen miles off. Barnet's house on the harbour-road, once so insistently new, had acquired a respectable mellowness, with ivy, Virginia creepers, lichens, damp patches, and even constitutional infirmities of its own like its elder fellows. Its architecture, once so very improved and modern, had already become stale in style, without having reached the dignity of being old-fashioned. Trees about the harbour-road had increased in circumference or disappeared under the saw; while the church had had such a tremendous practical joke played upon it by some facetious restorer or other as to be scarce recognizable by its dearest old friends.

During this long interval George Barnet had never once been seen or heard of in the town of his fathers.

It was in the evening of a market-day, and some half-dozen middle-aged farmers and dairymen were lounging round the bar of the Black Bull Hotel, occasionally dropping a remark to each other, and less frequently to the two barmaids who stood within the pewter-topped counter in a perfunctory attitude of attention, these latter sighing and making a private observation to one another at odd intervals, on more interesting experiences than the present.

'Days get shorter,' said one of the dairymen, as he looked towards the street, and noticed that the lamplighter was passing by.

The farmers merely acknowledged by their countenances the propriety of this remark, and finding that nobody else spoke, one of the barmaids said 'yes', in a tone of painful duty.

'Come fair-day we shall have to light up before we start for home-along.'

'That's true,' his neighbour conceded, with a gaze of blankness.

'And after that we shan't see much further difference all's winter.'

The rest were not unwilling to go even so far as this.

The barmaid sighed again, and raised one of her hands from the counter on which they rested to scratch the smallest surface of her face with the smallest of her fingers. She looked towards the door, and presently remarked, 'I think I hear the 'bus coming in from station.'

The eyes of the dairymen and farmers turned to the glass door dividing the hall from the porch, and in a minute or two the omnibus drew up outside. Then there was a lumbering down of luggage, and then a man came into the hall, followed by a porter with a portmanteau on his poll, which he deposited on a bench.

The stranger was an elderly person, with curly ashen-white hair, a deeply creviced outer corner to each eyelid, and a countenance baked by innumerable suns to the colour of terra-cotta, its hue and that of his hair contrasting like heat and cold respectively. He walked meditatively and gently, like one who was fearful of disturbing his own mental equilibrium. But whatever lay at the bottom of his breast had evidently made him so accustomed to its situation there that it caused him little practical inconvenience.

He paused in silence while, with his dubious eyes fixed on the barmaids, he seemed to consider himself. In a moment or two he addressed them, and asked to be accommodated for the night. As he waited he looked curiously round the hall, but said nothing. As soon as invited he disappeared up the staircase, preceded by a chambermaid and candle, and followed by a lad with his trunk. Not a soul had recognized him.

A quarter of an hour later, when the farmers and dairymen had driven off to their homesteads in the country, he came downstairs, took a biscuit and one glass of wine, and walked out into the town, where the radiance from the shop-windows had grown so in volume of late years as to flood with cheerfulness every standing cart, barrow, stall, and idler that occupied the wayside, whether shabby or genteel. His chief interest at present seemed to lie in the names painted over the shop-fronts and on doorways, as far as they were visible; these now differed to an ominous extent from what they had been one-and-twenty years before.

The traveller passed on till he came to the bookseller's, where he looked in through the glass door. A fresh-faced young man was standing behind the counter, otherwise the shop was empty. The grey-haired observer entered, asked for some periodical by way of paying for admission, and with his elbow on the counter began to turn over the pages he had bought, though that he read nothing was obvious.

At length he said, 'Is old Mr Watkins still alive?' in a voice which had a curious youthful cadence in it even now.

'My father is dead, sir,' said the young man.

'Ah, I am sorry to hear it,' said the stranger. 'But it is so many years since I last visited this town that I could hardly expect it should be otherwise.' After a short silence he continued – 'And is the firm of Barnet, Browse, and Company still in existence? – they used to be large flax-merchants and twine spinners here?'

'The firm is still going on, sir, but they have dropped the name of Barnet. I believe that was a sort of fancy name – at least, I never knew of any living Barnet. 'Tis now Browse and Co.'

'And does Andrew Jones still keep on as architect?'

'He's dead, sir.'

'And the vicar of St Mary's – Mr Melrose?'

'He's been dead a great many years.'

'Dear me!' He paused yet longer, and cleared his voice. 'Is Mr Downe, the solicitor, still in practice?'

'No, sir, he's dead. He died about seven years ago.'

Here it was a longer silence still; and an attentive observer would have noticed that the paper in the stranger's hand increased its imperceptible tremor to a visible shake. That grey-haired gentleman noticed it himself, and rested the paper on the counter. 'Is *Mrs* Downe still alive?' he asked, closing his lips firmly as soon as the words were out of his mouth, and dropping his eyes.

'Yes, sir, she's alive and well. She's living at the old place.'

'In East Street?'

'O no; at Château Ringdale. I believe it has been in the family for some generations.'

'She lives with her children, perhaps?'

'No; she has no children of her own. There were some Miss Downes; I think they were Mr Downe's daughters by a former wife; but they are married and living in other parts of the town. Mrs Downe lives alone.'

'Quite alone?'

'Yes, sir; quite alone.'

The newly arrived gentleman went back to the hotel and dined; after which he made some change in his dress, shaved back his beard to the fashion that had prevailed twenty years earlier, when he was young and interesting, and once more emerging, bent his steps in the direction of the harbour-road. Just before getting to the point where the pavement ceased and the houses isolated themselves, he overtook a shambling, stooping, unshaven man, who at first sight appeared like a professional tramp, his shoulders having a perceptible greasiness as they passed under the gaslight. Each pedestrian momentarily turned and regarded the other, and the tramp-like gentleman started back.

'Good – why – is that Mr Barnet? 'Tis Mr Barnet, surely!'

'Yes; and you are Charlson?'

'Yes – ah – you notice my appearance. The Fates have rather ill-used me. By the bye, that fifty pounds. I never paid it, did I? ... But I was not ungrateful!' Here the stooping man laid one hand emphatically on the palm of the other. 'I gave you a chance, Mr George Barnet, which many men would have thought full value received – the chance to marry your Lucy. As far as the world was concerned, your wife was a *drowned woman*, hey?'

'Heaven forbid all that, Charlson!'

'Well, well, 'twas a wrong way of showing gratitude, I suppose. And now a drop of something to drink for old acquaintance' sake! And Mr Barnet, she's again free – there's a chance now if you care for it – ha, ha!' And the speaker pushed his tongue into his hollow cheek and slanted his eye in the old fashion.

'I know all,' said Barnet quickly; and slipping a small present into the hands of the needy, saddening man, he stepped ahead and was soon in the outskirts of the town.

He reached the harbour-road, and paused before the entrance to a well-known house. It was so highly bosomed in trees and shrubs planted since the erection of the building that one would scarcely have recognized the spot as that which had been a mere neglected slope till chosen as a site for a dwelling. He opened the swing-gate, closed it noiselessly, and gently moved into the semicircular drive, which remained exactly as it had been marked out by Barnet on the morning when Lucy Savile ran in to thank him for procuring her the post of governess to Downe's children. But the growth of trees and bushes which revealed itself at every step was beyond all expectation; sun-proof and moon-proof bowers vaulted the walks, and the walls of the house were uniformly bearded with creeping plants as high as the first-floor windows.

After lingering for a few minutes in the dusk of the bending boughs, the visitor rang the door-bell, and on the servant appearing, he announced himself as 'an old friend of Mrs Downe's.'

The hall was lighted, but not brightly, the gas being turned low, as if visitors were rare. There was a stagnation in the dwelling; it seemed to be waiting. Could it really be waiting for him? The partitions which had been probed by Barnet's walking-stick when the mortar was green, were now quite brown with the antiquity of their varnish, and the ornamental woodwork of the staircase, which had glistened with a pale yellow newness when first erected, was now of a rich wine-colour. During the servant's absence the following colloquy could be dimly heard through the nearly closed door of the drawing-room.

'He didn't give his name?'

'He only said "an old friend", ma'am.'

'What kind of gentleman is he?'

'A staidish gentleman, with grey hair.'

The voice of the second speaker seemed to affect the listener greatly. After a pause, the lady said, 'Very well, I will see him.'

And the stranger was shown in face to face with the Lucy who had once been Lucy Savile. The round cheek of that formerly young lady had, of course, alarmingly flattened its curve in her modern representative; a pervasive greyness overspread her once dark brown hair, like morning rime on heather. The parting down the middle was wide and jagged; once it had been a thin white line, a narrow crevice between two high banks of shade. But there was still enough left to form a handsome knob behind, and some curls beneath inwrought with a few hairs like silver wires were very becoming. In her eyes the only modification was that their originally mild rectitude of expression had become a little more stringent than heretofore. Yet she was still girlish – a girl who had been gratuitously weighted by destiny with a burden of five-and-forty years instead of her proper twenty.

'Lucy, don't you know me?' he said, when the servant had closed the door.

'I knew you the instant I saw you!' she returned cheerfully. 'I don't know why, but I always thought you would come back to your old town again.'

She gave him her hand, and then they sat down. 'They said you were dead,' continued Lucy, 'but I never thought so. We should have heard of it for certain if you had been.'

'It is a very long time since we met.'

'Yes; what you must have seen, Mr Barnet, in all these roving years, in comparison with what I have seen in this quiet place!' Her face grew more serious. 'You know my husband has been dead a long time? I am a lonely old woman now, considering what I have been; though Mr Downe's daughters – all married – manage to keep me pretty cheerful.'

'And I am a lonely old man, and have been any time these twenty years.'

'But where have you kept yourself? And why did you go off so mysteriously?'

'Well, Lucy, I have kept myself a little in America, and a little in Australia, a little in India, a little at the Cape, and so on; I have not stayed in any place for a long time, as it seems to me, and yet more than twenty years have flown. But when people get to my age two years go like one! – Your second question, why did I go away so mysteriously, is surely not necessary. You guessed why, didn't you?'

'No, I never once guessed,' she said simply; 'nor did Charles, nor did anybody as far as I know.'

'Well, indeed! Now think it over again, and then look at me, and say if you can't guess?'

She looked him in the face with an inquiring smile. 'Surely not because of me?' she said, pausing at the commencement of surprise.

Barnet nodded, and smiled again; but his smile was sadder than hers.

'Because I married Charles?' she asked.

'Yes; solely because you married him on the day I was free to ask you to marry me. My wife died four-and-twenty hours before you went to church with Downe. The fixing of my journey at that particular moment was because of her funeral; but once away I knew I should have no inducement to come back, and took my steps accordingly.'

Her face assumed an aspect of gentle reflection, and she looked up and down his form with great interest in her eyes. 'I never thought of it!' she said. 'I knew, of course, that you had once implied some warmth of feeling towards me, but I concluded that it passed off. And I have always been under the impression that your wife was alive at the time of my marriage. Was it not stupid of me! – But you will have some tea or something? I have never dined late, you know, since my husband's death. I have got into the way of making a regular meal of tea. You will have some tea with me, will you not?'

The travelled man assented quite readily, and tea was brought in. They sat and chatted over the tray, regardless of the flying hour. 'Well, well!' said Barnet presently, as for the first time he leisurely surveyed the room; 'how like it all is, and yet how different! Just where your piano stands was a board on a couple of trestles, bearing the patterns of wall-papers, when I was last here. I was choosing them – standing in this way, as it might be. Then my servant came in at the door, and handed me a note, so. It was from Downe, and announced that you were just going to be married to him. I chose no more wall-papers – tore up all those I had selected, and left the house. I never entered it again till now.'

'Ah, at last I understand it all,' she murmured.

They had both risen and gone to the fireplace. The mantel came almost on a level with her shoulder, which gently rested against it, and Barnet laid his hand upon the shelf close beside her shoulder. 'Lucy,' he said, 'better late than never. Will you marry me now?'

She started back, and the surprise which was so obvious in her wrought even greater surprise in him that it should be so. It was difficult to believe that she had been quite blind to the situation, and yet all reason and common sense went to prove that she was not acting.

'You take me quite unawares by such a question!' she said, with a forced laugh of uneasiness. It was the first time she had shown any embarrassment at all. 'Why,' she added, 'I couldn't marry you for the world.'

'Not after all this! Why not?'

'It is – I would – I really think I may say it – I would upon the whole rather marry you, Mr Barnet, than any other man

I have ever met, if I ever dreamed of marriage again. But I don't dream of it – it is quite out of my thoughts; I have not the least intention of marrying again.'

'But – on my account – couldn't you alter your plans a little? Come!'

'Dear Mr Barnet,' she said with a little flutter, 'I would on your account if on anybody's in existence. But you don't know in the least what it is you are asking – such an impractical thing – I won't say ridiculous, of course, because I see that you are really in earnest, and earnestness is never ridiculous to my mind.'

'Well, yes,' said Barnet more slowly, dropping her hand, which he had taken at the moment of pleading, 'I am in earnest. The resolve, two months ago, at the Cape, to come back once more was, it is true, rather sudden, and as I see now, not well considered. But I am in earnest in asking.'

'And I in declining. With all good feeling and all kindness, let me say that I am quite opposed to the idea of marrying a second time.'

'Well, no harm has been done,' he answered, with the same subdued and tender humorousness that he had shown on such occasions in early life. 'If you really won't accept me, I must put up with it, I suppose.' His eye fell on the clock as he spoke. 'Had you any notion that it was so late?' he asked. 'How absorbed I have been!'

She accompanied him to the hall, helped him to put on his overcoat, and let him out of the house herself.

'Goodnight,' said Barnet, on the doorstep, as the lamp shone in his face. 'You are not offended with me?'

'Certainly not. Nor you with me?'

'I'll consider whether I am or not,' he pleasantly replied. 'Goodnight.'

She watched him safely through the gate; and when his footsteps had died away upon the road, closed the door softly and returned to the room. Here the modest widow long pondered his speeches, with eyes dropped to an unusually low level. Barnet's urbanity under the blow of her refusal greatly impressed her. After having his long period of probation rendered useless by her decision, he had shown no anger, and had philosophically taken her words as if he deserved no better ones. It was very gentlemanly of him, certainly; it was more than gentlemanly; it was heroic and grand. The more she meditated, the more she questioned the virtue of her conduct in checking him so peremptorily; and went to her bedroom in a mood of dissatisfaction. On looking in the glass she was reminded that there was not so much remaining of her former beauty as to make his frank declaration an impulsive natural homage to her cheeks and eyes; it must undoubtedly have arisen from an old staunch feeling of his, deserving tenderest consideration. She recalled to her mind with much pleasure that he had told her he was staying at the Black Bull Hotel; so that if, after waiting a day or two, he should not, in his modesty, call again, she might then send him a nice little note. To alter her views for the present was far from her intention; but she would allow herself to be induced to reconsider the case, as any generous woman ought to do.

The morrow came and passed, and Mr Barnet did not drop in. At every knock, light youthful hues flew across her cheek; and she was abstracted in the presence of her other visitors. In the evening she walked about the house, not knowing what to do with herself; the conditions of existence seemed totally different from those which ruled only four-and-twenty short hours ago. What had been at first a tantalizing elusive sentiment was getting acclimatized within her as a definite hope, and her person was so informed by that emotion that she might almost have stood as its emblematical representative by the time the clock struck ten. In short, an interest in Barnet precisely resembling that of her early youth led her present heart to belie her yesterday's words to him, and she longed to see him again.

The next day she walked out early, thinking she might meet him in the street. The growing beauty of her romance absorbed her, and she went from the street to the fields, and from the fields to the shore, without any consciousness of distance, till reminded by her weariness that she could go no further. He had nowhere appeared. In the evening she took a step which under the circumstances seemed justifiable; she wrote a note to him at the hotel, inviting him to tea with her at six precisely, and signing her note 'Lucy'.

In a quarter of an hour the messenger came back. Mr Barnet had left the hotel early in the morning of the day before, but he had stated that he would probably return in the course of the week.

The note was sent back, to be given to him immediately on his arrival.

There was no sign from the inn that this desired event had occurred, either on the next day or the day following. On both nights she had been restless, and had scarcely slept half an hour.

On the Saturday, putting off all diffidence, Lucy went herself to the Black Bull, and questioned the staff closely.

Mr Barnet had cursorily remarked when leaving that he might return on the Thursday or Friday, but they were directed not to reserve a room for him unless he should write.

He had left no address.

Lucy sorrowfully took back her note, went home, and resolved to wait.

She did wait – years and years – but Barnet never reappeared.

April 1880

A Tragedy of Two Ambitions

———◆◆◆◆◆———

I

THE shouts of the village-boys came in at the window, accompanied by broken laughter from loungers at the inn-door; but the brothers Halborough worked on.

They were sitting in a bedroom of the master-millwright's house, engaged in the untutored reading of Greek and Latin. It was no tale of Homeric blows and knocks, Argonautic voyaging, or Theban family woe that inflamed their imaginations and spurred them onward. They were plodding away at the Greek Testament, immersed in a chapter of the idiomatic and difficult Epistle to the Hebrews.

The Dog-day sun in its decline reached the low ceiling with slanting sides, and the shadows of the great goat's-willow swayed and interchanged upon the walls like a spectral army manoeuvring. The open casement which admitted the remoter sounds now brought the voice of some-one close at hand. It was their sister, a pretty girl of fourteen, who stood in the court below.

'I can see the tops of your heads! What's the use of staying up there? I like you not to go out with the street-boys; but do come and play with me!'

They treated her as an inadequate interlocutor, and put her off with some slight word. She went away disappointed. Presently there was a dull noise of heavy footsteps at the side of the house, and one of the brothers sat up. 'I fancy I hear him coming,' he murmured, his eyes on the window.

A man in the light drab clothes of an old-fashioned country tradesman approached from round the corner, reeling as he came. The elder son flushed with anger, rose from his books, and descended the stairs. The younger sat on, till, after the lapse of a few minutes, his brother re-entered the room.

'Did Rosa see him?'

'No.'

'Nor anybody?'

'No.'

'What have you done with him?'

'He's in the straw-shed. I got him in with some trouble, and he has fallen asleep. I thought this would be the explanation of his absence! No stones dressed for Miller Kench, the great wheel of the saw-mills waiting for new float-boards, even the poor folk not able to get their wagons wheeled.'

'What *is* the use of poring over this!' said the younger, shutting up Donnegan's *Lexicon* with a slap. 'O if we had only been able to keep mother's nine hundred pounds, what we could have done!'

'How well she had estimated the sum necessary! Four hundred and fifty each, she thought. And I have no doubt that we could have done it on that, with care.'

This loss of the nine hundred pounds was the sharp thorn of their crown. It was a sum which their mother had amassed with great exertion and self-denial, by adding to a chance legacy such other small amounts as she could lay hands on from time to time; and she had intended with the hoard to indulge the dear wish of her heart – that of sending her sons, Joshua and Cornelius, to one of the Universities, having been informed that from four hundred to four hundred and fifty each might carry them through their terms with such great economy as she knew she could trust them to practise. But she had died a year or two before this time, worn out by too keen a strain towards these ends; and the money, coming unreservedly into the hands of their father, had been nearly dissipated. With its exhaustion went all opportunity and hope of a university degree for the sons.

'It drives me mad when I think of it,' said Joshua, the elder. 'And here we work and work in our own bungling way, and the utmost we can hope for is a term of years as national schoolmasters, and possible admission to a theological college, and ordination as despised licentiates.'

The anger of the elder was reflected as simple sadness in the face of the other. 'We can preach the Gospel as well without a hood on our surplices as with one,' he said with feeble consolation.

'Preach the Gospel – true,' said Joshua with a slight pursing of mouth. 'But we can't rise!'

'Let us make the best of it, and grind on.'

The other was silent, and they drearily bent over their books again.

The cause of all this gloom, the millwright Halborough, now snoring in the shed, had been a thriving master-machinist, notwithstanding his free and careless disposition, till a taste for a more than adequate quantity of strong liquor took hold of him; since when his habits had interfered with his business sadly. Already millers went elsewhere for their gear, and only one set of hands was now kept going, though there were formerly two. Already he found a difficulty in meeting his men at the week's end, and though they had been reduced in number there was barely enough work to do for those who remained.

The sun dropped lower and vanished, the shouts of the village children ceased to resound, darkness cloaked the students' bedroom, and all the scene outwardly breathed peace. None knew of the fevered youthful ambitions that throbbed in two breasts within the quiet creeper-covered walls of the millwright's house.

In a few months the brothers left the village of their birth to enter themselves as students in a training college for schoolmasters; first having placed their young sister Rosa under as efficient a tuition at a fashionable watering-place as the means at their disposal could command.

II

A man in semi-clerical dress was walking along the road which led from the railway-station into a provincial town. As he walked he read persistently, only looking up once now and then to see that he was keeping on the foot-track and to avoid other passengers. At those moments, whoever had known the former students at the millwright's would have perceived that one of them, Joshua Halborough, was the peripatetic reader here.

What had been simple force in the youth's face was energized judgement in the man's. His character was gradually writing itself out in his countenance. That he was watching his own career with deeper and deeper interest, that he continually 'heard his days before him', and cared to hear little else, might have been hazarded from what was seen there. His ambitions were, in truth, passionate, yet controlled; so that the germs of many more plans than ever blossomed to maturity had place in him; and forward visions were kept purposely in twilight, to avoid distraction.

Events so far had been encouraging. Shortly after assuming the mastership of his first school he had obtained an introduction to the Bishop of a diocese far from his native county, who had looked upon him as a promising young man and taken him in hand. He was now in the second year of his residence at the theological college of the cathedral-town, and would soon be presented for ordination.

He entered the town, turned into a back street, and then into a yard, keeping his book before him till he set foot under the arch of the latter place. Round the arch was written 'National School', and the stonework of the jambs was worn away as nothing but boys and the waves of ocean will wear it. He was soon amid the sing-song accents of the scholars.

His brother Cornelius, who was the schoolmaster here, laid down the pointer with which he was directing attention to the Capes of Europe, and came forward.

'That's his brother Jos!' whispered one of the sixth-standard boys. 'He's going to be a pa'son. He's now at college.'

'Corney is going to be one too, when he's saved enough money,' said another.

After greeting his brother, whom he had not seen for several months, the junior began to explain his system of teaching geography.

But Halborough the elder took no interest in the subject. 'How about your own studies?' he asked. 'Did you get the books I sent?'

Cornelius had received them, and he related what he was doing.

'Mind you work in the morning. What time do you get up?'

The younger replied: 'Half past five.'

'Half past four is not a minute too soon this time of the year. There is no time like the morning for construing. I don't know why, but when I feel even too dreary to read a novel I can translate – there is something mechanical about it, I suppose. Now, Cornelius, you are rather behindhand, and have some heavy reading before you if you mean to get out of this next Christmas.'

'I am afraid I have.'

'We must soon sound the Bishop. I am sure you will get a title without difficulty when he has heard all. The sub-dean, the principal of my college, says that the best plan will be for you to come there when his lordship is present at an examination, and he'll get you a personal interview with him. Mind you make a good impression upon him. I found in my case that that was everything, and doctrine almost nothing. You'll do for a deacon, Corney, if not for a priest.'

The younger remained thoughtful. 'Have you heard from Rosa lately?' he asked; 'I had a letter this morning.'

'Yes. The little minx writes rather too often. She is homesick – though Brussels must be an attractive place enough. But she must make the most of her time over there. I thought a year would be enough for her, after that high-class school at Sandbourne, but I have decided to give her two, and make a good job of it, expensive as the establishment is.'

Their two rather harsh faces had softened directly they began to speak of their sister, whom they loved more ambitiously than they loved themselves.

'But where is the money to come from, Joshua?'

'I have already got it.' He looked round, and finding that some boys were near withdrew a few steps. 'I have borrowed it at five per cent from the farmer who used to occupy the farm next to our field. You remember him.'

'But about paying him?'

'I shall pay him by degrees out of my stipend. No, Cornelius, it was no use to do the thing by halves. She promises to be a most attractive, not to say beautiful, girl. I have seen that for years; and if her face is not her fortune, her face and her brains together will be, if I observe and contrive aright. That she should be, every inch of her, an accomplished and refined woman, was indispensable for the fulfilment of her destiny, and for moving onwards and upwards with us; and she'll do it, you will see. I'd half starve myself rather than take her away from that school now.'

They looked round the school they were in. To Cornelius it was natural and familiar enough, but to Joshua, with his limited human sympathies, who had just dropped in from a superior sort of place, the sight jarred unpleasantly, as being that of something he had left behind. 'I shall be glad when you are out of this,' he said, 'and in your pulpit, and well through your first sermon.'

'You may as well say inducted into my fat living, while you are about it.'

'Ah, well – don't think lightly of the Church. There's a fine work for any man of energy in the Church, as you'll find,' he said fervidly. 'Torrents of infidelity to be stemmed, new views of old subjects to be expounded, truths in spirit to be substituted for truths in the letter . . .' He lapsed into reverie with the vision of his career, persuading himself that it was ardour for Christianity which spurred him on, and not pride of place. He had shouldered a body of doctrine, and was prepared to defend it tooth and nail, solely for the honour and glory that warriors win.

'If the Church is elastic, and stretches to the shape of the time, she'll last, I suppose,' said Cornelius. 'If not—. Only think, I bought a copy of Paley's *Evidences*, best edition, broad margins, excellent preservation, at a bookstall the other day for – ninepence; and I thought that at this rate Christianity must be in rather a bad way.'

'No, no!' said the other almost angrily. 'It only shows that such defences are no longer necessary. Men's eyes can see the truth without extraneous assistance. Besides, we are in for Christianity, and must stick to her whether or no. I am just now going right through Pusey's *Library of the Fathers*.'

'You'll be a bishop, Joshua, before you have done!'

'Ah!' said the other bitterly, shaking his head. 'Perhaps I might have been – I might have been! But where is my DD or LLD; and how be a bishop without that kind of appendage? Archbishop Tillotson was the son of a Sowerby clothier, but he was sent to Clare College. To hail Oxford or Cambridge as *alma mater* is not for me – for us! My God! when I think of what we should have been – what fair promise has been blighted by that cursed, worthless—'

'Hush, hush! . . . But I feel it, too, as much as you. I have seen it more forcibly lately. You would have obtained your degree long before this time – possibly fellowship – and I should have been on my way to mine.'

'Don't talk of it,' said the other. 'We must do the best we can.'

They looked out of the window sadly, through the dusty panes, so high up that only the sky was visible. By degrees the haunting trouble loomed again, and Cornelius broke the silence with a whisper: 'He has called on me!'

The living pulses died on Joshua's face, which grew arid as a clinker. 'When was that?' he asked quickly.

'Last week.'

'How did he get here – so many miles?'

'Came by railway. He came to ask for money.'

'Ah!'

'He says he will call on you.'

Joshua replied resignedly. The theme of their conversation spoilt his buoyancy for that afternoon. He returned in the evening, Cornelius accompanying him to the station; but he did not read in the train which took him back to the Fountall Theological College, as he had done on the way out. That ineradicable trouble still remained as a squalid spot in the expanse of his life. He sat with the other students in the cathedral choir next day; and the recollection of the trouble obscured the purple splendour thrown by the panes upon the floor.

It was afternoon. All was as still in the Close as a cathedral-green can be between the Sunday services, and the incessant cawing of the rooks was the only sound. Joshua Halborough had finished his ascetic lunch, and had gone into the library, where he stood for a few moments looking out of the large window facing the green. He saw walking slowly across it a man in a fustian coat and a battered white hat with a much-ruffled nap, having upon his arm a tall gipsy-woman wearing long brass earrings. The man was staring quizzically at the west front of the cathedral, and Halborough recognized in him the form and features of his father. Who the woman was he knew not. Almost as soon as Joshua became conscious of these things, the sub-dean, who was also the principal of the college, and of whom the young man stood in more awe than of the Bishop himself, emerged from the gate and entered a path across the Close. The pair met the dignitary, and to Joshua's horror his father turned and addressed the sub-dean.

What passed between them he could not tell. But as he stood in a cold sweat he saw his father place his hand familiarly on the sub-dean's shoulder; the shrinking response of the latter, and his quick withdrawal, told his feeling. The woman seemed to say nothing, but when the sub-dean had passed by they came on towards the college gate.

Halborough flew along the corridor and out at the side door, so as to intercept them before they could reach the front entrance, for which they were making. He caught them behind a clump of laurel.

'By Jerry, here's the very chap! Well, you're a fine fellow, Jos, never to send your father as much as a twist o' baccy on such an occasion, and to leave him to travel all these miles to find 'ee out!'

'First, who is this?' said Joshua Halborough with pale dignity, waving his hand towards the buxom woman with the great earrings.

'Dammy, the mis'ess! Your step-mother! Didn't you know I'd married? She helped me home from market one night, and we came to terms, and struck the bargain. Didn't we, Selinar?'

'Oi, by the great Lord an' we did!' simpered the lady.

'Well, what sort of a place is this you are living in?' asked the millwright. 'A kind of house-of-correction, apparently?'

Joshua listened abstractedly, his features set to resignation. Sick at heart he was going to ask them if they were in want of any necessary, any meal, when his father cut him short by saying, 'Why, we've called to ask ye to come round and take pot-luck with us at the Cock-and-Bottle, where we've put up for the day, on our way to see mis'ess's friends at Binegar Fair, where they'll be lying under canvas for a night or two. As for the victuals at the Cock I can't testify to 'em at all; but for the drink, they've the rarest drop of Old Tom that I've tasted for many a year.'

'Thanks; but I am a teetotaller; and I have lunched,' said Joshua, who could fully believe his father's testimony to the gin, from the odour of his breath. 'You see we have to observe regular habits here; and I couldn't be seen at the Cock-and-Bottle just now.'

'O dammy, then don't come, your reverence. Perhaps

you won't mind standing treat for those who can be seen there?'

'Not a penny,' said the younger firmly. 'You've had enough already.'

'Thank you for nothing. By the bye, who was that spindle-legged, shoe-buckled parson feller we met by now? He seemed to think we should poison him!'

Joshua remarked coldly that it was the principal of his college, guardedly inquiring, 'Did you tell him whom you were come to see?'

His father did not reply. He and his strapping gipsy wife – if she were his wife – stayed no longer, and disappeared in the direction of the High Street. Joshua Halborough went back to the library. Determined as was his nature, he wept hot tears upon the books, and was immeasurably more wretched that afternoon than the unwelcome millwright. In the evening he sat down and wrote a letter to his brother, in which, after stating what had happened, and expatiating upon this new disgrace in the gipsy wife, he propounded a plan for raising money sufficient to induce the couple to emigrate to Canada. 'It is our only chance,' he said. 'The case as it stands is maddening. For a successful painter, sculptor, musician, author, who takes society by storm, it is no drawback, it is sometimes even a romantic recommendation, to hail from outcasts and profligates. But for a clergyman of the Church of England! Cornelius, it is fatal! To succeed in the Church, people must believe in you, first of all, as a gentleman, secondly as a man of means, thirdly as a scholar, fourthly as a preacher, fifthly, perhaps, as a Christian – but always first as a gentleman, with all their heart and soul and strength. I would have faced the fact of being a small machinist's son, and have taken my chance, if he'd been in any sense respectable and decent. The essence of Christianity is humility, and by the help of God I would have brazened it out. But this terrible vagabondage and disreputable connection! If he does not accept my terms and leave the country, it will extinguish us and kill me. For how can we live, and relinquish our high aim, and bring down our dear sister Rosa to the level of a gipsy's step-daughter?'

III

THERE was excitement in the parish of Narrobourne one day. The congregation had just come out from morning service, and the whole conversation was of the new curate, Mr Halborough, who had officiated for the first time, in the absence of the rector.

Never before had the feeling of the villagers approached a level which could be called excitement on such a matter as this. The droning which had been the rule in that quiet old place for a century seemed ended at last. They repeated the text to each other as a refrain: 'O Lord, be thou my helper!' Not within living memory till today had the subject of the sermon formed the topic of conversation from the church door to the churchyard gate, to the exclusion of personal remarks on those who had been present, and on the week's news in general.

The thrilling periods of the preacher hung about their minds all that day. The parish being steeped in indifferentism, it happened that when the youths and maidens, middle-aged and old people, who had attended church that morning, recurred as by a fascination to what Halborough had said, they did so more or less indirectly, and even with the subterfuge of a light laugh that was not real, so great was their shyness under the novelty of their sensations.

What was more curious than that these unconventional villagers should have been excited by a preacher of a new school after forty years of familiarity with the old hand who had had charge of their souls, was the effect of Halborough's address upon the occupants of the manor-house pew, including the owner of the estate. These thought they knew how to discount the mere sensational sermon, how to minimize flash oratory to its bare proportions; but they had yielded like the rest of the assembly to the charm of the newcomer.

Mr Fellmer, the landowner, was a young widower, whose mother, still in the prime of life, had returned to her old position in the family mansion since the death of her son's wife in the year after her marriage, at the birth of a fragile little girl. From the date of his loss to the present time, Fellmer had led an inactive existence in the seclusion of the parish; a lack of motive seemed to leave him listless. He had gladly reinstated his mother in the gloomy house, and his main occupation now lay in stewarding his estate, which was not large. Mrs Fellmer, who had sat beside him under Halborough this morning, was a cheerful, straightforward woman, who did her marketing and her alms-giving in person, was fond of old-fashioned flowers, and walked about the village on very wet days visiting the parishioners. These, the only two great ones of Narrobourne, were impressed by Joshua's eloquence as much as the cottagers.

Halborough had been briefly introduced to them on his arrival some days before, and, their interest being kindled, they waited a few moments till he came out of the vestry, to walk down the churchyard-path with him. Mrs Fellmer spoke warmly of the sermon, of the good fortune of the parish in his advent, and hoped he had found comfortable quarters.

Halborough, faintly flushing, said that he had obtained very fair lodgings in the roomy house of a farmer, whom he named.

She feared he would find it very lonely, especially in the evenings, and hoped they would see a good deal of him. When would he dine with them? Could he not come that day – it must be so dull for him the first Sunday evening in country lodgings?

Halborough replied that it would give him much pleasure but that he feared he must decline. 'I am not altogether alone,' he said. 'My sister, who has just returned from Brussels, and who felt, as you do, that I should be rather dismal by myself, has accompanied me hither to stay a few days till she has put my rooms in order and set me going. She was too fatigued to come to church, and is waiting for me now at the farm.'

'O, but bring your sister – that will be still better! I shall be delighted to know her. How I wish I had been aware! Do tell her, please, that we had no idea of her presence.'

Halborough reassured Mrs Fellmer that he would certainly bear the message; but as to her coming he was not so sure. The real truth was, however, that the matter would be decided by him, Rosa having an almost filial respect for his wishes. But he was uncertain as to the state of her wardrobe, and had determined that she should not enter the manor-house at a disadvantage that evening, when there would probably be plenty of opportunities in the future of her doing so becomingly.

He walked to the farm in long strides. This, then, was the outcome of his first morning's work as curate here. Things had gone fairly well with him. He had been ordained; he was in a comfortable parish, where he would exercise almost sole supervision, the rector being infirm. He had made a deep impression at starting, and the absence of a hood seemed to have done him no harm. Moreover, by considerable persuasion and payment, his father and the dark woman had been shipped off to Canada, where they were not likely to interfere greatly with his interests.

Rosa came out to meet him. 'Ah! You should have gone to church like a good girl,' he said.

'Yes – I wished I had afterwards. But I do so hate church as a rule that even your preaching was underestimated in my mind. It was too bad of me!'

The girl who spoke thus playfully was fair, tall, and sylph-like, in a muslin dress, and with just the coquettish *désinvolture* which an English girl brings home from abroad, and loses again after a few months of native life. Joshua was the reverse of playful; the world was too important a concern for him to indulge in light moods. He told her in decided, practical phraseology of the invitation.

'Now, Rosa, we must go – that's settled – if you've a dress

that can be made fit to wear all on the hop like this. You didn't, of course, think of bringing an evening dress to such an out-of-the-way place?'

But Rosa had come from the wrong city to be caught napping in those matters. 'Yes, I did,' said she. 'One never knows what may turn up.'

'Well done! Then off we go at seven.'

The evening drew on, and at dusk they started on foot, Rosa pulling up the edge of her skirt under her cloak out of the way of the dews, so that it formed a great wind-bag all round her, and carrying her satin shoes under her arm. Joshua would not let her wait till she got indoors before changing them, as she proposed, but insisted on her performing that operation under a tree, so that they might enter as if they had not walked. He was nervously formal about such trifles, while Rosa took the whole proceeding – walk, dressing, dinner, and all – as a pastime. To Joshua it was a serious step in life.

A more unexpected kind of person for a curate's sister was never presented at a dinner. The surprise of Mrs Fellmer was unconcealed. She had looked forward to a Dorcas, or Martha, or Rhoda at the outside, and a shade of misgiving crossed her face. It was possible that, had the young lady accompanied her brother to church, there would have been no dining at Narrobourne House that day.

Not so with the young widower, her son. He resembled a sleeper who had awakened in a summer noon expecting to find it only dawn. He could scarcely help stretching his arms and yawning in their faces, so strong was his sense of being suddenly aroused to an unforeseen thing. When they had sat down to table he at first talked to Rosa somewhat with the air of a ruler in the land; but the woman lurking in the acquaintance soon brought him to his level, and the girl from Brussels saw him looking at her mouth, her hands, her contour, as if he could not quite comprehend how they got created: then he dropped into the more satisfactory stage which discerns no particulars.

He talked but little; she said much. The homeliness of

the Fellmers, to her view, though they were regarded with such awe down here, quite disembarrassed her. The squire had become so unpractised, had dropped so far into the shade during the last year or so of his life, that he had almost forgotten what the world contained till this evening reminded him. His mother, after her first moments of doubt, appeared to think that he must be left to his own guidance, and gave her attention to Joshua.

With all his foresight and doggedness of aim, the result of that dinner exceeded Halborough's expectations. In weaving his ambitions he had viewed his sister Rosa as a slight, bright thing to be helped into notice by his abilities; but it now began to dawn upon him that the physical gifts of nature to her might do more for them both than nature's intellectual gifts to himself. While he was patiently boring the tunnel Rosa seemed about to fly over the mountain.

He wrote the next day to his brother, now occupying his own old rooms in the theological college, telling him exultingly of the unanticipated *début* of Rosa at the manor-house. The next post brought him a reply of congratulation, dashed with the counteracting intelligence that his father did not like Canada – that his gipsy wife had deserted him, which made him feel so dreary that he thought of returning home.

In his recent satisfaction at his own successes Joshua Halborough had well-nigh forgotten his chronic trouble – latterly screened by distance. But it now returned upon him; he saw more in this brief announcement than his brother seemed to see. It was the cloud no bigger than a man's hand.

IV

THE following December, a day or two before Christmas, Mrs Fellmer and her son were walking up and down the broad gravel path which bordered the east front of the house. Till within the last half-hour the morning had been a drizzling one, and they had just emerged for a short turn before luncheon.

'You see, dear Mother,' the son was saying, 'it is the peculiarity of my position which makes her appear to me in such a desirable light. When you consider how I have been crippled at starting, how my life has been maimed; that I feel anything like publicity distasteful, that I have no political ambition, and that my chief aim and hope lie in the education of the little thing Annie has left me, you must see how desirable a wife like Miss Halborough would be, to prevent my becoming a mere vegetable.'

'If you adore her, I suppose you must have her!' replied his mother with dry indirectness. 'But you'll find that she will not be content to live on here as you do, giving her whole mind to a young child.'

'That's just where we differ. Her very disqualification, that of being a nobody, as you call it, is her recommendation in my eyes. Her lack of influential connections limits her ambition. From what I know of her, a life in this place is all that she would wish for. She would never care to go outside the park-gates if it were necessary to stay within.'

'Being in love with her, Albert, and meaning to marry her, you invent your practical reasons to make the case respectable. Well, do as you will; I have no authority over you, so why should you consult me? You mean to propose on this very occasion, no doubt. Don't you, now?'

'By no means. I am merely revolving the idea in my mind. If on further acquaintance she turns out to be as good as she has hitherto seemed – well, I shall see. Admit, now, that you like her.'

'I readily admit it. She is very captivating at first sight. But as a stepmother to your child! You seem mighty anxious, Albert, to get rid of me!'

'Not at all. And I am not so reckless as you think. I don't make up my mind in a hurry. But the thought having occurred to me, I mention it to you at once, Mother. If you dislike it, say so.'

'I don't say anything. I will try to make the best of it if you are determined. When does she come?'

'Tomorrow.'

All this time there were great preparations in train at the curate's, who was now a householder. Rosa, whose two or three weeks' stay on two occasions earlier in the year had so affected the squire, was coming again, and at the same time her younger brother Cornelius, to make up a family party. Rosa, who journeyed from the Midlands, could not arrive till late in the evening, but Cornelius was to get there in the afternoon, Joshua going out to meet him in his walk across the fields from the railway.

Everything being ready in Joshua's modest abode he started on his way, his heart buoyant and thankful, if ever it was in his life. He was of such good report himself that his brother's path into holy orders promised to be unexpectedly easy; and he longed to compare experiences with him, even though there was on hand a more exciting matter still. From his youth he had held that, in old-fashioned country places, the Church conferred social prestige up to a certain point at a cheaper price than any other profession or pursuit; and events seemed to be proving him right.

He had walked about half an hour when he saw Cornelius coming along the path; and in a few minutes the two brothers met. The experiences of Cornelius had been less immediately interesting than those of Joshua, but his personal position was satisfactory, and there was nothing to account for the singularly subdued manner that he exhibited, which at first Joshua set down to the fatigue of over-study; and he proceeded to the subject of Rosa's arrival in the evening, and the probable consequences of this her third visit. 'Before next Easter she'll be his wife, my boy,' said Joshua with grave exultation.

Cornelius shook his head. 'She comes too late!' he returned.

'What do you mean?'

'Look here.' He produced the Fountall paper, and placed his finger on a paragraph, which Joshua read. It appeared under the report of Petty Sessions, and was a commonplace case of disorderly conduct, in which a man was sent to prison for seven days for breaking windows in that town.

'Well?' said Joshua.

'It happened during an evening that I was in the street; and the offender is our father.'

'Not – how – I sent him more money on his promising to stay in Canada?'

'He is home, safe enough.' Cornelius in the same gloomy tone gave the remainder of his information. He had witnessed the scene, unobserved of his father, and had heard him say that he was on his way to see his daughter, who was going to marry a rich gentleman. The only good fortune attending the untoward incident was that the millwright's name had been printed as Joshua Alborough.

'Beaten! We are to be beaten on the eve of our expected victory!' said the elder brother. 'How did he guess that Rosa was likely to marry? Good Heaven! Cornelius, you seem doomed to bring bad news always, do you not!'

'I do,' said Cornelius. 'Poor Rosa!'

It was almost in tears, so great was their heart-sickness and shame, that the brothers walked the remainder of the way to Joshua's dwelling. In the evening they set out to meet Rosa, bringing her to the village in a fly; and when she had come into the house, and was sitting down with them, they almost forgot their secret anxiety in contemplating her, who knew nothing about it.

Next day the Fellmers came, and the two or three days after that were a lively time. That the squire was yielding to his impulses – making up his mind – there could be no doubt. On Sunday Cornelius read the service, and Joshua preached. Mrs Fellmer was quite maternal towards Rosa, and it appeared that she had decided to welcome the inevitable with a good grace. The pretty girl was to spend yet another afternoon with the elder lady, superintending some parish treat at the house in observance of Christmas, and afterwards to stay on to dinner, her brothers to fetch her in the evening. They were also invited to dine, but they could not accept owing to an engagement.

The engagement was of a sombre sort. They were going to meet their father, who would that day be released from Fountall Gaol, and try to persuade him to keep away from Narrobourne. Every exertion was to be made to get him back to Canada, to his old home in the Midlands – anywhere, so that he would not impinge disastrously upon their courses, and blast their sister's prospects of the auspicious marriage which was just then hanging in the balance.

As soon as Rosa had been fetched away by her friends at the manor-house her brothers started on their expedition, without waiting for dinner or tea. Cornelius, to whom the millwright always addressed his letters when he wrote any, drew from his pocket and re-read as he walked the curt note which had led to this journey being undertaken; it was dispatched by their father the night before, immediately upon his liberation, and stated that he was setting out for Narrobourne at the moment of writing; that having no money he would be obliged to walk all the way; that he calculated on passing through the intervening town of Ivell about six on the following day, where he should sup at the Castle Inn, and where he hoped they would meet him with a carriage-and-pair, or some other such conveyance, that he might not disgrace them by arriving like a tramp.

'That sounds as if he gave a thought to our position,' said Cornelius.

Joshua knew the satire that lurked in the paternal words, and said nothing. Silence prevailed during the greater part of their journey. The lamps were lighted in Ivell when they entered the streets, and Cornelius, who was quite unknown in this neighbourhood, and who, moreover, was not in clerical attire, decided that he should be the one to call at the Castle Inn. Here, in answer to his inquiry under the darkness of the archway, they told him that such a man as he had described left the house about a quarter of an hour earlier, after making a meal in the kitchen-settle. He was rather the worse for liquor.

'Then,' said Joshua, when Cornelius joined him outside with this intelligence, 'we must have met and passed him! And now that I think of it, we did meet someone who was unsteady in his gait, under the trees on the other side of Hendford Hill, where it was too dark to see him.'

They rapidly retraced their steps; but for a long stretch of the way home could discern nobody. When, however, they had gone about three-quarters of the distance, they became conscious of an irregular footfall in front of them, and could see a whitish figure in the gloom. They followed dubiously. The figure met another wayfarer – the single one that had been encountered upon this lonely road – and they distinctly heard him ask the way to Narrobourne. The stranger replied – what was quite true – that the nearest way was by turning in at the stile by the next bridge, and following the footpath which branched thence across the meadows.

When the brothers reached the stile they also entered the path, but did not overtake the subject of their worry till they had crossed two or three meads, and the lights from Narrobourne manor-house were visible before them through the trees. Their father was no longer walking; he was seated against the wet bank of an adjoining hedge. Observing their forms he shouted, 'I'm going to Narrobourne; who may you be?'

They went up to him, and revealed themselves, reminding him of the plan which he had himself proposed in his note, that they should meet him at Ivell.

'By Jerry, I'd forgot it!' he said. 'Well, what do you want me to do?' His tone was distinctly quarrelsome.

A long conversation followed, which became embittered at the first hint from them that he should not come to the village. The millwright drew a quart bottle from his pocket, and challenged them to drink if they meant friendly and called themselves men. Neither of the two had touched alcohol for years, but for once they thought it best to accept, so as not to needlessly provoke him.

'What's in it?' said Joshua.

'A drop of weak gin-and-water. It won't hurt 'ee. Drink

from the bottle.' Joshua did so, and his father pushed up the bottom of the vessel so as to make him swallow a good deal in spite of himself. It went down into his stomach like molten lead.

'Ha, ha, that's right!' said old Halborough. 'But 'twas raw spirit – ha, ha!'

'Why should you take me in so!' said Joshua, losing his self-command, try as he would to keep calm.

'Because you took me in, my lad, in banishing me to that cursed country under pretence that it was for my good. You were a pair of hypocrites to say so. It was done to get rid of me – no more nor less. But, by Jerry, I'm a match for ye now! I'll spoil your souls for preaching. My daughter is going to be married to the squire here. I've heard the news – I saw it in a paper!'

'It is premature—'

'I know it is true; and I'm her father, and I shall give her away, or there'll be a hell of a row, I can assure 'ee! Is that where the gennleman lives?'

Joshua Halborough writhed in impotent despair. Fellmer had not yet positively declared himself, his mother was hardly won round; a scene with their father in the parish would demolish as fair a palace of hopes as was ever builded. The millwright rose. 'If that's where the squire lives I'm going to call. Just arrived from Canady with her fortune – ha, ha! I wish no harm to the gennleman, and the gennleman will wish no harm to me. But I like to take my place in the family, and stand upon my rights, and lower people's pride!'

'You've succeeded already! Where's that woman you took with you—'

'Woman! She was my wife as lawful as the Constitution – a sight more lawful than your mother was till some time after you were born!'

Joshua had for many years before heard whispers that his father had cajoled his mother in their early acquaintance, and had made somewhat tardy amends; but never from his father's lips till now. It was the last stroke, and he could not bear it. He sank back against the hedge. 'It is over!' he said. 'He ruins us all!'

The millwright moved on, waving his stick triumphantly, and the two brothers stood still. They could see his drab figure stalking along the path, and over his head the lights from the conservatory of Narrobourne House, inside which Albert Fellmer might possibly be sitting with Rosa at that moment, holding her hand, and asking her to share his home with him.

The staggering whitey-brown form, advancing to put a blot on all this, had been diminishing in the shade; and now suddenly disappeared beside a weir. There was the noise of a flounce in the water.

'He has fallen in!' said Cornelius, starting forward to run for the place at which his father had vanished.

Joshua, awaking from the stupefied reverie into which he had sunk, rushed to the other's side before he had taken ten steps. 'Stop, stop, what are you thinking of?' he whispered hoarsely, grasping Cornelius's arm.

'Pulling him out!'

'Yes, yes – so am I. But – wait a moment—'

'But, Joshua!'

'Her life and happiness, you know – Cornelius – and your reputation and mine – and our chance of rising together, all three—'

He clutched his brother's arm to the bone; and as they stood breathless the splashing and floundering in the weir continued; over it they saw the hopeful lights from the manor-house conservatory winking through the trees as their bare branches waved to and fro. In their pause there had been time to save him twice over.

The floundering and splashing grew weaker, and they could hear gurgling words: 'Help – I'm drownded! Rosie – Rosie!'

'We'll go – we *must* save him. O Joshua!'

'Yes, yes! we must!'

Still they did not move, but waited, holding each other, each thinking the same thought. Weights of lead seemed to be affixed to their feet, which would no longer obey their wills. The mead became silent. Over it they fancied they could see figures moving in the conservatory. The air up there seemed to emit gentle kisses.

Cornelius started forward at last, and Joshua almost simultaneously. Two or three minutes brought them to the brink of the stream. At first they could see nothing in the water, though it was not so deep nor the night so dark but that their father's light kerseymere coat would have been visible if he had lain at the bottom. Joshua looked this way and that.

'He has drifted into the culvert,' he said.

Below the foot-bridge of the weir the stream suddenly narrowed to half its width, to pass under a barrel arch or culvert constructed for wagons to cross into the middle of the mead in haymaking time. It being at present the season of high water the arch was full to the crown, against which the ripples clucked every now and then. At this point he had just caught sight of a pale object slipping under. In a moment it was gone.

They went to the lower end, but nothing emerged. For a long time they tried at both ends to effect some communication with the interior, but to no purpose.

'We ought to have come sooner!' said the conscience-stricken Cornelius, when they were quite exhausted, and dripping wet.

'I suppose we ought,' replied Joshua heavily. He perceived his father's walking-stick on the bank; hastily picking it up he stuck it into the mud among the sedge. Then they went on.

'Shall we – say anything about this accident?' whispered Cornelius as they approached the door of Joshua's house.

'What's the use? It can do no good. We must wait until he is found.'

They went indoors and changed their clothes; after which they started for the manor-house, reaching it about ten o'clock. Besides their sister there were only three guests; an adjoining landowner and his wife, and the infirm old rector.

Rose, although she had parted from them so recently, grasped their hands in an ecstatic, brimming, joyful manner, as if she had not seen them for years. 'You look pale,' she said.

The brothers answered that they had had a long walk, and were somewhat tired. Everybody in the room seemed charged full with some sort of interesting knowledge: the squire's neighbour and neighbour's wife looked wisely around; and Fellmer himself played the part of host with a preoccupied bearing which approached fervour. They left at eleven, not accepting the carriage offered, the distance being so short and the roads dry. The squire came rather further into the dark with them than he need have done, and wished Rose goodnight in a mysterious manner, slightly apart from the rest.

When they were walking along Joshua said, with a desperate attempt at joviality, 'Rosa, what's going on?'

'O, I—' she began between a gasp and a bound. 'He—'

'Never mind – if it disturbs you.'

She was so excited that she could not speak connectedly at first, the practised air which she had brought home with her having disappeared. Calming herself she added, 'I am not disturbed and nothing has happened. Only he said he wanted to ask me *something*, some day; and I said never mind that now. He hasn't asked yet, and is coming to speak to you about it. He would have done so tonight, only I asked him not to be in a hurry. But he will come tomorrow, I am sure!'

V

IT was summer-time, six months later, and mowers and haymakers were at work in the meads. The manor-house, being opposite them, frequently formed a peg for conversation during these operations; and the doings of the squire, and the squire's young wife, the curate's sister – who was at present the admired of most of them, and the interest of all – met with their due amount of criticism.

Rosa was happy, if ever woman could be said to be so. She had not learnt the fate of her father, and sometimes wondered – perhaps with a sense of relief – why he did not write to her from his supposed home in Canada. Her brother Joshua had been presented to a living in a small town, shortly after her marriage, and Cornelius had thereupon succeeded to the vacant curacy of Narrobourne.

These two had awaited in deep suspense the discovery of their father's body; and yet the discovery had not been made. Every day they expected a man or a boy to run up from the meads with the intelligence; but he had never come. Days had accumulated to weeks and months; the wedding had come and gone: Joshua had tolled and read himself in at his new parish; and never a shout of amazement over the millwright's remains.

But now, in June, when they were mowing the meads, the hatches had to be drawn and the water let out of its channels for the convenience of the mowers. It was thus that the discovery was made. A man, stooping low with his scythe, caught a view of the culvert lengthwise, and saw something entangled in the recently bared weeds of its bed. A day or two after there was an inquest; but the body was unrecognizable. Fish and flood had been busy with the millwright; he had no watch or marked article which could be identified; and a verdict of the accidental drowning of a person unknown settled the matter.

As the body was found in Narrobourne parish, there it had to be buried. Cornelius wrote to Joshua, begging him to come and read the service, or to send some one; he himself could not do it. Rather than let in a stranger Joshua came, and silently scanned the coroner's order handed him by the undertaker:

'I, Henry Giles, Coroner for the Mid-Division of Outer Wessex, do hereby order the Burial of the Body now shown to the Inquest Jury as the Body of an Adult Male Person Unknown . . .' etc.

Joshua Halborough got through the service in some way,

and rejoined his brother Cornelius at his house. Neither accepted an invitation to lunch at their sister's; they wished to discuss parish matters together. In the afternoon she came down, though they had already called on her, and had not expected to see her again. Her bright eyes, brown hair, flowery bonnet, lemon-coloured gloves, and flush beauty, were like an irradiation into the apartment, which they in their gloom could hardly bear.

'I forgot to tell you,' she said, 'of a curious thing which happened to me a month or two before my marriage – something which I have thought may have had a connection with the accident to the poor man you have buried today. It was on that evening I was at the manor-house waiting for you to fetch me; I was in the winter-garden with Albert, and we were sitting silent together, when we fancied we heard a cry in the distant meadow. We opened the door, and while Albert ran to fetch his hat, leaving me standing there, the cry was repeated, and my excited senses made me think I heard my own name. When Albert came back all was silent, and we decided that it was only a drunken shout, and not a cry for help. We both forgot the incident, and it never has occurred to me till since the funeral today that it might have been this stranger's cry. The name of course was only fancy, or he might have had a wife or child with a name something like mine, poor man!'

When she had gone the brothers were silent till Cornelius said, 'Now mark this, Joshua. Sooner or later she'll know.'

'How?'

'From one of us. Do you think human hearts are iron-cased safes, that you suppose we can keep this secret for ever?'

'Yes, I think they are, sometimes,' said Joshua.

'No. It will out. We shall tell.'

'What, and ruin her – kill her? Disgrace her children, and pull down the whole auspicious house of Fellmer about our ears? No! May I – drown where he was drowned before I do it! Never, never. Surely you can say the same, Cornelius!'

Cornelius seemed fortified, and no more was said. For a long time after that day he did not see Joshua, and before the next year was out a son and heir was born to the Fellmers. The villagers rang the three bells every evening for a week and more, and were made merry by Mr Fellmer's ale; and when the christening came on Joshua paid Narrobourne another visit.

Among all the people who assembled on that day the brother clergymen were the least interested. Their minds were haunted by a spirit in kerseymere. In the evening they walked together in the fields.

'She's all right,' said Joshua. 'But here are you doing journey-work, Cornelius, and likely to continue at it till the end of the day, as far as I can see. I, too, with my petty living – what am I, after all? ... To tell the truth, the Church is a poor forlorn hope for people without influence, particularly when their enthusiasm begins to flag. A social regenerator has a better chance outside, where he is unhampered by dogma and tradition. As for me, I would rather have gone on mending mills, with my crust of bread and liberty.'

Almost automatically they had bent their steps along the margin of the river; they now paused. They were standing on the brink of the well-known weir. There were the hatches, there was the culvert; they could see the pebbly bed of the stream through the pellucid water. The notes of the church-bells were audible, still jangled by the enthusiastic villagers.

'Why see – it was there I hid his walking-stick!' said Joshua, looking towards the sedge. The next moment, during a passing breeze, something flashed white on the spot to which the attention of Cornelius was drawn.

From the sedge rose a straight little silver-poplar, and it was the leaves of this sapling which caused the flicker of whiteness.

'His walking-stick has grown!' Joshua added. 'It was a rough one – cut from the hedge, I remember.'

At every puff of wind the tree turned white, till they could not bear to look at it; and they walked away.

'I see him every night,' Cornelius murmured ... 'Ah, we read our *Hebrews* to little account, Jos! Ὑπέμεινε σταυρὸν, αἰσχύνης καταφρονήσας. To have *endured* the cross, *despising* the shame – there lay greatness! But now I often feel that I should like to put an end to trouble here in this self-same spot.'

'I have thought of it myself,' said Joshua.

'Perhaps we shall, some day,' murmured his brother.

'Perhaps,' said Joshua moodily.

With that contingency to consider in the silence of their nights and days they bent their steps homewards.

December 1888

An Imaginative Woman

WHEN William Marchmill had finished his inquiries for lodgings at the well-known watering-place of Solentsea in Upper Wessex, he returned to the hotel to find his wife. She, with the children, had rambled along the shore, and March-mill followed in the direction indicated by the military-look-ing hall-porter.

'By Jove, how far you've gone! I'm quite out of breath,' Marchmill said, rather impatiently, when he came up with his wife, who was reading as she walked, the three children being considerably further ahead with the nurse.

Mrs Marchmill started out of the reverie into which the book had thrown her. 'Yes,' she said, 'you've been such a long time. I was tired of staying in that dreary hotel. But I am sorry if you have wanted me, Will?'

'Well, I have had trouble to suit myself. When you see the airy and comfortable rooms heard of, you find they are stuffy and uncomfortable. Will you come and see if what I've fixed on will do? There is not much room, I am afraid; but I can light on nothing better. The town is rather full.'

The pair left the children and nurse to continue their ramble, and went back together.

In age well-balanced, in personal appearance fairly

matched, and in domestic requirements conformable, in temper this couple differed, though even here they did not often clash, he being equable, if not lymphatic, and she decidedly nervous and sanguine. It was to their tastes and fancies, those smallest, greatest particulars, that no common denominator could be applied. Marchmill considered his wife's likes and inclinations somewhat silly; she considered his sordid and material. The husband's business was that of a gunmaker in a thriving city northwards, and his soul was in that business always; the lady was best characterized by that superannuated phrase of elegance 'a votary of the muse'. An impressionable, palpitating creature was Ella, shrinking humanely from detailed knowledge of her husband's trade whenever she reflected that everything he manufactured had for its purpose the destruction of life. She could only recover her equanimity by assuring herself that some, at least, of his weapons were sooner or later used for the extermination of horrid vermin and animals almost as cruel to their inferiors in species as human beings were to theirs.

She had never antecedently regarded this occupation of his as any objection to having him for a husband. Indeed, the necessity of getting life-leased at all cost, a cardinal virtue which all good mothers teach, kept her from thinking of it at all till she had closed with William, had passed the honeymoon, and reached the reflecting stage. Then, like a person who has stumbled upon some object in the dark, she wondered what she had got; mentally walked round it, estimated it; whether it were rare or common; contained gold, silver, or lead; were a clog or a pedestal, everything to her or nothing.

She came to some vague conclusions, and since then had kept her heart alive by pitying her proprietor's obtuseness and want of refinement, pitying herself, and letting off her delicate and ethereal emotions in imaginative occupations, day-dreams, and night-sighs, which perhaps would not much have disturbed William if he had known of them.

Her figure was small, elegant, and slight in build, tripping, or rather bounding, in movement. She was dark-eyed, and had that marvellously bright and liquid sparkle in each pupil which characterizes persons of Ella's cast of soul, and is too often a cause of heartache to the possessor's male friends, ultimately sometimes to herself. Her husband was a tall, long-featured man, with a brown beard; he had a pondering regard; and was, it must be added, usually kind and tolerant to her. He spoke in squarely shaped sentences, and was supremely satisfied with a condition of sublunary things which made weapons a necessity.

Husband and wife walked till they had reached the house they were in search of, which stood in a terrace facing the sea, and was fronted by a small garden of wind-proof and salt-proof evergreens, stone steps leading up to the porch. It had its number in the row, but, being rather larger than the rest, was in addition sedulously distinguished as Coburg House by its landlady, though everybody else called it 'Thirteen, New Parade.' The spot was bright and lively now; but in winter it became necessary to place sandbags against the door, and to stuff up the keyhole against the wind and rain, which had worn the paint so thin that the priming and knotting showed through.

The householder, who had been watching for the gentleman's return, met them in the passage, and showed the rooms. She informed them that she was a professional man's widow, left in needy circumstances by the rather sudden death of her husband, and she spoke anxiously of the conveniences of the establishment.

Mrs Marchmill said that she liked the situation and the house; but, it being small, there would not be accommodation enough, unless she could have all the rooms.

The landlady mused with an air of disappointment. She wanted the visitors to be her tenants very badly, she said, with obvious honesty. But unfortunately two of the rooms were occupied permanently by a bachelor gentleman. He did not pay season prices, it was true; but as he kept on his apartments all the year round, and was an extremely nice and interesting young man, who gave no trouble, she did not like to turn him out for a month's 'let', even at a high figure. 'Perhaps, however,' she added, 'he might offer to go for a time.'

They would not hear of this, and went back to the hotel, intending to proceed to the agent's to inquire further. Hardly had they sat down to tea when the landlady called. Her gentleman, she said, had been so obliging as to offer to give up his rooms for three or four weeks rather than to drive the new-comers away.

'It is very kind, but we won't inconvenience him in that way,' said the Marchmills.

'O, it won't inconvenience him, I assure you!' said the landlady eloquently. 'You see, he's a different sort of young man from most – dreamy, solitary, rather melancholy – and he cares more to be here when the south-westerly gales are beating against the door, and the sea washes over the Parade, and there's not a soul in the place, than he does now in the season. He'd just as soon be where, in fact, he's going temporarily, to a little cottage on the Island opposite, for a change.' She hoped therefore that they would come.

The Marchmill family accordingly took possession of the house next day, and it seemed to suit them very well. After luncheon Mr Marchmill strolled out towards the pier, and Mrs Marchmill, having dispatched the children to their outdoor amusements on the sands, settled herself in more completely, examining this and that article, and testing the reflecting powers of the mirror in the wardrobe door.

In the small back sitting-room, which had been the young bachelor's, she found furniture of a more personal nature than in the rest. Shabby books, of correct rather than rare editions, were piled up in a queerly reserved manner in corners, as if the previous occupant had not conceived the possibility that any incoming person of the season's bringing could care to look inside them. The landlady hovered on the threshold to rectify anything that Mrs Marchmill might not find to her satisfaction.

'I'll make this my own little room,' said the latter, 'because the books are here. By the way, the person who has left seems to have a good many. He won't mind my reading some of them, Mrs Hooper, I hope?'

'O dear no, ma'am. Yes, he has a good many. You see, he is in the literary line himself somewhat. He is a poet – yes, really a poet – and he has a little income of his own, which is enough to write verses on, but not enough for cutting a figure, even if he cared to.'

'A poet! O, I did not know that.'

Mrs Marchmill opened one of the books, and saw the owner's name written on the title-page. 'Dear me!' she continued; 'I know his name very well – Robert Trewe – of course I do; and his writings! And it is *his* rooms we have taken, and *him* we have turned out of his home?'

Ella Marchmill, sitting down alone a few minutes later, thought with interested surprise of Robert Trewe. Her own latter history will best explain that interest. Herself the only daughter of a struggling man of letters, she had during the last year or two taken to writing poems, in an endeavour to find a congenial channel in which to let flow her painfully embayed emotions, whose former limpidity and sparkle seemed departing in the stagnation caused by the routine of a practical household and the gloom of bearing children to a commonplace father. These poems, subscribed with a masculine pseudonym, had appeared in various obscure magazines, and in two cases in rather prominent ones. In the second of the latter the page which bore her effusion at the bottom, in smallish print, bore at the top, in large print, a few verses on the same subject by this very man, Robert Trewe. Both of them had, in fact, been struck by a tragic incident reported in the daily papers, and had used it simultaneously as an inspiration, the editor remarking in a note upon the coincidence, and that the excellence of both poems prompted him to give them together.

After that event Ella, otherwise 'John Ivy', had watched with much attention the appearance anywhere in print of verse bearing the signature Robert Trewe, who, with a man's unsusceptibility on the question of sex, had never once thought of passing himself off as a woman. To be sure, Mrs

Marchmill had satisfied herself with a sort of reason for doing the contrary in her case; since nobody might believe in her inspiration if they found that the sentiments came from a pushing tradesman's wife, from the mother of three children by a matter-of-fact small-arms manufacturer.

Trewe's verse contrasted with that of the rank and file of recent minor poets in being impassioned rather than ingenious, luxuriant rather than finished. Neither *symboliste* nor *décadent*, he was a pessimist in so far as that character applies to a man who looks at the worst contingencies as well as the best in the human condition. Being little attracted by excellences of form and rhythm apart from content, he sometimes, when feeling outran his artistic speed, perpetrated sonnets in the loosely rhymed Elizabethan fashion, which every right-minded reviewer said he ought not to have done.

With sad and hopeless envy Ella Marchmill had often and often scanned the rival poet's work, so much stronger as it always was than her own feeble lines. She had imitated him, and her inability to touch his level would send her into fits of despondency. Months passed away thus, till she observed from the publishers' list that Trewe had collected his fugitive pieces into a volume, which was duly issued, and was much or little praised according to chance, and had a sale quite sufficient to pay for the printing.

This step onward had suggested to John Ivy the idea of collecting her pieces also, or at any rate of making up a book of her rhymes by adding many in manuscript to the few that had seen the light, for she had been able to get no great number into print. A ruinous charge was made for costs of publication; a few reviews noticed her poor little volume; but nobody talked of it, nobody bought it, and it fell dead in a fortnight – if it had ever been alive.

The author's thoughts were diverted to another groove just then by the discovery that she was going to have a third child, and the collapse of her poetical venture had perhaps less effect upon her mind than it might have done if she had been domestically unoccupied. Her husband had paid the publisher's bill with the doctor's, and there it all had ended for the time. But, though less than a poet of her century, Ella was more than a mere multiplier of her kind, and latterly she had begun to feel the old afflatus once more. And now by an odd conjunction she found herself in the rooms of Robert Trewe.

She thoughtfully rose from her chair and searched the apartment with the interest of a fellow-tradesman. Yes, the volume of his own verse was among the rest. Though quite familiar with its contents, she read it here as if it spoke aloud to her, then called up Mrs Hooper, the landlady, for some trivial service, and inquired again about the young man.

'Well, I'm sure you'd be interested in him, ma'am, if you could see him, only he's so shy that I don't suppose you will.' Mrs Hooper seemed nothing loth to minister to her tenant's curiosity about her predecessor. 'Lived here long? Yes, nearly two years. He keeps on his rooms even when he's not here: the soft air of this place suits his chest, and he likes to be able to come back at any time. He is mostly writing or reading, and doesn't see many people, though, for the matter of that, he is such a good, kind young fellow that folks would only be too glad to be friendly with him if they knew him. You don't meet kind-hearted people every day.'

'Ah, he's kind-hearted ... and good.'

'Yes; he'll oblige me in anything if I ask him. "Mr Trewe," I say to him sometimes, "you are rather out of spirits." "Well, I am, Mrs Hooper," he'll say, "though I don't know how you should find it out." "Why not take a little change?" I ask. Then in a day or two he'll say that he will take a trip to Paris, or Norway, or somewhere; and I assure you he comes back all the better for it.'

'Ah, indeed! His is a sensitive nature, no doubt.'

'Yes. Still he's odd in some things. Once when he had finished a poem of his composition late at night he walked up and down the room rehearsing it; and the floors being so thin – jerry-built houses, you know, though I say it myself – he kept me awake up above him till I wished him further ... But we get on very well.'

This was but the beginning of a series of conversations about the rising poet as the days went on. On one of these occasions Mrs Hooper drew Ella's attention to what she had not noticed before: minute scribblings in pencil on the wall-paper behind the curtains at the head of the bed.

'O! let me look,' said Mrs Marchmill, unable to conceal a rush of tender curiosity as she bent her pretty face close to the wall.

'These,' said Mrs Hooper, with the manner of a woman who knew things, 'are the very beginnings and first thoughts of his verses. He has tried to rub most of them out, but you can read them still. My belief is that he wakes up in the night, you know, with some rhyme in his head, and jots it down there on the wall lest he should forget it by the morning. Some of these very lines you see here I have seen afterwards in print in the magazines. Some are newer; indeed, I have not seen that one before. It must have been done only a few days ago.'

'O yes! ...'

Ella Marchmill flushed without knowing why, and suddenly wished her companion would go away, now that the information was imparted. An indescribable consciousness of personal interest rather than literary made her anxious to read the inscription alone; and she accordingly waited till she could do so, with a sense that a great store of emotion would be enjoyed in the act.

Perhaps because the sea was choppy outside the Island, Ella's husband found it much pleasanter to go sailing and steaming about without his wife, who was a bad sailor, than with her. He did not disdain to go thus alone on board the steamboats of the cheap-trippers, where there was dancing by moonlight, and where the couples would come suddenly down with a lurch into each other's arms; for, as he blandly told her, the company was too mixed for him to take her amid such scenes. Thus, while this thriving manufacturer got a great deal of change and sea-air out of his sojourn here, the life, external at least, of Ella was monotonous enough, and mainly consisted in passing a certain number of hours each day in bathing and walking up and down a stretch of shore. But the poetic impulse having again waxed strong, she was possessed by an inner flame which left her hardly conscious of what was proceeding around her.

She had read till she knew by heart Trewe's last little volume of verses, and spent a great deal of time in vainly attempting to rival some of them, till, in her failure, she burst into tears. The personal element in the magnetic attraction exercised by this circumambient unapproachable master of hers was so much stronger than the intellectual and abstract that she could not understand it. To be sure, she was surrounded noon and night by his customary environment, which literally whispered of him to her at every moment; but he was a man she had never seen, and that all that moved her was the instinct to specialize a waiting emotion on the first fit thing that came to hand did not, of course, suggest itself to Ella.

In the natural way of passion under the too practical conditions which civilization has devised for its fruition, her husband's love for her had not survived, except in the form of fitful friendship, any more than, or even so much as, her own for him; and, being a woman of very living ardours, that required sustenance of some sort, they were beginning to feed on this chancing material, which was, indeed, of a quality far better than chance usually offers.

One day the children had been playing hide-and-seek in a closet, whence, in their excitement, they pulled out some clothing. Mrs Hooper explained that it belonged to Mr Trewe, and hung it up in the closet again. Possessed of her fantasy, Ella went later in the afternoon, when nobody was in that part of the house, opened the closet, unhitched one of the articles, a mackintosh, and put it on, with the waterproof cap belonging to it.

'The mantle of Elijah!' she said. 'Would it might inspire me to rival him, glorious genius that he is!'

Her eyes always grew wet when she thought like that, and she turned to look at herself in the glass. *His* heart had beat inside that coat, and *his* brain had worked under that hat at levels of thought she would never reach. The consciousness of her weakness beside him made her feel quite sick. Before she had got the things off her the door opened, and her husband entered the room.

'What the devil—'

She blushed, and removed them.

'I found them in the closet here,' she said, 'and put them on in a freak. What have I else to do? You are always away!'

'Always away? Well . . .'

That evening she had a further talk with the landlady, who might herself have nourished a half-tender regard for the poet, so ready was she to discourse ardently about him.

'You are interested in Mr Trewe, I know, ma'am,' she said; 'and he has just sent to say that he is going to call to-morrow afternoon to look up some books of his that he wants, if I'll be in, and he may select them from your room?'

'O yes!'

'You could very well meet Mr Trewe then, if you'd like to be in the way!'

She promised with secret delight, and went to bed musing of him.

Next morning her husband observed: 'I've been thinking of what you said, Ell: that I have gone about a good deal and left you without much to amuse you. Perhaps it's true. Today, as there's not much sea, I'll take you with me on board the yacht.'

For the first time in her experience of such an offer Ella was not glad. But she accepted it for the moment. The time for setting out drew near, and she went to get ready. She stood reflecting. The longing to see the poet she was now distinctly in love with overpowered all other considerations.

'I don't want to go,' she said to herself. 'I can't bear to be away! And I won't go.'

She told her husband that she had changed her mind about wishing to sail. He was indifferent, and went his way.

For the rest of the day the house was quiet, the children having gone out upon the sands. The blinds waved in the sunshine to the soft, steady stroke of the sea beyond the wall;

and the notes of the Green Silesian band, a troop of foreign gentlemen hired for the season, had drawn almost all the residents and promenaders away from the vicinity of Coburg House. A knock was audible at the door.

Mrs Marchmill did not hear any servant go to answer it, and she became impatient. The books were in the room where she sat; but nobody came up. She rang the bell.

'There is some person waiting at the door,' she said.

'O no, ma'am! He's gone long ago. I answered it,' the servant replied, and Mrs Hooper came in herself. 'So disappointing!' she said. 'Mr Trewe not coming after all!'

'But I heard him knock, I fancy!'

'No; that was somebody inquiring for lodgings who came to the wrong house. I forgot to tell you that Mr Trewe sent a note just before lunch to say I needn't get any tea for him, as he should not require the books, and wouldn't come to select them.'

Ella was miserable, and for a long time could not even re-read his mournful ballad on 'Severed Lives', so aching was her erratic little heart, and so tearful her eyes. When the children came in with wet stockings, and ran up to her to tell her of their adventures, she could not feel that she cared about them half as much as usual.

'Mrs Hooper, have you a photograph of – the gentleman who lived here?' She was getting to be curiously shy in mentioning his name.

'Why, yes. It's in the ornamental frame on the mantelpiece in your own bedroom, ma'am.'

'No; the Royal Duke and Duchess are in that.'

'Yes, so they are; but he's behind them. He belongs rightly to that frame, which I bought on purpose; but as he went away he said: "Cover me up from those strangers that are coming, for God's sake. I don't want them staring at me, and I am sure they won't want me staring at them." So I slipped in the Duke and Duchess temporarily in front of him, as they had no frame, and Royalties are more suitable for letting furnished than a private young man. If you take 'em out you'll

see him under. Lord, ma'am, he wouldn't mind if he knew
it! He didn't think the next tenant would be such an attractive lady as you, or he wouldn't have thought of hiding himself, perhaps.'.

'Is he handsome?' she asked timidly.

'*I* call him so. Some, perhaps, wouldn't.'

'Should I?' she asked, with eagerness.

'I think you would, though some would say he's more
striking than handsome; a large-eyed thoughtful fellow, you
know, with a very electric flash in his eye when he looks
round quickly, such as you'd expect a poet to be who
doesn't get his living by it.'

'How old is he?'

'Several years older than yourself, ma'am; about thirty-
one or two, I think.'

Ella was, as a matter of fact, a few months over thirty herself; but she did not look nearly so much. Though so im-
mature in nature, she was entering on that tract of life in
which emotional women begin to suspect that last love may
be stronger than first love; and she would soon, alas, enter on
the still more melancholy tract when at least the vainer ones
of her sex shrink from receiving a male visitor otherwise
than with their backs to the window or the blinds half down.
She reflected on Mrs Hooper's remark, and said no more
about age.

Just then a telegram was brought up. It came from her
husband, who had gone down the Channel as far as Bud-
mouth with his friends in the yacht, and would not be able
to get back till next day.

After her light dinner Ella idled about the shore with the
children till dusk, thinking of the yet uncovered photograph
in her room, with a serene sense of something ecstatic to
come. For, with the subtle luxuriousness of fancy in which
this young woman was an adept, on learning that her husband was to be absent that night she had refrained from in-
continently rushing upstairs and opening the picture-frame,
preferring to reserve the inspection till she could be alone,
and a more romantic tinge be imparted to the occasion by

silence, candles, solemn sea and stars outside, than was afforded by the garish afternoon sunlight.

The children had been sent to bed, and Ella soon followed, though it was not yet ten o'clock. To gratify her passionate curiosity she now made her preparations, first getting rid of superfluous garments and putting on her dressing-gown, then arranging a chair in front of the table and reading several pages of Trewe's tenderest utterances. Next she fetched the portrait-frame to the light, opened the back, took out the likeness, and set it up before her.

It was a striking countenance to look upon. The poet wore a luxuriant black moustache and imperial, and a slouched hat which shaded the forehead. The large dark eyes described by the landlady showed an unlimited capacity for misery; they looked out from beneath well-shaped brows as if they were reading the universe in the microcosm of the confronter's face, and were not altogether overjoyed at what the spectacle portended.

Ella murmured in her lowest, richest, tenderest tone: 'And it's *you* who've so cruelly eclipsed me these many times!'

As she gazed long at the portrait she fell into thought, till her eyes filled with tears, and she touched the cardboard with her lips. Then she laughed with a nervous lightness, and wiped her eyes.

She thought how wicked she was, a woman having a husband and three children, to let her mind stray to a stranger in this unconscionable manner. No, he was not a stranger! She knew his thoughts and feelings as well as she knew her own; they were, in fact, the self-same thoughts and feelings as hers, which her husband distinctly lacked; perhaps luckily for himself, considering that he had to provide for family expenses.

'He's nearer my real self, he's more intimate with the real me than Will is, after all, even though I've never seen him,' she said.

She laid his book and picture on the table at the bedside, and when she was reclining on the pillow she re-read those of Robert Trewe's verses which she had marked from time to time as most touching and true. Putting these aside she set up the photograph on its edge upon the coverlet, and contemplated it as she lay. Then she scanned again by the light of the candle the half-obliterated pencillings on the wall-paper beside her head. There they were – phrases, couplets, *bouts-rimés*, beginnings and middles of lines, ideas in the rough, like Shelley's scraps, and the least of them so intense, so sweet, so palpitating, that it seemed as if his very breath, warm and loving, fanned her cheeks from those walls, walls that had surrounded his head times and times as they surrounded her own now. He must often have put up his hand so – with the pencil in it. Yes, the writing was sideways, as it would be if executed by one who extends his arm thus.

These inscribed shapes of the poet's world,

> Forms more real than living man,
> Nurslings of immortality,

were, no doubt, the thoughts and spirit-strivings which had come to him in the dead of night, when he could let himself go and have no fear of the frost of criticism. No doubt they had often been written up hastily by the light of the moon, the rays of the lamp, in the blue-grey dawn, in full daylight perhaps never. And now her hair was dragging where his arm had lain when he secured the fugitive fancies; she was sleeping on a poet's limbs, immersed in the very essence of him, permeated by his spirit as by an ether.

While she was dreaming the minutes away thus, a footstep came upon the stairs, and in a moment she heard her husband's heavy step on the landing immediately without.

'Ell, where are you?'

What possessed her she could not have described, but, with an instinctive objection to let her husband know what she had been doing, she slipped the photograph under the pillow just as he flung open the door with the air of a man who had dined not badly.

'O, I beg pardon,' said William Marchmill. 'Have you a headache? I am afraid I have disturbed you.'

'No, I've not got a headache,' said she. 'How is it you've come?'

'Well, we found we could get back in very good time after all, and I didn't want to make another day of it, because of going somewhere else tomorrow.'

'Shall I come down again?'

'O no. I'm as tired as a dog. I've had a good feed and I shall turn in straight off. I want to get out at six o'clock tomorrow if I can ... I shan't disturb you by my getting up; it will be long before you are awake.' And he came forward into the room.

While her eyes followed his movements, Ella softly pushed the photograph further out of sight.

'Sure you're not ill?' he asked, bending over her.

'No, only wicked!'

'Never mind that.' And he stooped and kissed her. 'I wanted to be with you tonight.'

Next morning Marchmill was called at six o'clock; and in waking and yawning she heard him muttering to himself: 'What the deuce is this that's been crackling under me so?' Imagining her asleep he searched round him and withdrew something. Through her half-opened eyes she perceived it to be Mr Trewe.

'Well, I'm damned!' her husband exclaimed.

'What, dear?' said she.

'O, you are awake? Ha! ha!'

'What *do* you mean?'

'Some bloke's photograph – a friend of our landlady's, I suppose. I wonder how it came here; whisked off the mantelpiece by accident perhaps when they were making the bed.'

'I was looking at it yesterday, and it must have dropped in then.'

'O, he's a friend of yours? Bless his picturesque heart!'

Ella's loyalty to the object of her admiration could not endure to hear him ridiculed. 'He's a clever man!' she said, with a tremor in her gentle voice which she herself felt to be absurdly uncalled for. 'He is a rising poet – the gentleman who occupied two of these rooms before we came, though I've never seen him.'

'How do you know, if you've never seen him?'

'Mrs Hooper told me when she showed me the photograph.'

'O, well, I must up and be off. I shall be home rather early. Sorry I can't take you today, dear. Mind the children don't go getting drowned.'

That day Mrs Marchmill inquired if Mr Trewe were likely to call at any other time.

'Yes,' said Mrs Hooper. 'He's coming this day week to stay with a friend near here till you leave. He'll be sure to call.'

Marchmill did return quite early in the afternoon; and, opening some letters which had arrived in his absence, declared suddenly that he and his family would have to leave a week earlier than they had expected to do – in short, in three days.

'Surely we can stay a week longer?' she pleaded. 'I like it here.'

'I don't. It is getting rather slow.'

'Then you might leave me and the children!'

'How perverse you are, Ell! What's the use? And have to come to fetch you! No: we'll all return together; and we'll make out our time in North Wales or Brighton a little later on. Besides, you've three days longer yet.'

It seemed to be her doom not to meet the man for whose rival talent she had a despairing admiration, and to whose person she was now absolutely attached. Yet she determined to make a last effort; and having gathered from her landlady that Trewe was living in a lonely spot not far from the fashionable town on the Island opposite, she crossed over in the packet from the neighbouring pier the following afternoon.

What a useless journey it was! Ella knew but vaguely where the house stood, and when she fancied she had found it, and ventured to inquire of a pedestrian if he lived there, the answer returned by the man was that he did not know. And if he did live there, how could she call upon him? Some women might have the assurance to do it, but she had not. How crazy he would think her. She might have asked him to call upon her, perhaps; but she had not the courage for that, either. She lingered mournfully about the picturesque seaside eminence till it was time to return to the town and enter the steamer for recrossing, reaching home for dinner without having been greatly missed.

At the last moment, unexpectedly enough, her husband said that he should have no objection to letting her and the children stay on till the end of the week, since she wished to do so, if she felt herself able to get home without him. She concealed the pleasure this extension of time gave her; and Marchmill went off the next morning alone.

But the week passed, and Trewe did not call.

On Saturday morning the remaining members of the Marchmill family departed from the place which had been productive of so much fervour in her. The dreary, dreary train; the sun shining in moted beams upon the hot cushions; the dusty permanent way; the mean rows of wire – these things were her accompaniment: while out of the window the deep blue sea-levels disappeared from her gaze, and with them her poet's home. Heavy-hearted, she tried to read, and wept instead.

Mr Marchmill was in a thriving way of business, and he and his family lived in a large new house, which stood in rather extensive grounds a few miles outside the Midland city wherein he carried on his trade. Ella's life was lonely here, as the suburban life is apt to be, particularly at certain seasons; and she had ample time to indulge her taste for lyric and elegiac composition. She had hardly got back when she encountered a piece by Robert Trewe in the new number of her favourite magazine, which must have been written almost immediately before her visit to Solentsea, for it contained the very couplet she had seen pencilled on the wall-paper by the bed, and Mrs Hooper had declared to be recent.

Ella could resist no longer, but seizing a pen impulsively, wrote to him as a brother-poet, using the name of John Ivy, congratulating him in her letter on his triumphant executions in metre and rhythm of thoughts that moved his soul, as compared with her own brow-beaten efforts in the same pathetic trade.

To this address there came a response in a few days, little as she had dared to hope for it – a civil and brief note, in which the young poet stated that, though he was not well acquainted with Mr Ivy's verse, he recalled the name as being one he had seen attached to some very promising pieces; that he was glad to gain Mr Ivy's acquaintance by letter, and should certainly look with much interest for his productions in the future.

There must have been something juvenile or timid in her own epistle, as one ostensibly coming from a man, she declared to herself; for Trewe quite adopted the tone of an elder and superior in this reply. But what did it matter? He had replied; he had written to her with his own hand from that very room she knew so well, for he was now back again in his quarters.

The correspondence thus begun was continued for two months or more, Ella Marchmill sending him from time to time some that she considered to be the best of her pieces, which he very kindly accepted, though he did not say he sedulously read them, nor did he send her any of his own in return. Ella would have been more hurt at this than she was if she had not known that Trewe laboured under the impression that she was one of his own sex.

Yet the situation was unsatisfactory. A flattering little voice told her that, were he only to see her, matters would be otherwise. No doubt she would have helped on this by making a frank confession of womanhood, to begin with, if something had not happened, to her delight, to render it unnecessary. A friend of her husband's, the editor of the most important newspaper in their city and county, who was dining with them one day, observed during their conversation about the poet that his (the editor's) brother the landscape-painter was a friend of Mr Trewe's, and that the two men were at that very moment in Wales together.

Ella was slightly acquainted with the editor's brother. The next morning down she sat and wrote, inviting him to stay at her house for a short time on his way back, and requesting him to bring with him, if practicable, his companion Mr Trewe, whose acquaintance she was anxious to make. The answer arrived after some days. Her correspondent and his friend Trewe would have much satisfaction in accepting her invitation on their way southward, which would be on such and such a day in the following week.

Ella was blithe and buoyant. Her scheme had succeeded; her beloved though as yet unseen one was coming. 'Behold, he standeth behind our wall; he looked forth at the windows, showing himself through the lattice,' she thought ecstatically. 'And, lo, the winter is past, the rain is over and gone, the flowers appear on the earth, the time of the singing of birds is come, and the voice of the turtle is heard in our land.'

But it was necessary to consider the details of lodging and feeding him. This she did most solicitously, and awaited the pregnant day and hour.

It was about five in the afternoon when she heard a ring at the door and the editor's brother's voice in the hall. Poetess as she was, or as she thought herself, she had not been too sublime that day to dress with infinite trouble in a fashionable robe of rich material, having a faint resemblance to the *chiton* of the Greeks, a style just then in vogue among ladies of an artistic and romantic turn, which had been obtained by Ella of her Bond Street dressmaker when she was last in London. Her visitor entered the drawing-room. She looked towards his rear; nobody else came through the door. Where, in the name of the God of Love, was Robert Trewe?

'O, I'm sorry,' said the painter, after their introductory words had been spoken. 'Trewe is a curious fellow, you know, Mrs Marchmill. He said he'd come; then he said he couldn't. He's rather dusty. We've been doing a few miles with knapsacks, you know; and he wanted to get on home.'

'He – he's not coming?'

'He's not; and he asked me to make his apologies.'

'When did you p-p-part from him?' she asked, her nether lip starting off quivering so much that it was like a *tremolo*-stop opened in her speech. She longed to run away from this dreadful bore and cry her eyes out.

'Just now, in the turnpike road yonder there.'

'What! he has actually gone past my gates?'

'Yes. When we got to them – handsome gates they are, too, the finest bit of modern wrought-iron work I have seen – when we came to them we stopped, talking there a little while, and then he wished me goodbye and went on. The truth is, he's a little bit depressed just now, and doesn't want to see anybody. He's a very good fellow, and a warm friend, but a little uncertain and gloomy sometimes; he thinks too much of things. His poetry is rather too erotic and passionate, you know, for some tastes; and he has just come in for a terrible slating from the — *Review* that was published yesterday; he saw a copy of it at the station by accident. Perhaps you've read it?'

'No.'

'So much the better. O, it is not worth thinking of; just one of those articles written to order, to please the narrow-minded set of subscribers upon whom the circulation depends. But he's upset by it. He says it is the misrepresentation that hurts him so; that, though he can stand a fair attack, he can't stand lies that he's powerless to refute and stop from spreading. That's just Trewe's weak point. He lives so much by himself that these things affect him much more than they would if he were in the bustle of fashionable or commercial life. So he wouldn't come here, making the excuse that it all looked so new and monied – if you'll pardon—'

'But – he must have known – there was sympathy here! Has he never said anything about getting letters from this address?'

'Yes, yes, he has, from John Ivy – perhaps a relative of yours, he thought, visiting here at the time?'

'Did he – like Ivy, did he say?'

'Well, I don't know that he took any great interest in Ivy.'

'Or in his poems?'

'Or in his poems – so far as I know, that is.'

Robert Trewe took no interest in her house, in her poems, or in their writer. As soon as she could get away she went into the nursery and tried to let off her emotion by unnecessarily kissing the children, till she had a sudden sense of disgust at being reminded how plain-looking they were, like their father.

The obtuse and single-minded landscape-painter never once perceived from her conversation that it was only Trewe she wanted, and not himself. He made the best of his visit, seeming to enjoy the society of Ella's husband, who also took a great fancy to him, and showed him everywhere about the neighbourhood, neither of them noticing Ella's mood.

The painter had been gone only a day or two when, while sitting upstairs alone one morning, she glanced over the London paper just arrived, and read the following paragraph:

SUICIDE OF A POET

Mr Robert Trewe, who has been favourably known for some years as one of our rising lyrists, committed suicide at his lodgings at Solentsea on Saturday evening last by shooting himself in the right temple with a revolver. Readers hardly need to be reminded that Mr Trewe has recently attracted the attention of a much wider public than had hitherto known him, by his new volume of verse, mostly of an impassioned kind, entitled *Lyrics to a Woman Unknown*, which has been already favourably noticed in these pages for the extraordinary gamut of feeling it traverses, and which has been made the subject of a severe, if not ferocious, criticism in the — *Review*. It is supposed, though not certainly known, that the article may have partially conduced to the sad act, as a copy of the review in question was found on his writing-table; and he had been observed to be in a somewhat depressed state of mind since the critique appeared.

Then came the report of the inquest, at which the following letter was read, it having been addressed to a friend at a distance:

DEAR—, Before these lines reach your hands I shall be delivered from the inconveniences of seeing, hearing, and knowing more of the things around me. I will not trouble you by giving my reasons for the step I have taken, though I can assure you they were sound and logical. Perhaps had I been blessed with a mother, or a sister, or a female friend of another sort tenderly devoted to me, I might have thought it worth while to continue my present existence. I have long dreamt of such an unattainable creature, as you know; and she, this undiscoverable, elusive one, inspired my last volume; the imaginary woman alone, for, in spite of what has been said in some quarters, there is no real woman behind the title. She has continued to the last unrevealed, unmet, unwon. I think it desirable to mention this in order that no blame may attach to any real woman as having been the cause of my decease by cruel or cavalier treatment of me. Tell my landlady that I am sorry to have caused her this unpleasantness; but my occupancy of the rooms will soon be forgotten. There are ample funds in my name at the bank to pay all expenses.

R. TREWE.

Ella sat for a while as if stunned, then rushed into the adjoining chamber and flung herself upon her face on the bed.

Her grief and distraction shook her to pieces; and she lay in this frenzy of sorrow for more than an hour. Broken words came every now and then from her quivering lips: 'O, if he had only known me – known of me – me! . . . O, if I had only once met him – only once; and put my hand upon his hot forehead – kissed him – let him know how I loved him – that I would have suffered shame and scorn, would have lived and died, for him! Perhaps it would have saved his dear life! ... But no – it was not allowed! God is a jealous God; and that happiness was not for him and me!'

All possibilities were over; the meeting was stultified. Yet it was almost visible to her in her fantasy even now, though it could never be substantiated – .

The hour which might have been, yet might not be,
Which man's and woman's heart conceived and bore,
Yet whereof life was barren.

She wrote to the landlady at Solentsea in the third person, in as subdued a style as she could command, enclosing a postal order for a sovereign, and informing Mrs Hooper that Mrs Marchmill had seen in the papers the sad account of the poet's death, and having been, as Mrs Hooper was aware, much interested in Mr Trewe during her stay at Coburg House, she would be obliged if Mrs Hooper could obtain a small portion of his hair before his coffin was closed down, and send it her as a memorial of him, as also the photograph that was in the frame.

By the return-post a letter arrived containing what had been requested. Ella wept over the portrait and secured it in her private drawer; the lock of hair she tied with white ribbon and put in her bosom, whence she drew it and kissed it every now and then in some unobserved nook.

'What's the matter?' said her husband, looking up from his newspaper on one of these occasions. 'Crying over something? A lock of hair? Whose is it?'

'He's dead!' she murmured.

'Who?'

'I don't want to tell you, Will, just now, unless you insist!' she said, a sob hanging heavy in her voice.

'O, all right.'

'Do you mind my refusing? I will tell you some day.'

'It doesn't matter in the least, of course.'

He walked away whistling a few bars of no tune in particular; and when he had got down to his factory in the city the subject came into Marchmill's head again.

He, too, was aware that a suicide had taken place recently at the house they had occupied at Solentsea. Having seen the volume of poems in his wife's hand of late, and heard fragments of the landlady's conversation about Trewe when they were her tenants, he all at once said to himself, 'Why of course it's he! ... How the devil did she get to know him? What sly animals women are!'

Then he placidly dismissed the matter, and went on with his daily affairs. By this time Ella at home had come to a determination. Mrs Hooper, in sending the hair and photograph, had informed her of the day of the funeral; and as the morning and noon wore on an overpowering wish to know where they were laying him took possession of the sympathetic woman. Caring very little now what her husband or any one else might think of her eccentricities, she wrote Marchmill a brief note, stating that she was called away for the afternoon and evening, but would return on the following morning. This she left on his desk, and having given the same information to the servants, went out of the house on foot.

When Mr Marchmill reached home early in the afternoon the servants looked anxious. The nurse took him privately aside, and hinted that her mistress's sadness during the past few days had been such that she feared she had gone out to drown herself. Marchmill reflected. Upon the whole he thought that she had not done that. Without saying whither he was bound he also started off, telling them not to sit up for him. He drove to the railway-station, and took a ticket for Solentsea.

It was dark when he reached the place, though he had come by a fast train, and he knew that if his wife had preceded him thither it could only have been by a slower train, arriving not a great while before his own. The season at Solentsea was now past: the parade was gloomy, and the flys were few and cheap. He asked the way to the Cemetery, and soon reached it. The gate was locked, but the keeper let him in, declaring, however, that there was nobody within the precincts. Although it was not late, the autumnal darkness had now become intense; and he found some difficulty in keeping to the serpentine path which led to the quarter where, as the man had told him, the one or two interments for the day had taken place. He stepped upon the grass, and stumbling over some pegs, stooped now and then to discern if possible a figure against the sky. He could see none; but lighting on a spot where the soil was trodden, beheld a crouching object beside a newly made grave. She heard him, and sprang up.

'Ell, how silly this is!' he said indignantly. 'Running away from your home – I never heard of such a thing! Of course I am not jealous of this unfortunate man; but it is too ridiculous that you, a married woman with three children and a fourth coming, should go losing your head like this over a dead lover! ... Do you know you were locked in? You might not have been able to get out all night.'

She did not answer.

'I hope it didn't go far between you and him, for your own sake.'

'Don't insult me, Will.'

'Mind, I won't have any more of this sort of thing; do you hear?'

'Very well,' she said.

He drew her arm within his own, and conducted her out of the Cemetery. It was impossible to get back that night; and not wishing to be recognized in their present sorry condition he took her to a miserable little coffee-house close to the station, whence they departed early in the morning, travelling almost without speaking, under the sense that it was one of those dreary situations occurring in married life which words could not mend, and reaching their own door at noon.

The months passed, and neither of the twain ever ventured to start a conversation upon this episode. Ella seemed to be only too frequently in a sad and listless mood, which might almost have been called pining. The time was approaching when she would have to undergo the stress of childbirth for a fourth time, and that apparently did not tend to raise her spirits.

'I don't think I shall get over it this time!' she said one day.

'Pooh! What a childish foreboding! Why shouldn't it be as well now as ever?'

She shook her head. 'I feel almost sure I am going to die; and I should be glad, if it were not for Nelly, and Frank, and Tiny.'

'And me!'

'You'll soon find somebody to fill my place,' she murmured, with a sad smile. 'And you'll have a perfect right to; I assure you of that.'

'Ell, you are not thinking still about that – poetical friend of yours?'

She neither admitted nor denied the charge. 'I am not going to get over my illness this time,' she reiterated. 'Something tells me I shan't.'

This view of things was rather a bad beginning, as it usually is; and, in fact, six weeks later, in the month of May, she was lying in her room, pulseless and bloodless, with hardly strength enough left to follow up one feeble breath with another, the infant for whose unnecessary life she was slowly parting with her own being fat and well. Just before her death she spoke to Marchmill softly:

'Will, I want to confess to you the entire circumstances of that – about you know what – that time we visited Solentsea. I can't tell what possessed me – how I could forget you so, my husband! But I had got into a morbid state: I thought you had been unkind; that you had neglected me; that you weren't up to my intellectual level, while he was, and far above it. I wanted a fuller appreciator, perhaps, rather than another lover—'

She could get no further then for very exhaustion; and she went off in a sudden collapse a few hours later, without having said anything more to her husband on the subject of her love for the poet. William Marchmill, in truth, like most husbands of several years' standing, was little disturbed by retrospective jealousies, and had not shown the least anxiety to press her for confessions concerning a man dead and gone beyond any power of inconveniencing him more.

But when she had been buried a couple of years it chanced one day that, in turning over some forgotten papers that he wished to destroy before his second wife entered the house, he lighted on a lock of hair in an envelope, with the photograph of the deceased poet, a date being written on the back in his late wife's hand. It was that of the time they spent at Solentsea.

Marchmill looked long and musingly at the hair and portrait, for something struck him. Fetching the little boy who had been the death of his mother, now a noisy toddler, he took him on his knee, held the lock of hair against the child's head, and set up the photograph on the table behind, so that he could closely compare the features each countenance presented. By a known but inexplicable trick of Nature there were undoubtedly strong traces of resemblance to the man Ella had never seen; the dreamy and peculiar expression of the poet's face sat, as the transmitted idea, upon the child's, and the hair was of the same hue.

'I'm damned if I didn't think so!' murmured Marchmill. 'Then she *did* play me false with that fellow at the lodgings! Let me see: the dates – the second week in August ... the third week in May ... Yes ... yes ... Get away, you poor little brat! You are nothing to me!'

1893

Barbara of the House of Grebe

———◆❖◆———

IT was apparently an idea, rather than a passion, that inspired Lord Uplandtowers's resolve to win her. Nobody ever knew when he formed it, or whence he got his assurance of success in the face of her manifest dislike of him. Possibly not until after that first important act of her life which I shall presently mention. His matured and cynical doggedness at the age of nineteen, when impulse mostly rules calculation, was remarkable, and might have owed its existence as much to his succession to the earldom and its accompanying local honours in childhood, as to the family character; an elevation which jerked him into maturity, so to speak, without his having known adolescence. He had only reached his twelfth year when his father, the fourth Earl, died, after a course of the Bath waters.

Nevertheless, the family character had a great deal to do with it. Determination was hereditary in the bearers of that escutcheon; sometimes for good, sometimes for evil.

The seats of the two families were about ten miles apart, the way between them lying along the now old, then new, turnpike-road connecting Havenpool and Warborne with the city of Melchester; a road which, though only a branch from what was known as the Great Western Highway, is probably, even at present, as it has been for the last hundred years, one of the finest examples of macadamized turnpike-track that can be found in England.

The mansion of the Earl, as well as that of his neighbour, Barbara's father, stood back about a mile from the highway, with which each was connected by an ordinary drive and lodge. It was along this particular highway that the young Earl drove on a certain evening at Christmastide some twenty years before the end of the last century, to attend a ball at Chene Manor, the home of Barbara and her parents Sir John and Lady Grebe. Sir John's was a baronetcy created a few years before the breaking out of the Civil War, and his lands were even more extensive than those of Lord Uplandtowers himself, comprising this Manor of Chene, another on the coast near, half the Hundred of Cockdene, and well-enclosed lands in several other parishes, notably Warborne and those contiguous. At this time Barbara was barely seventeen, and the ball is the first occasion on which we have any tradition of Lord Uplandtowers attempting tender relations with her; it was early enough, God knows.

An intimate friend – one of the Drenkhards – is said to have dined with him that day, and Lord Uplandtowers had, for a wonder, communicated to his guest the secret design of his heart.

'You'll never get her – sure; you'll never get her!' this friend had said at parting. 'She's not drawn to your lordship by love: and as for thought of a good match, why, there's no more calculation in her than in a bird.'

'We'll see,' said Lord Uplandtowers impassively.

He no doubt thought of his friend's forecast as he travelled along the highway in his chariot; but the sculptural repose of his profile against the vanishing daylight on his right hand would have shown his friend that the Earl's equanimity was undisturbed. He reached the solitary wayside tavern called Lornton Inn – the rendezvous of many a daring poacher for operations in the adjoining forest; and he might have observed, if he had taken the trouble, a strange post-chaise standing in the halting-space before the inn. He duly sped past it, and half an hour after through the little town of Warborne. Onward, a mile further, was the house of his entertainer.

At this date it was an imposing edifice – or, rather, congeries of edifices – as extensive as the residence of the Earl himself, though far less regular. One wing showed extreme antiquity, having huge chimneys, whose substructures projected from the external walls like towers; and a kitchen of vast dimensions, in which (it was said) breakfasts had been cooked for John of Gaunt. Whilst he was yet in the forecourt he could hear the rhythm of French horns and clarionets, the favourite instruments of those days at such entertainments.

Entering the long parlour, in which the dance had just been opened by Lady Grebe with a minuet – it being now seven o'clock, according to the tradition – he was received with a welcome befitting his rank, and looked around for Barbara. She was not dancing, and seemed to be preoccupied – almost, indeed, as though she had been waiting for him. Barbara at this time was a good and pretty girl, who never spoke ill of any one, and hated other pretty women the very least possible. She did not refuse him the country-dance which followed, and soon after was his partner in a second.

The evening wore on, and the horns and clarionets tootled merrily. Barbara evinced towards her lover neither distinct preference nor aversion; but old eyes would have seen that she pondered something. However, after supper she pleaded a headache, and disappeared. To pass the time of her absence, Lord Uplandtowers went into a little room adjoining the long gallery, where some elderly ones were sitting by the fire – for he had a phlegmatic dislike of dancing for its own sake – and, lifting the window-curtains, he looked out of the window into the park and wood, dark now as a cavern. Some of the guests appeared to be leaving even so soon as this, two lights showing themselves as turning away from the door and sinking to nothing in the distance.

His hostess put her head into the room to look for part- ners for the ladies, and Lord Uplandtowers came out. Lady Grebe informed him that Barbara had not returned to the ball-room: she had gone to bed in sheer necessity.

'She has been so excited over the ball all day,' her mother continued, 'that I feared she would be worn out early ... But sure, Lord Uplandtowers, you won't be leaving yet?'

He said that it was near twelve o'clock, and that some had already left.

'I protest nobody has gone yet,' said Lady Grebe.

To humour her he stayed till midnight, and then set out. He had made no progress in his suit; but he had assured him- self that Barbara gave no other guest the preference, and nearly everybody in the neighbourhood was there.

' 'Tis only a matter of time,' said the calm young philoso- pher.

The next morning he lay till near ten o'clock, and he had only just come out upon the head of the staircase when he heard hoofs upon the gravel without; in a few moments the door had been opened, and Sir John Grebe met him in the hall, as he set foot on the lowest stair.

'My lord – where's Barbara – my daughter?'

Even the Earl of Uplandtowers could not repress amaze- ment. 'What's the matter, my dear Sir John?' says he.

The news was startling, indeed. From the Baronet's dis- jointed explanation Lord Uplandtowers gathered that after his own and the other guests' departure Sir John and Lady Grebe had gone to rest without seeing any more of Barbara; it being understood by them that she had retired to bed when she sent word to say that she could not join the dancers again. Before then she had told her maid that she would dis- pense with her services for this night; and there was evidence to show that the young lady had never lain down at all, the bed remaining unpressed. Circumstances seemed to prove that the deceitful girl had feigned indisposition to get an ex- cuse for leaving the ball-room, and that she had left the house within ten minutes, presumably during the first dance after supper.

'I saw her go,' said Lord Uplandtowers.

'The devil you did!' says Sir John.

'Yes.' And he mentioned the retreating carriage-lights, and how he was assured by Lady Grebe that no guest had departed.

'Surely that was it!' said the father. 'But she's not gone alone, d'ye know!'

'Ah – who is the young man?'

'I can on'y guess. My worst fear is my most likely guess. I'll say no more. I thought – yet I would not believe – it possible that you was the sinner. Would that you had been! But 'tis t'other, 'tis t'other, by Heaven! I must e'en up and after 'em!'

'Whom do you suspect?'

Sir John would not give a name, and, stultified rather than agitated, Lord Uplandtowers accompanied him back to Chene. He again asked upon whom were the Baronet's suspicions directed; and the impulsive Sir John was no match for the insistence of Uplandtowers.

He said at length, 'I fear 'tis Edmond Willowes.'

'Who's he?'

'A young fellow of Shottsford-Forum – a widow-woman's son,' the other told him, and explained that Willowes's father, or grandfather, was the last of the old glass-painters in that place, where (as you may know) the art lingered on when it had died out in every other part of England.

'By God that's bad – mighty bad!' said Lord Uplandtowers, throwing himself back in the chaise in frigid despair.

They dispatched emissaries in all directions; one by the Melchester Road, another by Shottsford-Forum, another coastwards.

But the lovers had a ten-hours' start; and it was apparent that sound judgement had been exercised in choosing as their time of flight the particular night when the movements of a strange carriage would not be noticed, either in the park or on the neighbouring highway, owing to the general press of vehicles. The chaise which had been waiting at Lornton Inn was, no doubt, the one they had escaped in; and the pair of heads which had planned so cleverly thus far had probably contrived marriage ere now.

The fears of her parents were realized. A letter sent by special messenger from Barbara, on the evening of that day, briefly informed them that her lover and herself were on the way to London, and before this communication reached her home they would be united as husband and wife. She had taken this extreme step because she loved her dear Edmond as she could love no other man, and because she had seen closing round her the doom of marriage with Lord Uplandtowers, unless she put that threatened fate out of possibility by doing as she had done. She had well considered the step beforehand, and was prepared to live like any other country-townsman's wife if her father repudiated her for her action.

'Damn her!' said Lord Uplandtowers, as he drove homeward that night. 'Damn her for a fool!' – which shows the kind of love he bore her.

Well; Sir John had already started in pursuit of them as a matter of duty, driving like a wild man to Melchester, and thence by the direct highway to the capital. But he soon saw that he was acting to no purpose; and by and by, discovering that the marriage had actually taken place, he forbore all attempts to unearth them in the city, and returned and sat down with his lady to digest the event as best they could.

To proceed against this Willowes for the abduction of our heiress was, possibly, in their power; yet, when they considered the now unalterable facts, they refrained from violent retribution. Some six weeks passed, during which time Barbara's parents, though they keenly felt her loss, held no communication with the truant, either for reproach or condonation. They continued to think of the disgrace she had brought upon herself; for, though the young man was an honest fellow, and the son of an honest father, the latter had died so early, and his widow had had such struggles to maintain herself, that the son was very imperfectly educated. Moreover, his blood was, as far as they knew, of no distinction whatever, whilst hers, through her mother, was compounded of the best juices of ancient baronial distillation, containing tinctures of Maundeville, and Mohun, and Syward, and Peverell, and Culliford, and Talbot, and Plantagenet, and York, and Lancaster, and God knows what besides, which it was a thousand pities to throw away.

The father and mother sat by the fireplace that was spanned by the four-centred arch bearing the family shields on its haunches, and groaned aloud – the lady more than Sir John.

'To think this should have come upon us in our old age!' said he.

'Speak for yourself!' she snapped through her sobs, 'I am only one-and-forty! ... Why didn't ye ride faster and overtake 'em!'

In the meantime the young married lovers, caring no more about their blood than about ditch-water, were intensely happy – happy, that is, in the descending scale which, as we all know, Heaven in its wisdom has ordained for such rash cases; that is to say, the first week they were in the seventh heaven, the second in the sixth, the third week temperate, the fourth reflective, and so on; a lover's heart after possession being comparable to the earth in its geologic stages, as described to us sometimes by our worthy President; first a hot coal, then a warm one, then a cooling cinder, then chilly – the simile shall be pursued no further. The long and the short of it was that one day a letter, sealed with their daughter's own little seal, came into Sir John and Lady Grebe's hands; and, on opening it, they found it to contain an appeal from the young couple to Sir John to forgive them for what they had done, and they would fall on their naked knees and be most dutiful children for evermore.

Then Sir John and his lady sat down again by the fireplace with the four-centred arch, and consulted, and re-read the letter. Sir John Grebe, if the truth must be told, loved his daughter's happiness far more, poor man, than he loved his name and lineage; he recalled to his mind all her little ways, gave vent to a sigh; and, by this time acclimatized to the idea of the marriage, said that what was done could not be undone, and that he supposed they must not be too harsh with her. Perhaps Barbara and her husband were in actual need; and how could they let their only child starve?

A slight consolation had come to them in an unexpected manner. They had been credibly informed that an ancestor of plebeian Willowes was once honoured with intermarriage with a scion of the aristocracy who had gone to the dogs. In short, such is the foolishness of distinguished parents, and sometimes of others also, that they wrote that very day to the address Barbara had given them, informing her that she might return home and bring her husband with her; they would not object to see him, would not reproach her, and would endeavour to welcome both, and to discuss with them what could best be arranged for their future.

In three or four days a rather shabby post-chaise drew up at the door of Chene Manor-house, at sound of which the tender-hearted baronet and his wife ran out as if to welcome a prince and princess of the blood. They were overjoyed to see their spoilt child return safe and sound – though she was only Mrs Willowes, wife of Edmond Willowes of nowhere. Barbara burst into penitential tears, and both husband and wife were contrite enough, as well they might be, considering that they had not a guinea to call their own.

When the four had calmed themselves, and not a word of chiding had been uttered to the pair, they discussed the position soberly, young Willowes sitting in the background with great modesty till invited forward by Lady Grebe in no frigid tone.

'How handsome he is!' she said to herself. 'I don't won-der at Barbara's craze for him.'

He was, indeed, one of the handsomest men who ever set his lips on a maid's. A blue coat, murrey waistcoat, and breeches of drab set off a figure that could scarcely be sur-passed. He had large dark eyes, anxious now, as they glanced from Barbara to her parents and tenderly back again to her; observing whom, even now in her trepidation, one could see why the *sang froid* of Lord Uplandtowers had been raised to

more than lukewarmness. Her fair young face (according to
the tale handed down by old women) looked out from under
a grey conical hat, trimmed with white ostrich-feathers, and
her little toes peeped from a buff petticoat worn under a
puce gown. Her features were not regular: they were almost
infantine, as you may see from miniatures in possession of
the family, her mouth showing much sensitiveness, and one
could be sure that her faults would not lie on the side of
bad temper unless for urgent reasons.

Well, they discussed their state as became them, and the
desire of the young couple to gain the goodwill of those
upon whom they were literally dependent for everything induced them to agree to any temporizing measure that was
not too irksome. Therefore, having been nearly two months
united, they did not oppose Sir John's proposal that he
should furnish Edmond Willowes with funds sufficient for
him to travel a year on the Continent in the company of a
tutor, the young man undertaking to lend himself with the
utmost diligence to the tutor's instructions, till he became
polished outwardly and inwardly to the degree required in
the husband of such a lady as Barbara. He was to apply
himself to the study of languages, manners, history, society,
ruins, and everything else that came under his eyes, till he
should return to take his place without blushing by Barbara's side.

'And by that time,' said worthy Sir John, 'I'll get my little
place out at Yewsholt ready for you and Barbara to occupy
on your return. The house is small and out of the way; but
it will do for a young couple for a while.'

'If 'twere no bigger than a summer-house it would do!'
says Barbara.

'If 'twere no bigger than a sedan-chair!' says Willowes.
'And the more lonely the better.'

'We can put up with the loneliness,' said Barbara, with
less zest. 'Some friends will come, no doubt.'

All this being laid down, a travelled tutor was called in –
a man of many gifts and great experience – and on a fine
morning away tutor and pupil went. A great reason urged

against Barbara accompanying her youthful husband was that his attentions to her would naturally be such as to prevent his zealously applying every hour of his time to learning and seeing – an argument of wise prescience, and unanswerable. Regular days for letter-writing were fixed, Barbara and her Edmond exchanged their last kisses at the door, and the chaise swept under the archway into the drive.

He wrote to them from Le Havre, as soon as he reached that port, which was not for seven days, on account of adverse winds; he wrote from Rouen, and from Paris; described to her his sight of the King and Court at Versailles, and the wonderful marblework and mirrors in that palace; wrote next from Lyons; then, after a comparatively long interval, from Turin, narrating his fearful adventures in crossing Mont Cenis on mules, and how he was overtaken with a terrific snowstorm, which had well-nigh been the end of him, and his tutor, and his guides. Then he wrote glowingly of Italy; and Barbara could see the development of her husband's mind reflected in his letters month by month; and she much admired the forethought of her father in suggesting this education for Edmond. Yet she sighed sometimes – her husband being no longer in evidence to fortify her in her choice of him – and timidly dreaded what mortifications might be in store for her by reason of this *mésalliance*. She went out very little; for on the one or two occasions on which she had shown herself to former friends she noticed a distinct difference in their manner, as though they should say, 'Ah, my happy swain's wife; you're caught!'

Edmond's letters were as affectionate as ever; even more affectionate, after a while, than hers were to him. Barbara observed this growing coolness in herself; and like a good and honest lady was horrified and grieved, since her only wish was to act faithfully and uprightly. It troubled her so much that she prayed for a warmer heart, and at last wrote to her husband to beg him, now that he was in the land of Art, to send her his portrait, ever so small, that she might look at it all day and every day, and never for a moment forget his features.

Willowes was nothing loth, and replied that he would do more than she wished : he had made friends with a sculptor in Pisa, who was much interested in him and his story; and he had commissioned this artist to make a bust of himself in marble, which when finished he would send her. What Barbara had wanted was something immediate; but she expressed no objection to the delay; and in his next communication Edmond told her that the sculptor, of his own choice, had decided to extend the bust to a full-length statue, so anxious was he to get a specimen of his skill introduced to the notice of the English aristocracy. It was progressing well, and rapidly.

Meanwhile, Barbara's attention began to be occupied at home with Yewsholt Lodge, the house that her kind-hearted father was preparing for her residence when her husband returned. It was a small place on the plan of a large one – a cottage built in the form of a mansion, having a central hall with a wooden gallery running round it, and rooms no bigger than closets to support this introduction. It stood on a slope so solitary, and surrounded by trees so dense, that the birds who inhabited the boughs sang at strange hours, as if they hardly could distinguish night from day.

During the progress of repairs at this bower Barbara frequently visited it. Though so secluded by the dense growth, it was near the high road, and one day while looking over the fence she saw Lord Uplandtowers riding past. He saluted her courteously, yet with mechanical stiffness, and did not halt. Barbara went home, and continued to pray that she might never cease to love her husband. After that she sickened, and did not come out of doors again for a long time.

The year of education had extended to fourteen months, and the house was in order for Edmond's return to take up his abode there with Barbara, when, instead of the accustomed letter for her, came one to Sir John Grebe in the handwriting of the said tutor, informing him of a terrible catastrophe that had occurred to them at Venice. Mr Willowes and himself had attended the theatre one night during the

Carnival of the preceding week, to witness the Italian comedy, when, owing to the carelessness of one of the candle-snuffers, the theatre had caught fire, and been burnt to the ground. Few persons had lost their lives, owing to the superhuman exertions of some of the audience in getting out the senseless sufferers; and, among them all, he who had risked his own life the most heroically was Mr Willowes. In re-entering for the fifth time to save his fellow-creatures some fiery beams had fallen upon him, and he had been given up for lost. He was, however, by the blessing of Providence, recovered, with the life still in him, though he was fearfully burnt; and by almost a miracle he seemed likely to survive, his constitution being wondrously sound. He was, of course, unable to write, but he was receiving the attention of several skilful surgeons. Further report would be made by the next mail or by private hand.

The tutor said nothing in detail of poor Willowes's sufferings, but as soon as the news was broken to Barbara she realized how intense they must have been, and her immediate instinct was to rush to his side, though, on consideration, the journey seemed impossible to her. Her health was by no means what it had been, and to post across Europe at that season of the year, or to traverse the Bay of Biscay in a sailing-craft, was an undertaking that would hardly be justified by the result. But she was anxious to go till, on reading to the end of the letter, her husband's tutor was found to hint very strongly against such a step if it should be contemplated, this being also the opinion of the surgeons. And though Willowes's comrade refrained from giving his reasons, they disclosed themselves plainly enough in the sequel.

The truth was that the worst of the wounds resulting from the fire had occurred to his head and face – that handsome face which had won her heart from her – and both the tutor and the surgeons knew that for a sensitive young woman to see him before his wounds had healed would cause more misery to her by the shock than happiness to him by her ministrations.

Lady Grebe blurted out what Sir John and Barbara had thought, but had had too much delicacy to express.

'Sure, 'tis mighty hard for you, poor Barbara, that the one little gift he had to justify your rash choice of him – his wonderful good looks – should be taken away like this, to leave 'ee no excuse at all for your conduct in the world's eyes ... Well, I wish you'd married t'other – that I do!' And the lady sighed.

'He'll soon get right again,' said her father soothingly.

Such remarks as the above were not often made; but they were frequent enough to cause Barbara an uneasy sense of self-stultification. She determined to hear them no longer; and the house at Yewsholt being ready and furnished, she withdrew thither with her maids, where for the first time she could feel mistress of a home that would be hers and her husband's exclusively, when he came.

After long weeks Willowes had recovered sufficiently to be able to write himself, and slowly and tenderly he enlightened her upon the full extent of his injuries. It was a mercy, he said, that he had not lost his sight entirely; but he was thankful to say that he still retained full vision in one eye, though the other was dark for ever. The sparing manner in which he meted out particulars of his condition told Barbara how appalling had been his experience. He was grateful for her assurance that nothing could change her; but feared she did not fully realize that he was so sadly disfigured as to make it doubtful if she would recognize him. However, in spite of all, his heart was as true to her as it ever had been.

Barbara saw from his anxiety how much lay behind. She replied that she submitted to the decrees of Fate, and would welcome him in any shape as soon as he could come. She told him of the pretty retreat in which she had taken up her abode, pending their joint occupation of it, and did not reveal how much she had sighed over the information that all his good looks were gone. Still less did she say that she felt a certain strangeness in awaiting him, the weeks they had lived together having been so short by comparison with the length of his absence.

Slowly drew on the time when Willowes found himself well enough to come home. He landed at Southampton, and posted thence towards Yewsholt. Barbara arranged to go out to meet him as far as Lornton Inn – the spot between the Forest and the Chase at which he had waited for night on the evening of their elopement. Thither she drove at the appointed hour in a little pony-chaise, presented her by her father on her birthday for her especial use in her new house; which vehicle she sent back on arriving at the inn, the plan agreed upon being that she should perform the return journey with her husband in his hired coach.

There was not much accommodation for a lady at this wayside tavern; but, as it was a fine evening in early summer, she did not mind – walking about outside, and straining her eyes along the highway for the expected one. But each cloud of dust that enlarged in the distance and drew near was found to disclose a conveyance other than his post-chaise. Barbara remained till the appointment was two hours passed, and then began to fear that owing to some adverse wind in the Channel he was not coming that night.

While waiting she was conscious of a curious trepidation that was not entirely solicitude, and did not amount to dread; her tense state of incertitude bordered both on disappointment and on relief. She had lived six or seven weeks with an imperfectly educated yet handsome husband whom now she had not seen for seventeen months, and who was so changed physically by an accident that she was assured she would hardly know him. Can we wonder at her compound state of mind?

But her immediate difficulty was to get away from Lornton Inn, for her situation was becoming embarrassing. Like too many of Barbara's actions, this drive had been undertaken without much reflection. Expecting to wait no more than a few minutes for her husband in his post-chaise, and to enter it with him, she had not hesitated to isolate herself by sending back her own little vehicle. She now found that, being so well known in this neighbourhood, her excursion to meet her long-absent husband was exciting great interest.

She was conscious that more eyes were watching her from the inn-windows than met her own gaze. Barbara had decided to get home by hiring whatever kind of conveyance the tavern afforded, when, straining her eyes for the last time over the now darkening highway, she perceived yet another dust-cloud drawing near. She paused; a chariot ascended to the inn, and would have passed had not its occupant caught sight of her standing expectantly. The horses were checked on the instant.

'You here – and alone, my dear Mrs Willowes?' said Lord Uplandtowers, whose carriage it was.

She explained what had brought her into this lonely situation; and, as he was going in the direction of her own home, she accepted his offer of a seat beside him. Their conversation was embarrassed and fragmentary at first; but when they had driven a mile or two she was surprised to find herself talking earnestly and warmly to him: her impulsiveness was in truth but the natural consequence of her late existence – a somewhat desolate one by reason of the strange marriage she had made; and there is no more indiscreet mood than that of a woman surprised into talk who has long been imposing upon herself a policy of reserve. Therefore her ingenuous heart rose with a bound into her throat when, in response to his leading questions, or rather hints, she allowed her troubles to leak out of her. Lord Uplandtowers took her quite to her own door, although he had driven three miles out of his way to do so; and in handing her down she heard from him a whisper of stern reproach: 'It need not have been thus if you had listened to me!'

She made no reply, and went indoors. There, as the evening wore away, she regretted more and more that she had been so friendly with Lord Uplandtowers. But he had launched himself upon her so unexpectedly: if she had only foreseen the meeting with him, what a careful line of conduct she would have marked out! Barbara broke into a perspiration of disquiet when she thought of her unreserve, and, in self-chastisement, resolved to sit up till midnight on the bare chance of Edmond's return; directing that supper should be laid for him, improbable as his arrival till the morrow was.

The hours went past, and there was a dead silence in and round about Yewsholt Lodge, except for the soughing of the trees; till, when it was near upon midnight, she heard the noise of hoofs and wheels approaching the door. Knowing that it could only be her husband, Barbara instantly went into the hall to meet him. Yet she stood there not without a sensation of faintness, so many were the changes since their parting! And, owing to her casual encounter with Lord Uplandtowers, his voice and image still remained with her, excluding Edmond, her husband, from the inner circle of her impressions.

But she went to the door, and the next moment a figure stepped inside, of which she knew the outline, but little besides. Her husband was attired in a flapping black cloak and slouched hat, appearing altogether as a foreigner, and not as the young English burgess who had left her side. When he came forward into the light of the lamp, she perceived with surprise, and almost with fright, that he wore a mask. At first she had not noticed this – there being nothing in its colour which would lead a casual observer to think he was looking on anything but a real countenance.

He must have seen her start of dismay at the unexpectedness of his appearance, for he said hastily: 'I did not mean to come in to you like this – I thought you would have been in bed. How good you are, dear Barbara!' He put his arm round her, but he did not attempt to kiss her.

'O Edmond – it *is* you? – it must be?' she said, with clasped hands, for though his figure and movement were almost enough to prove it, and the tones were not unlike the old tones, the enunciation was so altered as to seem that of a stranger.

'I am covered like this to hide myself from the curious eyes of the inn-servants and others,' he said, in a low voice. 'I will send back the carriage and join you in a moment.'

'You are quite alone?'

'Quite. My companion stopped at Southampton.'

The wheels of the post-chaise rolled away as she entered the dining-room, where the supper was spread; and presently he rejoined her there. He had removed his cloak and hat, but the mask was still retained; and she could now see that it was of special make, of some flexible material like silk, coloured so as to represent flesh; it joined naturally to the front hair, and was otherwise cleverly executed.

'Barbara – you look ill,' he said, removing his glove, and taking her hand.

'Yes – I have been ill,' said she.

'Is this pretty little house ours?'

'O – yes.' She was hardly conscious of her words, for the hand he had ungloved in order to take hers was contorted, and had one or two of its fingers missing; while through the mask she discerned the twinkle of one eye only.

'I would give anything to kiss you, dearest, now at this moment!' he continued, with mournful passionateness. 'But I cannot – in this guise. The servants are abed, I suppose?'

'Yes,' said she. 'But I can call them? You will have some supper?'

He said he would have some, but that it was not necessary to call anybody at that hour. Thereupon they approached the table, and sat down, facing each other.

Despite Barbara's scared state of mind, it was forced upon her notice that her husband trembled, as if he feared the impression he was producing, or was about to produce, as much as, or more than, she. He drew nearer, and took her hand again.

'I had this mask made at Venice,' he began, in evident embarrassment. 'My darling Barbara – my dearest wife – do you think you – will mind when I take it off? You will not dislike me – will you?'

'O Edmond, of course I shall not mind,' said she. 'What has happened to you is our misfortune; but I am prepared for it.'

'Are you sure you are prepared?'

'O yes! You are my husband.'

'You really feel quite confident that nothing external can

affect you?' he said again, in a voice rendered uncertain by his agitation.

'I think I am – quite,' she answered faintly.

He bent his head. 'I hope, I hope you are,' he whispered. In the pause which followed, the ticking of the clock in the hall seemed to grow loud; and he turned a little aside to remove the mask. She breathlessly awaited the operation, which was one of some tediousness, watching him one moment, averting her face the next; and when it was done she shut her eyes at the dreadful spectacle that was revealed. A quick spasm of horror had passed through her; but though she quailed she forced herself to regard him anew, repressing the cry that would naturally have escaped from her ashy lips. Unable to look at him longer, Barbara sank down on the floor beside her chair, covering her eyes.

'You cannot look at me!' he groaned in a hopeless way. 'I am too terrible an object even for you to bear! I knew it; yet I hoped against it. Oh, this is a bitter fate – curse the skill of those Venetian surgeons who saved me alive! ... Look up, Barbara,' he continued beseechingly; 'view me completely; say you loathe me, if you do loathe me, and settle the case between us for ever!'

His unhappy wife pulled herself together for a desperate strain. He was her Edmond; he had done her no wrong; he had suffered. A momentary devotion to him helped her, and lifting her eyes as bidden she regarded this human remnant, this *écorché*, a second time. But the sight was too much. She again involuntarily looked aside and shuddered.

'Do you think you can get used to this?' he said. 'Yes or no! Can you bear such a thing of the charnel-house near you? Judge for yourself, Barbara. Your Adonis, your matchless man, has come to this!'

The poor lady stood beside him motionless, save for the restlessness of her eyes. All her natural sentiments of affection and pity were driven clean out of her by a sort of panic; she had just the same sense of dismay and fearfulness that she would have had in the presence of an apparition. She could nohow fancy this to be her chosen one – the man she had loved; he was metamorphosed to a specimen of another species. 'I do not loathe you,' she said with trembling. 'But I am so horrified – so overcome! Let me recover myself. Will you sup now? And while you do so may I go to my room to – regain my old feeling for you? I will try, if I may leave you awhile? Yes, I will try!'

Without waiting for an answer from him, and keeping her gaze carefully averted, the frightened woman crept to the door and out of the room. She heard him sit down to the table, as if to begin supper; though, Heaven knows, his appetite was slight enough after a reception which had confirmed his worst surmises. When Barbara had ascended the stairs and arrived in her chamber she sank down, and buried her face in the coverlet of the bed.

Thus she remained for some time. The bed-chamber was over the dining-room, and presently as she knelt Barbara heard Willowes thrust back his chair, and rise to go into the hall. In five minutes that figure would probably come up the stairs and confront her again; it – this new and terrible form, that was not her husband's. In the loneliness of this night, with neither maid nor friend beside her, she lost all self-control, and at the first sound of his footsteps on the stairs, without so much as flinging a cloak round her, she flew from the room, ran along the gallery to the back staircase, which she descended, and, unlocking the back door, let herself out. She scarcely was aware what she had done till she found herself in the greenhouse, crouching on a flower-stand.

Here she remained, her great timid eyes strained through the glass upon the garden without, and her skirts gathered up, in fear of the field-mice which sometimes came there. Every moment she dreaded to hear footsteps which she ought by law to have longed for, and a voice that should have been as music to her soul. But Edmond Willowes came not that way. The nights were getting short at this season, and soon the dawn appeared, and the first rays of the sun. By daylight she had less fear than in the dark. She thought she could meet him, and accustom herself to the spectacle.

So the much-tried young woman unfastened the door of

the hot-house, and went back by the way she had emerged a few hours ago. Her poor husband was probably in bed and asleep, his journey having been long; and she made as little noise as possible in her entry. The house was just as she had left it, and she looked about in the hall for his cloak and hat, but she could not see them; nor did she perceive the small trunk which had been all that he brought with him, his heavier baggage having been left at Southampton for the road-wagon. She summoned courage to mount the stairs; the bedroom-door was open as she had left it. She fearfully peeped round; the bed had not been pressed. Perhaps he had lain down on the dining-room sofa. She descended and entered; he was not there. On the table beside his unsoiled plate lay a note, hastily written on the leaf of a pocket-book. It was something like this:

MY EVER-BELOVED WIFE – The effect that my forbidding appearance has produced upon you was one which I foresaw as quite possible. I hoped against it, but foolishly so. I was aware that no *human* love could survive such a catastrophe. I confess I thought yours *divine*; but, after so long an absence, there could not be left sufficient warmth to overcome the too natural first aversion. It was an experiment, and it has failed. I do not blame you; perhaps, even, it is better so. Goodbye. I leave England for one year. You will see me again at the expiration of that time, if I live. Then I will ascertain your true feeling; and, if it be against me, go away for ever.   E.W.

On recovering from her surprise, Barbara's remorse was such that she felt herself absolutely unforgiveable. She should have regarded him as an afflicted being, and not have been this slave to mere eyesight, like a child. To follow him and entreat him to return was her first thought. But on making inquiries she found that nobody had seen him: he had silently disappeared.

More than this, to undo the scene of last night was impossible. Her terror had been too plain, and he was a man unlikely to be coaxed back by her efforts to do her duty. She went and confessed to her parents all that had occurred; which, indeed, soon became known to more persons than those of her own family.

The year passed, and he did not return; and it was doubted if he were alive. Barbara's contrition for her unconquerable repugnance was now such that she longed to build a church-aisle, or erect a monument, and devote herself to deeds of charity for the remainder of her days. To that end she made inquiry of the excellent parson under whom she sat on Sundays, at a vertical distance of a dozen feet. But he could only adjust his wig and tap his snuff-box; for such was the lukewarm state of religion in those days, that not an aisle, steeple, porch, east window, Ten-Commandment board, lion-and-unicorn, or brass candlestick, was required anywhere at all in the neighbourhood as a votive offering from a distracted soul – the last century contrasting greatly in this respect with the happy times in which we live, when urgent appeals for contributions to such objects pour in by every morning's post, and nearly all churches have been made to look like new pennies. As the poor lady could not ease her conscience this way, she determined at least to be charitable, and soon had the satisfaction of finding her porch thronged every morning by the raggedest, idlest, most drunken, hypocritical, and worthless tramps in Christendom.

But human hearts are as prone to change as the leaves of the creeper on the wall, and in the course of time, hearing nothing of her husband, Barbara could sit unmoved whilst her mother and friends said in her hearing, 'Well, what has happened is for the best.' She began to think so herself, for even now she could not summon up that lopped and mutilated form without a shiver, though whenever her mind flew back to her early wedded days, and the man who had stood beside her then, a thrill of tenderness moved her, which if quickened by his living presence might have become strong. She was young and inexperienced, and had hardly on his late return grown out of the capricious fancies of girlhood.

But he did not come again, and when she thought of his word that he would return once more, if living, and how unlikely he was to break his word, she gave him up for dead. So did her parents; so also did another person – that man of silence, of irresistible incisiveness, of still countenance, who was as awake as seven sentinels when he seemed to be as sound asleep as the figures on his family monument. Lord Uplandtowers, though not yet thirty, had chuckled like a caustic fogey of threescore when he heard of Barbara's terror and flight at her husband's return, and of the latter's prompt departure. He felt pretty sure, however, that Willowes, despite his hurt feelings, would have reappeared to claim his bright-eyed property if he had been alive at the end of the twelve months.

As there was no husband to live with her, Barbara had relinquished the house prepared for them by her father, and taken up her abode anew at Chene Manor, as in the days of her girlhood. By degrees the episode with Edmond Willowes seemed but a fevered dream, and as the months grew to years Lord Uplandtowers's friendship with the people at Chene – which had somewhat cooled after Barbara's elopement – revived considerably, and he again became a frequent visitor there. He could not make the most trivial alteration or improvement at Knollingwood Hall, where he lived, without riding off to consult with his friend Sir John at Chene; and thus putting himself frequently under her eyes, Barbara grew accustomed to him, and talked to him as freely as to a brother. She even began to look up to him as a person of authority, judgement, and prudence; and though his severity on the bench towards poachers, smugglers, and turnip-stealers was matter of common notoriety, she trusted that much of what was said might be misrepresentation.

Thus they lived on till her husband's absence had stretched to years, and there could be no longer any doubt of his death. A passionless manner of renewing his addresses seemed no longer out of place in Lord Uplandtowers. Barbara did not love him, but hers was essentially one of those sweet-pea or with-wind natures which require a twig of stouter fibre than its own to hang upon and bloom. Now, too, she was older, and admitted to herself that a man whose ancestor had run scores of Saracens through and through in fighting for the site of the Holy Sepulchre was a more desirable husband, socially considered, than one who could only claim with certainty to know that his father and grandfather were respectable burgesses.

Sir John took occasion to inform her that she might legally consider herself a widow; and, in brief, Lord Uplandtowers carried his point with her, and she married him, though he could never get her to own that she loved him as she had loved Willowes. In my childhood I knew an old lady whose mother saw the wedding, and she said that when Lord and Lady Uplandtowers drove away from her father's house in the evening it was in a coach-and-four, and that my lady was dressed in green and silver, and wore the gayest hat and feather that ever were seen; though whether is was that the green did not suit her complexion, or otherwise, the Countess looked pale, and the reverse of blooming. After their marriage her husband took her to London, and she saw the gaieties of a season there; then they returned to Knollingwood Hall, and thus a year passed away.

Before their marriage her husband had seemed to care but little about her inability to love him passionately. 'Only let me win you,' he had said, 'and I will submit to all that.' But now her lack of warmth seemed to irritate him, and he conducted himself towards her with a resentfulness which led to her passing many hours with him in painful silence. The heir-presumptive to the title was a remote relative, whom Lord Uplandtowers did not exclude from the dislike he entertained towards many persons and things besides, and he had set his mind upon a lineal successor. He blamed her much that there was no promise of this, and asked her what she was good for.

On a particular day in her gloomy life a letter, addressed to her as Mrs Willowes, reached Lady Uplandtowers from an unexpected quarter. A sculptor in Pisa, knowing nothing of her second marriage, informed her that the long-delayed life-size statue of Mr Willowes, which, when her husband left that city, he had been directed to retain till it was sent for, was still in his studio. As his commission had not wholly been paid, and the statue was taking up room he could ill spare, he should be glad to have the debt cleared off, and directions where to forward the figure. Arriving at a time when the Countess was beginning to have little secrets (of a harmless kind, it is true) from her husband, by reason of their growing estrangement, she replied to this letter without saying a word to Lord Uplandtowers, sending off the balance that was owing to the sculptor, and telling him to dispatch the statue to her without delay.

It was some weeks before it arrived at Knollingwood Hall, and, by a singular coincidence, during the interval she received the first absolutely conclusive tidings of her Edmond's death. It had taken place years before, in a foreign land, about six months after their parting, and had been induced by the sufferings he had already undergone, coupled with much depression of spirit, which had caused him to succumb to a slight ailment. The news was sent her in a brief and formal letter from some relative of Willowes's in another part of England.

Her grief took the form of passionate pity for his misfortunes, and of reproach to herself for never having been able to conquer her aversion to his latter image by recollection of what Nature had originally made him. The sad spectacle that had gone from earth had never been her Edmond at all to her. O that she could have met him as he was at first! Thus Barbara thought. It was only a few days later that a wagon with two horses, containing an immense packing-case, was seen at breakfast-time both by Barbara and her husband to drive round to the back of the house, and by-and-by they were informed that a case labelled 'Sculpture' had arrived for her ladyship.

'What can that be?' said Lord Uplandtowers.

'It is the statue of poor Edmond, which belongs to me, but has never been sent till now,' she answered.

'Where are you going to put it?' asked he.

'I have not decided,' said the Countess. 'Anywhere, so that it will not annoy you.'

'Oh, it won't annoy me,' says he.

When it had been unpacked in a back room of the house, they went to examine it. The statue was a full-length figure, in the purest Carrara marble, representing Edmond Willowes in all his original beauty, as he had stood at parting from her when about to set out on his travels; a specimen of manhood almost perfect in every line and contour. The work had been carried out with absolute fidelity.

'Phœbus-Apollo, sure,' said the Earl of Uplandtowers, who had never seen Willowes, real or represented, till now.

Barbara did not hear him. She was standing in a sort of trance before the first husband, as if she had no consciousness of the other husband at her side. The mutilated features of Willowes had disappeared from her mind's eye; this perfect being was really the man she had loved, and not that later pitiable figure; in whom tenderness and truth should have seen this image always, but had not done so.

It was not till Lord Uplandtowers said roughly, 'Are you going to stay here all the morning worshipping him?' that she roused herself.

Her husband had not till now the least suspicion that Edmond Willowes originally looked thus, and he thought how deep would have been his jealousy years ago if Willowes had been known to him. Returning to the Hall in the afternoon he found his wife in the gallery, whither the statue had been brought.

She was lost in reverie before it, just as in the morning.

'What are you doing?' he asked.

She started and turned. 'I am looking at my husb— my statue, to see if it is well done,' she stammered. 'Why should I not?'

'There's no reason why,' he said. 'What are you going to do with the monstrous thing? It can't stand here for ever.'

'I don't wish it,' she said. 'I'll find a place.'

In her boudoir there was a deep recess, and while the

Earl was absent from home for a few days in the following week, she hired joiners from the village, who under her directions enclosed the recess with a panelled door. Into the tabernacle thus formed she had the statue placed, fastening the door with a lock, the key of which she kept in her pocket.

When her husband returned he missed the statue from the gallery, and, concluding that it had been put away out of deference to his feelings, made no remark. Yet at moments he noticed something on his lady's face which he had never noticed there before. He could not construe it; it was a sort of silent ecstasy, a reserved beatification. What had become of the statue he could not divine, and growing more and more curious, looked about here and there for it till, thinking of her private room, he went towards that spot. After knocking he heard the shutting of a door, and the click of a key; but when he entered his wife was sitting at work, on what was in those days called knotting. Lord Uplandtowers's eye fell on the newly painted door where the recess had formerly been.

'You have been carpentering in my absence then, Bar-bara,' he said carelessly.

'Yes, Uplandtowers.'

'Why did you go putting up such a tasteless enclosure as that – spoiling the handsome arch of the alcove?'

'I wanted more closet-room; and I thought that as this was my own apartment—'

'Of course,' he returned. Lord Uplandtowers knew now where the statue of young Willowes was.

One night, or rather in the smallest hours of the morning, he missed the Countess from his side. Not being a man of nervous imaginings he fell asleep again before he had much considered the matter, and the next morning had forgotten the incident. But a few nights later the same circumstances occurred. This time he fully roused himself; but before he had moved to search for her she returned to the chamber in her dressing-gown, carrying a candle, which she extinguished as she approached, deeming him asleep. He could discover from her breathing that she was strangely moved; but not on this occasion either did he reveal that he had seen her. Presently, when she had lain down, affecting to wake, he asked her some trivial questions. 'Yes, *Edmond*,' she replied absently.

Lord Uplandtowers became convinced that she was in the habit of leaving the chamber in this queer way more frequently than he had observed, and he determined to watch. The next midnight he feigned deep sleep, and shortly after perceived her stealthily rise and let herself out of the room in the dark. He slipped on some clothing and followed. At the further end of the corridor, where the clash of flint and steel would be out of the hearing of one in the bed-chamber, she struck a light. He stepped aside into an empty room till she had lit a taper and had passed on to her boudoir. In a minute or two he followed. Arrived at the door of the boudoir, he beheld the door of the private recess open, and Barbara within it, standing with her arms clasped tightly round the neck of her Edmond, and her mouth on his. The shawl which she had thrown round her nightclothes had slipped from her shoulders, and her long white robe and pale face lent her the blanched appearance of a second statue embracing the first. Between her kisses, she apostrophized it in a low murmur of infantine tenderness :

'My only love – how could I be so cruel to you, my perfect one – so good and true – I am ever faithful to you, despite my seeming infidelity! I always think of you – dream of you – during the long hours of the day, and in the night-watches! O Edmond, I am always yours!' Such words as these, intermingled with sobs, and streaming tears, and dishevelled hair, testified to an intensity of feeling in his wife which Lord Uplandtowers had not dreamed of her possessing.

'Ha, ha!' says he to himself. 'This is where we evaporate – this is where my hopes of a successor in the title dissolve – ha! ha! This must be seen to, verily!'

Lord Uplandtowers was a subtle man when once he set himself to strategy; though in the present instance he never thought of the simple stratagem of constant tenderness. Nor did he enter the room and surprise his wife as a blunderer would have done, but went back to his chamber as silently as he had left it. When the Countess returned thither, shaken by spent sobs and sighs, he appeared to be soundly sleeping as usual. The next day he began his countermoves by making inquiries as to the whereabouts of the tutor who had travelled with his wife's first husband; this gentleman, he found, was now master of a grammar-school at no great distance from Knollingwood. At the first convenient moment Lord Uplandtowers went thither and obtained an interview with the said gentleman. The schoolmaster was much gratified by a visit from such an influential neighbour, and was ready to communicate anything that his lordship desired to know.

After some general conversation on the school and its progress, the visitor observed that he believed the schoolmaster had once travelled a good deal with the unfortunate Mr Willowes, and had been with him on the occasion of his accident. He, Lord Uplandtowers, was interested in knowing what had really happened at that time, and had often thought of inquiring. And then the Earl not only heard by word of mouth as much as he wished to know, but, their chat becoming more intimate, the schoolmaster drew upon paper a sketch of the disfigured head, explaining with bated breath various details in the representation.

'It was very strange and terrible!' said Lord Uplandtowers, taking the sketch in his hand. 'Neither nose nor ears, nor lips scarcely!'

A poor man in the town nearest to Knollingwood Hall, who combined the art of sign-painting with ingenious mechanical occupations, was sent for by Lord Uplandtowers to come to the Hall on a day in that week when the Countess had gone on a short visit to her parents. His employer made the man understand that the business in which his assistance was demanded was to be considered private, and money insured the observance of this request. The lock of the cupboard was picked, and the ingenious mechanic and painter, assisted by the schoolmaster's sketch, which

Lord Uplandtowers had put in his pocket, set to work upon the god-like countenance of the statue under my lord's direction. What the fire had maimed in the original the chisel maimed in the copy. It was a fiendish disfigurement, ruthlessly carried out, and was rendered still more shocking by being tinted to the hues of life, as life had been after the wreck.

Six hours after, when the workman was gone, Lord Uplandtowers looked upon the result, and smiled grimly, and said:

'A statue should represent a man as he appeared in life, and that's as he appeared. Ha! ha! But 'tis done to good purpose, and not idly.'

He locked the door of the closet with a skeleton key, and went his way to fetch the Countess home.

That night she slept, but he kept awake. According to the tale, she murmured soft words in her dream; and he knew that the tender converse of her imaginings was held with one whom he had supplanted but in name. At the end of her dream the Countess of Uplandtowers awoke and arose, and then the enactment of former nights was repeated. Her husband remained still and listened. Two strokes sounded from the clock in the pediment without, when, leaving the chamber-door ajar, she passed along the corridor to the other end, where, as usual, she obtained a light. So deep was the silence that he could even from his bed hear her softly blowing the tinder to a glow after striking the steel. She moved on into the boudoir, and he heard, or fancied he heard, the turning of the key in the closet-door. The next moment there came from that direction a loud and prolonged shriek, which resounded to the furthest corners of the house. It was repeated, and there was the noise of a heavy fall.

Lord Uplandtowers sprang out of bed. He hastened along the dark corridor to the door of the boudoir, which stood ajar, and, by the light of the candle within, saw his poor young Countess lying in a heap in her nightdress on the floor of the closet. When he reached her side he found that she had fainted, much to the relief of his fears that matters were worse. He quickly shut up and locked in the hated image which had done the mischief, and lifted his wife in his arms, where in a few instants she opened her eyes. Pressing her face to his without saying a word, he carried her back to her room, endeavouring as he went to disperse her terrors by a laugh in her ear, oddly compounded of causticity, predilection, and brutality.

'Ho – ho – ho!' says he. 'Frightened, dear one, hey? What a baby 'tis! Only a joke, sure, Barbara – a splendid joke! But a baby should not go to closets at midnight to look for the ghost of the dear departed! If it do it must expect to be terrified at his aspect – ho – ho – ho!'

When she was in her bed-chamber, and had quite come to herself, though her nerves were still much shaken, he spoke to her more sternly. 'Now, my lady, answer me: do you love him – eh?'

'No – no!' she faltered, shuddering, with her expanded eyes fixed on her husband. 'He is too terrible – no, no!'

'You are sure?'

'Quite sure!' replied the poor broken-spirited Countess.

But her natural elasticity asserted itself. Next morning he again inquired of her: 'Do you love him now?' She quailed under his gaze, but did not reply.

'That means that you do still, by God!' he continued.

'It means that I will not tell an untruth, and do not wish to incense my lord,' she answered, with dignity.

'Then suppose we go and have another look at him?' As he spoke, he suddenly took her by the wrist, and turned as if to lead her towards the ghastly closet.

'No – no! O – no!' she cried, and her desperate wriggle out of his hand revealed that the fright of the night had left more impression upon her delicate soul than superficially appeared.

'Another dose or two, and she will be cured,' he said to himself.

It was now so generally known that the Earl and Countess were not in accord, that he took no great trouble to disguise his deeds in relation to this matter. During the day he ordered four men with ropes and rollers to attend him in the boudoir. When they arrived, the closet was open, and the upper part of the statue tied up in canvas. He had it taken to the sleeping-chamber. What followed is more or less matter of conjecture. The story, as told to me, goes on to say that, when Lady Uplandtowers retired with him that night, she saw facing the foot of the heavy oak four-poster, a tall dark wardrobe, which had not stood there before; but she did not ask what its presence meant.

'I have had a little whim,' he explained when they were in the dark.

'Have you?' says she.

'To erect a little shrine, as it may be called.'

'A little shrine?'

'Yes; to one whom we both equally adore – eh? I'll show you what it contains.'

He pulled a cord which hung covered by the bed-curtains, and the doors of the wardrobe slowly opened, disclosing that the shelves within had been removed throughout, and the interior adapted to receive the ghastly figure, which stood there as it had stood in the boudoir, but with a wax candle burning on each side of it to throw the cropped and distorted features into relief. She clutched him, uttered a low scream, and buried her head in the bedclothes. 'O, take it away – please take it away!' she implored.

'All in good time; namely, when you love me best,' he returned calmly. 'You don't quite yet – eh?'

'I don't know – I think – O Uplandtowers, have mercy – I cannot bear it – O, in pity, take it away!'

'Nonsense; one gets accustomed to anything. Take another gaze.'

In short, he allowed the doors to remain unclosed at the foot of the bed, and the wax-tapers burning; and such was the strange fascination of the grisly exhibition that a morbid curiosity took possession of the Countess as she lay, and, at his repeated request, she did again look out from the coverlet, shuddered, hid her eyes, and looked again, all the while begging him to take it away, or it would drive her out of her senses. But he would not do so yet, and the wardrobe was not locked till dawn.

The scene was repeated the next night. Firm in enforcing his ferocious correctives, he continued the treatment till the nerves of the poor lady were quivering in agony under the virtuous tortures inflicted by her lord, to bring her truant heart back to faithfulness.

The third night, when the scene had opened as usual, and she lay staring with immense wild eyes at the horrid fascination, on a sudden she gave an unnatural laugh; she laughed more and more, staring at the image, till she literally shrieked with laughter: then there was silence, and he found her to have become insensible. He thought she had fainted, but soon saw that the event was worse: she was in an epileptic fit. He started up, dismayed by the sense that, like many other subtle personages, he had been too exacting for his own interests. Such love as he was capable of, though rather a selfish gloating than a cherishing solicitude, was fanned into life on the instant. He closed the wardrobe with the pulley, clasped her in his arms, took her gently to the window, and did all he could to restore her.

It was a long time before the Countess came to herself, and when she did so, a considerable change seemed to have taken place in her emotions. She flung her arms around him, and with gasps of fear abjectly kissed him many times, at last bursting into tears. She had never wept in this scene before.

'You'll take it away, dearest – you will!' she begged plaintively.

'If you love me.'

'I do – oh, I do!'

'And hate him, and his memory?'

'Yes – yes!'

'Thoroughly?'

'I cannot endure recollection of him!' cried the poor Countess slavishly. 'It fills me with shame – how could I ever be so depraved! I'll never behave badly again, Uplandtowers; and you will never put the hated statue again before my eyes?'

He felt that he could promise with perfect safety. 'Never,' said he.

'And then I'll love you,' she returned eagerly, as if dreading lest the scourge should be applied anew. 'And I'll never, never dream of thinking a single thought that seems like faithlessness to my marriage vow.'

The strange thing now was that this fictitious love wrung from her by terror took on, through mere habit of enactment, a certain quality of reality. A servile mood of attachment to the Earl became distinctly visible in her contemporaneously with an actual dislike for her late husband's memory. The mood of attachment grew and continued when the statue was removed. A permanent revulsion was operant in her, which intensified as time wore on. How fright could have effected such a change of idiosyncrasy learned physicians alone can say; but I believe such cases of reactionary instinct are not unknown.

The upshot was that the cure became so permanent as to be itself a new disease. She clung to him so tightly that she would not willingly be out of his sight for a moment. She would have no sitting-room apart from his, though she could not help starting when he entered suddenly to her. Her eyes were well-nigh always fixed upon him. If he drove out, she wished to go with him; his slightest civilities to other women made her frantically jealous; till at length her very fidelity became a burden to him, absorbing his time, and curtailing his liberty, and causing him to curse and swear. If he ever spoke sharply to her now, she did not revenge herself by flying off to a mental world of her own; all that affection for another, which had provided her with a resource, was now a cold black cinder.

From that time the life of this scared and enervated lady – whose existence might have been developed to so much higher purpose but for the ignoble ambition of her parents and the conventions of the time – was one of obsequious amativeness towards a perverse and cruel man. Little personal events came to her in quick succession – half a dozen, eight, nine, ten such events – in brief, she bore him no less than eleven children in the nine following years, but half of them came prematurely into the world, or died a few days old; only one, a girl, attained to maturity; she in after years became the wife of the Honourable Mr Beltonleigh, who was created Lord d'Almaine, as may be remembered.

There was no living son and heir. At length, completely worn out in mind and body, Lady Uplandtowers was taken abroad by her husband, to try the effect of a more genial climate upon her wasted frame. But nothing availed to strengthen her, and she died at Florence, a few months after her arrival in Italy.

Contrary to expectation, the Earl of Uplandtowers did not marry again. Such affection as existed in him – strange, hard, brutal as it was – seemed untransferable, and the title, as is known, passed at his death to his nephew. Perhaps it may not be so generally known that, during the enlargement of the Hall for the sixth Earl, while digging in the grounds for the new foundations, the broken fragments of a marble statue were unearthed. They were submitted to various antiquaries, who said that, so far as the damaged pieces would allow them to form an opinion, the statue seemed to be that of a mutilated Roman satyr; or, if not, an allegorical figure of Death. Only one or two old inhabitants guessed whose statue those fragments had composed.

I should have added that, shortly after the death of the Countess, an excellent sermon was preached by the Dean of Melchester, the subject of which, though names were not mentioned, was unquestionably suggested by the aforesaid events. He dwelt upon the folly of indulgence in sensuous love for a handsome form merely; and showed that the only rational and virtuous growths of that affection were those based upon intrinsic worth. In the case of the tender but somewhat shallow lady whose life I have related, there is no doubt that an infatuation for the person of young Willowes was the chief feeling that induced her to marry him; which was the more deplorable in that his beauty, by all tradition, was the least of his recommendations, every report bearing out the inference that he must have been a man of steadfast nature, bright intelligence, and promising life.

The company thanked the old surgeon for his story, which the rural dean declared to be a far more striking one than anything he could hope to tell. An elderly member of the Club, who was mostly called the Bookworm, said that a woman's natural instinct of fidelity would, indeed, send back her heart to a man after his death in a truly wonderful manner sometimes – if anything occurred to put before her forcibly the original affection between them, and his original aspect in her eyes – whatever his inferiority may have been, social or otherwise; and then a general conversation ensued upon the power that a woman has of seeing the actual in the representation, the reality in the dream – a power which (according to the sentimental member) men have no faculty of equalling.

The rural dean thought that such cases as that related by the surgeon were rather an illustration of passion electrified back to life than of a latent, true affection. The story had suggested that he should try to recount to them one which he had used to hear in his youth, and which afforded an instance of the latter and better kind of feeling, his heroine being also a lady who had married beneath her, though he feared his narrative would be of a much slighter kind than the surgeon's. The Club begged him to proceed, and the parson began.

The Melancholy Hussar of the
German Legion

———◆———

I

HERE stretch the downs, high and breezy and green, absolutely unchanged since those eventful days. A plough has never disturbed the turf, and the sod that was uppermost then is uppermost now. Here stood the camp; here are distinct traces of the banks thrown up for the horses of the cavalry, and spots where the midden-heaps lay are still to be observed. At night, when I walk across the lonely place, it is impossible to avoid hearing, amid the scourings of the wind over the grass-bents and thistles, the old trumpet and bugle calls, the rattle of the halters; to help seeing rows of spectral tents and the *impedimenta* of the soldiery. From within the canvases come guttural syllables of foreign tongues, and broken songs of the fatherland; for they were mainly regiments of the King's German Legion that slept round the tent-poles hereabout at that time.

It was nearly ninety years ago. The British uniform of that period, with its immense epaulettes, queer cocked-hat, breeches, gaiters, ponderous cartridge-box, buckled shoes, and what not, would look strange and barbarous now. Ideas have changed; invention has followed invention. Soldiers were monumental objects then. A divinity still hedged kings here and there; and war was considered a glorious thing.

Secluded old manor-houses and hamlets lie in the ravines and hollows among these hills, where a stranger had hardly ever been seen till the King chose to take the baths yearly at the sea-side watering-place a few miles to the south; as a consequence of which battalions descended in a cloud upon the open country around. Is it necessary to add that the echoes of many characteristic tales, dating from that picturesque time, still linger about here in more or less fragmentary form, to be caught by the attentive ear? Some of them I have repeated; most of them I have forgotten; one I have never repeated, and assuredly can never forget.

Phyllis told me the story with her own lips. She was then an old lady of seventy-five, and her auditor a lad of fifteen. She enjoined silence as to her share in the incident, till she should be 'dead, buried, and forgotten'. Her life was prolonged twelve years after the day of her narration, and she has now been dead nearly twenty. The oblivion which in her modesty and humility she courted for herself has only partially fallen on her, with the unfortunate result of inflicting an injustice upon her memory; since such fragments of her story as got abroad at the time, and have been kept alive ever since, are precisely those which are most unfavourable to her character.

It all began with the arrival of the York Hussars, one of the foreign regiments above alluded to. Before that day scarcely a soul had been seen near her father's house for weeks. When a noise like the brushing skirt of a visitor was heard on the doorstep, it proved to be a scudding leaf; when a carriage seemed to be nearing the door, it was her father grinding his sickle on the stone in the garden for his favourite relaxation of trimming the box-tree borders to the plots. A sound like luggage thrown down from the coach was a gun far away at sea; and what looked like a tall man by the gate at dusk was a yew bush cut into a quaint and attenuated shape. There is no such solitude in country places now as there was in those old days.

Yet all the while King George and his court were at his favourite sea-side resort, not more than five miles off.

The daughter's seclusion was great, but beyond the seclusion of the girl lay the seclusion of the father. If her social condition was twilight, his was darkness. Yet he enjoyed his darkness, while her twilight oppressed her. Dr Grove had been a professional man whose taste for lonely meditation over metaphysical questions had diminished his practice till it no longer paid him to keep it going; after which he had relinquished it and hired at a nominal rent the small, dilapidated, half farm – half manor-house of this obscure inland nook, to make a sufficiency of an income which in a town would have been inadequate for their maintenance. He stayed in his garden the greater part of the day, growing more and more irritable with the lapse of time, and the increasing perception that he had wasted his life in the pursuit of illusions. He saw his friends less and less frequently. Phyllis became so shy that if she met a stranger anywhere in her short rambles she felt ashamed at his gaze, walked awkwardly, and blushed to her shoulders.

Yet Phyllis was discovered even here by an admirer, and her hand most unexpectedly asked in marriage.

The King, as aforesaid, was at the neighbouring town, where he had taken up his abode at Gloucester Lodge; and his presence in the town naturally brought many county people thither. Among these idlers – many of whom professed to have connections and interests with the Court – was one Humphrey Gould, a bachelor, a personage neither young nor old, neither good-looking nor positively plain. Too steady-going to be 'a buck' (as fast and unmarried men were then called), he was an approximately fashionable man of a mild type. This bachelor of thirty found his way to the village on the down; beheld Phyllis; made her father's acquaintance in order to make hers; and by some means or other she sufficiently inflamed his heart to lead him in that direction almost daily; till he became engaged to marry her.

As he was of an old local family, some of whose members were held in respect in the county, Phyllis, in bringing him to her feet, had accomplished what was considered a brilliant move for one in her constrained position. How she had done it was not quite known to Phyllis herself. In those days unequal marriages were regarded rather as a violation of the laws of nature than as a mere infringement of convention, the more modern view, and hence when Phyllis, of the watering-place *bourgeoisie*, was chosen by such a gentlemanly fellow, it was as if she were going to be taken to heaven, though perhaps the uninformed would have seen no great difference in the respective positions of the pair, the said Gould being as poor as a crow.

This pecuniary condition was his excuse – probably a true one – for postponing their union, and as the winter drew nearer, and the King departed for the season, Mr Humphrey Gould set out for Bath, promising to return to Phyllis in a few weeks. The winter arrived, the date of his promise passed, yet Gould postponed his coming, on the ground that he could not very easily leave his father in the city of their sojourn, the elder having no other relative near him. Phyllis, though lonely in the extreme, was content. The man who had asked her in marriage was a desirable husband for her in many ways; her father highly approved of his suit; but this neglect of her was awkward, if not painful, for Phyllis. Love him in the true sense of the word she assured me she never did, but she had a genuine regard for him; admired a certain methodical and dogged way in which he sometimes took his pleasure; valued his knowledge of what the Court was doing, had done, or was about to do; and she was not without a feeling of pride that he had chosen her when he might have exercised a more ambitious choice.

But he did not come; and the spring developed. His letters were regular though formal; and it is not to be wondered that the uncertainty of her position, linked with the fact that there was not much passion in her thoughts of Humphrey, bred an indescribable dreariness in the heart of Phyllis Grove. The spring was soon summer, and the summer brought the King; but still no Humphrey Gould. All this while the engagement by letter was maintained intact.

At this point of time a golden radiance flashed in upon the lives of people here, and charged all youthful thought with emotional interest. This radiance was the aforesaid York Hussars.

II

The present generation has probably but a very dim notion of the celebrated York Hussars of ninety years ago. They were one of the regiments of the King's German Legion, and (though they somewhat degenerated later on) their brilliant uniform, their splendid horses, and, above all, their foreign air and mustachios (rare appendages then), drew crowds of admirers of both sexes wherever they went. These with other regiments had come to encamp on the downs and pastures, because of the presence of the King in the neighbouring town.

The spot was high and airy, and the view extensive, commanding Portland – the Isle of Slingers – in front, and reaching to St Aldhelm's Head eastward, and almost to the Start on the west.

Phyllis, though not precisely a girl of the village, was as interested as any of them in this military investment. Her father's home stood somewhat apart, and on the highest point of ground to which the lane ascended, so that it was almost level with the top of the church tower in the lower part of the parish. Immediately from the outside of the garden-wall the grass spread away to a great distance, and it was crossed by a path which came close to the wall. Ever since her childhood it had been Phyllis's pleasure to clamber up this fence and sit on the top – a feat not so difficult as it may seem, the walls in this district being built of rubble, without mortar, so that there were plenty of crevices for small toes.

She was sitting up here one day, listlessly surveying the

pasture without, when her attention was arrested by a solitary figure walking along the path. It was one of the renowned German Hussars, and he moved onward with his eyes on the ground, and with the manner of one who wished to escape company. His head would probably have been bent like his eyes but for his stiff neck-gear. On nearer view she perceived that his face was marked with deep sadness. Without observing her, he advanced by the footpath till it brought him almost immediately under the wall.

Phyllis was much surprised to see a fine, tall soldier in such a mood as this. Her theory of the military, and of the York Hussars in particular (derived entirely from hearsay, for she had never talked to a soldier in her life), was that their hearts were as gay as their accoutrements.

At this moment the Hussar lifted his eyes and noticed her on her perch, the white muslin neckerchief which covered her shoulders and neck where left bare by her low gown, and her white raiment in general, showing conspicuously in the bright sunlight of this summer day. He blushed a little at the suddenness of the encounter, and without halting a moment from his pace passed on.

All that day the foreigner's face haunted Phyllis; its aspect was so striking, so handsome, and his eyes were so blue, and sad, and abstracted. It was perhaps only natural that on some following day at the same hour she should look over that wall again, and wait till he had passed a second time. On this occasion he was reading a letter, and at the sight of her his manner was that of one who had half expected or hoped to discover her. He almost stopped, smiled, and made a courteous salute. The end of the meeting was that they exchanged a few words. She asked him what he was reading, and he readily informed her that he was re-perusing letters from his mother in Germany; he did not get them often, he said, and was forced to read the old ones a great many times. This was all that passed at the present interview, but others of the same kind followed.

Phyllis used to say that his English, though not good, was quite intelligible to her, so that their acquaintance was never hindered by difficulties of speech. Whenever the subject became too delicate, subtle, or tender, for such words of English as were at his command, the eyes no doubt helped out the tongue, and – though this was later on – the lips helped out the eyes. In short this acquaintance, unguardedly made, and rash enough on her part, developed and ripened. Like Desdemona, she pitied him, and learnt his history.

His name was Matthäus Tina, and Saarbrück his native town, where his mother was still living. His age was twenty-two, and he had already risen to the grade of corporal, though he had not long been in the army. Phyllis used to assert that no such refined or well-educated young man could have been found in the ranks of the purely English regiments, some of these foreign soldiers having rather the graceful manner and presence of our native officers than of our rank and file.

She by degrees learnt from her foreign friend a circumstance about himself and his comrades which Phyllis would least have expected of the York Hussars. So far from being as gay as its uniform, the regiment was pervaded by a dreadful melancholy, a chronic home-sickness, which depressed many of the men to such an extent that they could hardly attend to their drill. The worst sufferers were the younger soldiers who had not been over here long. They hated England and English life; they took no interest whatever in King George and his island kingdom, and they only wished to be out of it and never to see it any more. Their bodies were here, but their hearts and minds were always far away in their dear fatherland, of which – brave men and stoical as they were in many ways – they would speak with tears in their eyes. One of the worst of the sufferers from this home-woe, as he called it in his own tongue, was Matthäus Tina, whose dreamy musing nature felt the gloom of exile still more intensely from the fact that he had left a lonely mother at home with nobody to cheer her.

Though Phyllis, touched by all this, and interested in his history, did not disdain her soldier's acquaintance, she declined (according to her own account, at least) to permit the young man to overstep the line of friendship for a long while – as long, indeed, as she considered herself likely to become the possession of another; though it is probable that she had lost her heart to Matthäus before she was herself aware. The stone wall of necessity made anything like intimacy difficult; and he had never ventured to come, or to ask to come, inside the garden, so that all their conversation had been overtly conducted across this boundary.

III

But news reached the village from a friend of Phyllis's father concerning Mr Humphrey Gould, her remarkably cool and patient betrothed. This gentleman had been heard to say in Bath that he considered his overtures to Miss Phyllis Grove to have reached only the stage of a half-understanding; and in view of his enforced absence on his father's account, who was too great an invalid now to attend to his affairs, he thought it best that there should be no definite promise as yet on either side. He was not sure, indeed, that he might not cast his eyes elsewhere.

This account – though only a piece of hearsay, and as such entitled to no absolute credit – tallied so well with the infrequency of his letters and their lack of warmth, that Phyllis did not doubt its truth for one moment; and from that hour she felt herself free to bestow her heart as she should choose. Not so her father; he declared the whole story to be a fabrication. He had known Mr Gould's family from his boyhood; and if there was one proverb which expressed the matrimonial aspect of that family, it was 'Love me little, love me long'. Humphrey was an honourable man, who would not think of treating his engagement so lightly. 'Do you wait in patience,' he said; 'all will be right enough in time.'

From these words Phyllis at first imagined that her father was in correspondence with Mr Gould, and her heart sank within her; for in spite of her original intentions she had been relieved to hear that her engagement had come to nothing. But she presently learnt that her father had heard no more of Humphrey Gould than she herself had done; while he would not write and address her affianced directly on the subject, lest it should be deemed an imputation on that bachelor's honour.

'You want an excuse for encouraging one or other of those foreign fellows to flatter you with his unmeaning attentions,' her father exclaimed, his mood having of late been a very unkind one towards her. 'I see more than I say. Don't you ever set foot outside that garden-fence without my permission. If you want to see the camp I'll take you myself some Sunday afternoon.'

Phyllis had not the smallest intention of disobeying him in her actions, but she assumed herself to be independent with respect to her feelings. She no longer checked her fancy for the Hussar, though she was far from regarding him as her lover in the serious sense in which an Englishman might have been regarded as such. The young foreign soldier was almost an ideal being to her, with none of the appurtenances of an ordinary house-dweller; one who had descended she knew not whence, and would disappear she knew not whither; the subject of a fascinating dream – no more.

They met continually now – mostly at dusk – during the brief interval between the going down of the sun and the minute at which the last trumpet-call summoned him to his tent. Perhaps her manner had become less restrained latterly; at any rate that of the Hussar was so; he had grown more tender every day, and at parting after these hurried interviews she reached down her hand from the top of the wall that he might press it. One evening he held it such a while that she exclaimed, 'The wall is white, and somebody in the field may see your shape against it!'

He lingered so long that night that it was with the greatest difficulty that he could run across the intervening stretch of ground and enter the camp in time. On the next occasion of his awaiting her she did not appear in her usual place at the usual hour. His disappointment was unspeakably keen; he remained staring blankly at the spot, like a man in a trance. The trumpets and tattoo sounded, and still he did not go.

She had been delayed purely by an accident. When she arrived she was anxious because of the lateness of the hour, having heard as well as he the sounds denoting the closing of the camp. She implored him to leave immediately.

'No,' he said gloomily. 'I shall not go in yet – the moment you come – I have thought of your coming all day.'

'But you may be disgraced at being after time?'

'I don't mind that. I should have disappeared from the world some time ago if it had not been for two persons – my beloved, here, and my mother in Saarbrück. I hate the army. I care more for a minute of your company than for all the promotion in the world.'

Thus he stayed and talked to her, and told her interesting details of his native place, and incidents of his childhood, till she was in a simmer of distress at his recklessness in remaining. It was only because she insisted on bidding him good-night and leaving the wall that he returned to his quarters.

The next time that she saw him he was without the stripes that had adorned his sleeve. He had been broken to the level of private for his lateness that night; and as Phyllis considered herself to be the cause of his disgrace her sorrow was great. But the position was now reversed; it was his turn to cheer her.

'Don't grieve, meine Liebliche!' he said. 'I have got a remedy for whatever comes. First, even supposing I regain my stripes, would your father allow you to marry a non-commissioned officer in the York Hussars?'

She flushed. This practical step had not been in her mind in relation to such an unrealistic person as he was; and a moment's reflection was enough for it. 'My father would not – certainly would not,' she answered unflinchingly. 'It cannot be thought of! My dear friend, please do forget me: I fear I am ruining you and your prospects!'

'Not at all!' said he. 'You are giving this country of yours just sufficient interest to me to make me care to keep alive in it. If my dear land were here also, and my old parent, with you, I could be happy as I am, and would do my best as a soldier. But it is not so. And now listen. This is my plan. That you go with me to my own country, and be my wife there, and live there with my mother and me. I am not a Hanoverian, as you know, though I entered the army as such; my country is by the Saar, and is at peace with France, and if I were once in it I should be free.'

'But how get there?' she asked. Phyllis had been rather amazed than shocked at his proposition. Her position in her father's house was growing irksome and painful in the extreme; his parental affection seemed to be quite dried up. She was not a native of the village, like all the joyous girls around her; and in some way Matthäus Tina had affected her with his own passionate longing for his country, and mother, and home.

'But how?' she repeated, finding that he did not answer. 'Will you buy your discharge?'

'Ah, no,' he said. 'That's impossible in these times. No; I came here against my will; why should I not escape? Now is the time, as we shall soon be striking camp, and I might see you no more. This is my scheme. I will ask you to meet me on the highway two miles off, on some calm night next week that may be appointed. There will be nothing unbecoming in it, or to cause you shame; you will not fly alone with me, for I will bring with me my devoted young friend Christoph, an Alsatian, who has lately joined the regiment, and who has agreed to assist in this enterprise. We shall have come from yonder harbour, where we shall have examined the boats, and found one suited to our purpose. Christoph has already a chart of the Channel, and we will then go to the harbour, and at midnight cut the boat from her moorings, and row away round the point out of sight; and by the next morning we are on the coast of France, near Cherbourg. The rest is easy, for I have saved money for the land journey, and can get a change of clothes. I will write to my mother, who will meet us on the way.'

He added details in reply to her inquiries, which left no doubt in Phyllis's mind of the feasibility of the undertaking. But its magnitude almost appalled her; and it is questionable if she would ever have gone further in the wild adventure if, on entering the house that night, her father had not accosted her in the most significant terms.

'How about the York Hussars?' he said.

'They are still at the camp; but they are soon going away, I believe.'

'It is useless for you to attempt to cloak your actions in that way. You have been meeting one of those fellows; you have been seen walking with him – foreign barbarians, not much better than the French themselves! I have made up my mind – don't speak a word till I have done, please! – I have made up my mind that you shall stay here no longer while they are on the spot. You shall go to your aunt's.'

It was useless for her to protest that she had never taken a walk with any soldier or man under the sun except himself. Her protestations were feeble, too, for though he was not literally correct in his assertion, he was virtually only half in error.

The house of her father's sister was a prison to Phyllis. She had quite recently undergone experience of its gloom; and when her father went on to direct her to pack what would be necessary for her to take, her heart died within her. In after years she never attempted to excuse her conduct during this week of agitation; but the result of her self-communing was that she decided to join in the scheme of her lover and his friend, and fly to the country which he had coloured with such lovely hues in her imagination. She always said that the one feature in his proposal which overcame her hesitation was the obvious purity and straightforwardness of his intentions. He showed himself to be so virtuous and kind; he treated her with a respect to which she had never before been accustomed; and she was braced to the obvious risks of the voyage by her confidence in him.

IV

It was on a soft, dark evening of the following week that they engaged in the adventure. Tina was to meet her at a point in the highway at which the lane to the village branched off. Christoph was to go ahead of them to the harbour where the boat lay, row it round the Nothe – or Look-out as it was called in those days – and pick them up on the other side of the promontory, which they were to reach by crossing the harbour-bridge on foot, and climbing over the Look-out hill.

As soon as her father had ascended to his room she left the house, and, bundle in hand, proceeded at a trot along the lane. At such an hour not a soul was afoot anywhere in the village, and she reached the junction of the lane with the highway unobserved. Here she took up her position in the obscurity formed by the angle of a fence, whence she could discern everyone who approached along the turnpike-road, without being herself seen.

She had not remained thus waiting for her lover longer than a minute – though from the tension of her nerves the lapse of even that short time was trying – when, instead of the expected footsteps, the stage-coach could be heard descending the hill. She knew that Tina would not show himself till the road was clear, and waited impatiently for the coach to pass. Nearing the corner where she was it slackened speed, and, instead of going by as usual, drew up within a few yards of her. A passenger alighted, and she heard his voice. It was Humphrey Gould's.

He had brought a friend with him, and luggage. The luggage was deposited on the grass, and the coach went on its route to the royal watering-place.

'I wonder where that young man is with the horse and trap?' said her former admirer to his companion. 'I hope we shan't have to wait here long. I told him half past nine o'clock precisely.'

'Have you got her present safe?'

'Phyllis's? O, yes. It is in this trunk. I hope it will please her.'

'Of course it will. What woman would not be pleased with such a handsome peace-offering?'

'Well – she deserves it. I've treated her rather badly. But she has been in my mind these last two days much more than I should care to confess to everybody. Ah, well; I'll say no more about that. It cannot be that she is so bad as they make out. I am quite sure that a girl of her good wit would know better than to get entangled with any of those Hanoverian soldiers. I won't believe it of her, and there's an end on't.'

More words in the same strain were casually dropped as the two men waited; words which revealed to her, as by a sudden illumination, the enormity of her conduct. The conversation was at length cut off by the arrival of the man with the vehicle. The luggage was placed in it, and they mounted, and were driven on in the direction from which she had just come.

Phyllis was so conscious-stricken that she was at first inclined to follow them; but a moment's reflection led her to feel that it would only be bare justice to Matthäus to wait till he arrived, and explain candidly that she had changed her mind – difficult as the struggle would be when she stood face to face with him. She bitterly reproached herself for having believed reports which represented Humphrey Gould as false to his engagement, when, from what she now heard from his own lips, she gathered that he had been living full of trust in her. But she knew well enough who had won her love. Without him her life seemed a dreary prospect, yet the more she looked at his proposal the more she feared to accept it – so wild as it was, so vague, so venturesome. She had promised Humphrey Gould, and it was only his assumed faithlessness which had led her to treat that promise as nought. His solicitude in bringing her these gifts touched her; her promise must be kept, and esteem must take the place of love. She would preserve her self-respect. She would stay at home, and marry him, and suffer.

Phyllis had thus braced herself to an exceptional fortitude when, a few minutes later, the outline of Matthäus Tina appeared behind a field-gate, over which he lightly leapt as she stepped forward. There was no evading it; he pressed her to his breast.

'It is the first and last time!' she wildly thought as she stood encircled by his arms.

How Phyllis got through the terrible ordeal of that night she could never clearly recollect. She always attributed her success in carrying out her resolve to her lover's honour, for as soon as she declared to him in feeble words that she had changed her mind, and felt that she could not, dared not, fly with him, he forbore to urge her, grieved as he was at her decision. Unscrupulous pressure on his part, seeing how romantically she had become attached to him, would no doubt have turned the balance in his favour. But he did nothing to tempt her unduly or unfairly.

On her side, fearing for his safety, she begged him to remain. This, he declared, could not be. 'I cannot break faith with my friend,' said he. Had he stood alone he would have abandoned his plan. But Christoph, with the boat and compass and chart, was waiting on the shore; the tide would soon turn; his mother had been warned of his coming; go he must.

Many precious minutes were lost while he tarried, unable to tear himself away; Phyllis held to her resolve, though it cost her many a bitter pang. At last they parted, and he went down the hill. Before his footsteps had quite died away she felt a desire to behold at least his outline once more, and running noiselessly after him regained view of his diminishing figure. For one moment she was sufficiently excited to be on the point of rushing forward and linking her fate with his. But she could not. The courage which at the critical instant failed Cleopatra of Egypt could scarcely be expected of Phyllis Grove.

A dark shape, similar to his own, joined him in the highway. It was Christoph, his friend. She could see no more; they had hastened on in the direction of the town and harbour, four miles ahead. With a feeling akin to despair she turned and slowly pursued her way homeward.

Tattoo sounded in the camp; but there was no camp for her now. It was as dead as the camp of the Assyrians after the passage of the Destroying Angel.

She noiselessly entered the house, seeing nobody, and went to bed. Grief, which kept her awake at first, ultimately wrapped her in a heavy sleep. The next morning her father met her at the foot of the stairs.

'Mr Gould is come!' he said triumphantly.

Humphrey was staying at the inn, and had already called to inquire for her. He had brought her a present of a very handsome looking-glass in a frame of *repoussé* silverwork, which her father held in his hand. He had promised to call again in the course of an hour, to ask Phyllis to walk with him.

Pretty mirrors were rarer in country-houses at that day than they are now, and the one before her won Phyllis's admiration. She looked into it, saw how heavy her eyes were, and endeavoured to brighten them. She was in that wretched state of mind which leads a woman to move mechanically onward in what she conceives to be her allotted path. Mr Humphrey had, in his undemonstrative way, been adhering all along to the old understanding; it was for her to do the same, and to say not a word of her own lapse. She put on her bonnet and tippet, and when he arrived at the hour named she was at the door awaiting him.

V

Phyllis thanked him for his beautiful gift; but the talking was soon entirely on Humphrey's side as they walked along. He told her of the latest movements of the world of fashion – a subject which she willingly discussed to the exclusion of anything more personal – and his measured language helped to still her disquieted heart and brain. Had not her own sadness been what it was she must have observed his embarrassment. At last he abruptly changed the subject.

'I am glad you are pleased with my little present,' he said. 'The truth is that I brought it to propitiate 'ee, and to get you to help me out of a mighty difficulty.'

It was inconceivable to Phyllis that this independent bachelor – whom she admired in some respects – could have a difficulty.

'Phyllis – I'll tell you my secret at once; for I have a monstrous secret to confide before I can ask your counsel. The case is, then, that I am married: yes, I have privately married a dear young belle; and if you knew her, and I hope you will, you would say everything in her praise. But she is not quite the one that my father would have chose for me – you know the paternal idea as well as I – and I have kept it secret. There will be a terrible noise, no doubt; but I think with your help I may get over it. If you would only do me this good turn – when I have told my father, I mean – say that you never could have married me, you know, or something of that sort – 'pon my life, it will help to smooth the way vastly. I am so anxious to win him round to my point of view, and not to cause any estrangement.'

What Phyllis replied she scarcely knew, or how she counselled him as to his unexpected situation. Yet the relief that his announcement brought her was perceptible. To have confided her trouble in return was what her aching heart longed to do; and had Humphrey been a woman she would instantly have poured out her tale. But to him she feared to confess; and there was a real reason for silence, till a sufficient time had elapsed to allow her lover and his comrade to get out of harm's way.

As soon as she reached home again she sought a solitary place, and spent the time in half regretting that she had not gone away, and in dreaming over the meetings with Matthäus Tina from their beginning to their end. In his own country, amongst his own countrywomen, he would possibly soon forget her, even to her very name.

Her listlessness was such that she did not go out of the

house for several days. There came a morning which broke in fog and mist, behind which the dawn could be discerned in greenish grey; and the outlines of the tents, and the rows of horses at the ropes. The smoke from the canteen fires drooped heavily.

The spot at the bottom of the garden where she had been accustomed to climb the wall to meet Matthäus, was the only inch of English ground in which she took any interest; and in spite of the disagreeable haze prevailing she walked out there till she reached the well-known corner. Every blade of grass was weighted with little liquid globes, and slugs and snails had crept out upon the plots. She could hear the usual faint noises from the camp, and in the other direction the trot of farmers on the road to the town, for it was market-day. She observed that her frequent visits to this corner had quite trodden down the grass in the angle of the wall, and left marks of garden soil on the stepping-stones by which she had mounted to look over the top. Seldom having gone there till dusk, she had not considered that her traces might be visible by day. Perhaps it was these which had revealed her trysts to her father.

While she paused in melancholy regard, she fancied that the customary sounds from the tents were changing their character. Indifferent as Phyllis was to camp doings now, she mounted by the steps to the old place. What she beheld at first awed and perplexed her; then she stood rigid, her fingers hooked to the wall, her eyes staring out of her head, and her face as if hardened to stone.

On the open green stretching before her all the regiments in the camp were drawn up in line, in the mid-front of which two empty coffins lay on the ground. The unwonted sounds which she had noticed came from an advancing procession. It consisted of the band of the York Hussars playing a dead march; next two soldiers of that regiment in a mourning coach, guarded on each side, and accompanied by two priests. Behind came a crowd of rustics who had been attracted by the event. The melancholy procession marched along the front of the line, returned to the centre, and halted beside the coffins, where the two condemned men were blindfolded, and each placed kneeling on his coffin; a few minutes' pause was now given, while they prayed.

A firing-party of twenty-four men stood ready with levelled carbines. The commanding officer, who had his sword drawn, waved it through some cuts of the sword-exercise till he reached the downward stroke, whereat the firing party discharged their volley. The two victims fell, one upon his face across his coffin, the other backwards.

As the volley resounded there arose a shriek from the wall of Dr Grove's garden, and some one fell down inside; but nobody among the spectators without noticed it at the time. The two executed Hussars were Matthäus Tina and his friend Christoph. The soldiers on guard placed the bodies in the coffins almost instantly; but the colonel of the regiment, an Englishman, rode up and exclaimed in a stern voice: 'Turn them out – as an example to the men!'

The coffins were lifted endwise, and the dead Germans flung out upon their faces on the grass. Then all the regiments wheeled in sections, and marched past the spot in slow time. When the survey was over the corpses were again coffined, and borne away.

Meanwhile Dr Grove, attracted by the noise of the volley, had rushed out into his garden, where he saw his wretched daughter lying motionless against the wall. She was taken indoors, but it was long before she recovered consciousness; and for weeks they despaired of her reason.

It transpired that the luckless deserters from the York Hussars had cut the boat from her moorings in the adjacent harbour, according to their plan, and, with two other comrades who were smarting under ill-treatment from their colonel, had sailed in safety across the Channel. But mistaking their bearings they had steered into Jersey, thinking that island the French coast. Here they were perceived to be deserters, and delivered up to the authorities. Matthäus and Christoph interceded for the other two at the court-martial, saying that it was entirely by the former's representations that these were induced to go. Their sentence was accordingly commuted to flogging, the death punishment being reserved for their leaders.

The visitor to the well-worn old Georgian watering-place, who may well care to ramble to the neighbouring village under the hills, and examine the register of burials, will there find two entries in these words:

Matth: Tina (Corpl.) in His Majesty's Regmt. of York Hussars, and Shot for Desertion, was Buried June 30th, 1801, aged 22 years. Born in the town of Saarbruck, Germany.

Christoph Bless, belonging to His Majesty's Regmt. of York Hussars, who was Shot for Desertion, was Buried June 30th, 1801, aged 22 years. Born at Lothaargen, Alsatia.

Their graves were dug at the back of the little church, near the wall. There is no memorial to mark the spot, but Phyllis pointed it out to me. While she lived she used to keep their mounds neat; but now they are overgrown with nettles, and sunk nearly flat. The older villagers, however, who know of the episode from their parents, still recollect the place where the soldiers lie. Phyllis lies near.

October 1889

Hugh Walpole

ROGUE HERRIES 35p

The first volume of the Herries Chronicle.

A magnificent history of a divided family which mirrors the heart and pulse of eighteenth-century England.

Here is fiction in glorious, sweeping measure, set against the wild and beautiful scenery of the Lake District, crowded with fairs, balls, weddings, duels, revels, witches, abductions, murder, strolling players and Jacobite agents.

Bestriding these events like a Colossus is proud, intolerant Francis Herries – the Dark Angel of Borrowdale – who despised his wife and sold his mistress at a public fair, yet came to love sixteen-year-old Mirabell Starr more than life itself . . .

'A superb work of fiction. There is not one tired, listless page' – J. B. PRIESTLEY

Also available in Pan are the remaining three volumes of the Herries Chronicle:

JUDITH PARIS 35p

THE FORTRESS 35p

VANESSA 35p

Lewis Grassic Gibbon

SUNSET SONG   40p
Book One of the trilogy A SCOTS QUAIR

Filled with loving warmth and rich humanity, this magnificent novel, set in the years of World War One, encompasses the life of a woman, and the life of a people – a story to hold all Scotland in its telling.

CLOUD HOWE   35p
Book Two of the trilogy A SCOTS QUAIR

Vivid in its panoramic canvas, this compelling story of Scottish life continues the saga of Chris Guthrie into the turbulent 1920s, moving from the hills of Kinraddie to the jute mills by Segget Water.

GREY GRANITE   35p
Book Three of the trilogy A SCOTS QUAIR

This powerful and evocative novel of Scotland in the hungry thirties takes a twice-widowed Chris Guthrie to the granite walls of Duncairn.

'His three great novels have the impetus and music of mountain burns in spate' – Ivor Brown, OBSERVER

'All three novels are magnificent pieces of writing' – J. M. Reid, GLASGOW HERALD

Alexander Cordell

An enthralling anthology of mid-nineteenth-century Wales.

RAPE OF THE FAIR COUNTRY   35p
Here begins the story of the Mortymer family, brave men, beautiful women, fighters all, whom nothing can daunt as they live, and starve, and fight, and make love, and above all slave for the cruel English ironmasters.

THE HOSTS OF REBECCA   35p
A lusty, brawling novel where strong and angry men use the cover of night to burn the hated toll-gates that bring them to the edge of starvation.
It is also the story of young Jethro Mortymer, miner by day and rebel by night, who struggles to conceal a terrible, hungry love for the gentle Mari, his brother's widow . . .

SONG OF THE EARTH   35p
Concludes the superb trilogy. Mostyn Evan and family, miners turned bargees, pray as hard as they fight, sing as passionately as they love, and face the threat of the railways with irrepressible humour and a stubbornness as hard as their native hills.